A. BAGUS

PLAN B

ISBN: 9798573340906

ACKNOWLEDGMENTS...i
Prologue 1
1 The Project 4
2 Genesis 31
3 Apocalypse.. 37
4 Creation... 38
5 Evolved men 41
6 First discontinuity 43
7 The history begins 51
8 Cultural revolutions.. 66
9 Divine intervention 75
10 Technological progress.. 78
11 Galactic Era... 94
12 Rough Men of space 110
13 Mythology.. 119
14 Edge Adventure... 126
15 The Galactic Warfare... 144
16 The domain of the gna 152
17 Chattering from the Nucleus 164
18 The Plan B 167
19 The Heroes of Bettie Page 172
20 Fiesta in Space.. 181
21 The GNA reacts 185
22 The Journey of the Vie en Rose....................... 189
23 The decline of the nucleus 209
24 The wrath of the CH.A.O.S................................ 211
25 Intersection... 221
26 The first true galactic hero 226
27 The rebirth of arms... 229
28 In the Current 234
29 Myths and Legends 251
30 Birth of the Universal Species 253
About the author.. 256

ACKNOWLEDGMENTS

Thanks to all the women who have greatly contributed to the
inspiration of this book with their behavior

PROLOGUE

"Did it ever occur to you that we are basically nothing more than a big garbage truck?" said the Captain to his Second.

"Well, in short, it seems to me a somewhat trivial way to define our activity of earth-formation" replied the boatswain Da Silva.

"Don't bullshit Da Silva, earth-formation is a word invented by space adventure writers before we really went into space. Earth-formation is impossible! Planets are as they are because they have reached equilibrium and any change would only be a temporary change until the planet returns to its equilibrium condition. What we do is pollute them. Let's put it bluntly, we just find a planet that is already suitable and we dump on it a wagon of organic garbage."

"So somehow we modify its ecosystem" insisted the Second.

"But not even that. Before filling it with garbage you can't even talk about ecosystem. All we have found so far are planets with water and organic matter. Hydrocarbons, organic acids, aromatic complexes, amino acids, but no shade of proteins, in short only turbid and smelly broths. At that point we infect them with bacteria of all kinds and those do thrive in those primordial broths. Bacteria, algae, microorganisms, plankton, spores, seeds, larvae; we throw down everything without standing there watching what is better and what is worse. Only then can we talk about an ecosystem."

"Then we could at least say that we create an ecosystem, right?" insisted the Second.

"But not even that. We spread only the system we come from. We transport all this crap to form worlds, I mean our hold is a real cesspool, but in reality we could just go down to the planets, you and me, and shit on it and we will get the same result."

"You Captain have a true noble soul" replied the Second annoyed, "I would rather say that we sow on fertile ground."

"Yes yes, continue with the poetry, you. So, do we have a new course?" the Captain cut him off.

"I'm reading the results of the long-range sensors but so far nothing."

"All right, when you find something, call me; I'm going to my cabin to take a nap."

The Tiger's deep space telescopes ceaselessly photographed the surrounding space while the on-board computer compared photo sequences in search of the slightest fluctuations in the position of the stars that revealed the presence of planetary systems. The computer was able to discover the existence of planets within a radius of hundreds of light years, even if most of them were only gaseous planets. From a distance, however, there was no way to know what was what and the choice on which systems to explore fell from the computer to the crew, in this case the Captain, who chose with the only possible method, that was random.

But there at the edge of the galaxy there were very few stars and in most cases, spaceships like the Tiger stood in space without finding anything even for months.

The Captain's nap became a sound sleep, then a prolonged absence and for a few days there was no more news of him. In the meantime the Second had camped on the command bridge of the huge spaceship, transforming it in a short time into a campground, also because in addition to him and the Captain, the Tiger housed only the onboard computer, which since the time of Admiral Berg, everyone called Katjusa.

More than ten days had passed when the onboard computer finally announced with its persuasive voice that she had identified a possible target.

"Planetary system identified at alpha 312 degrees 12 minutes and 47 seconds, theta minus 8 degrees and 26 seconds, distance two hundred and twelve light years, stellar mass index 0.98, planetary mass index 0.04".

The Second stretched out long before reacting to the news. "Hey, Cap" he said on the intercom, "Katjusa found something."

"How much stuff?"

"Only one system, we are not even spoiled of choice."

"Okay, tell her to calculate a course while I get there."

When the Captain arrived on the bridge, Katjusa announced with a voice in which it seemed to sense a hint of satisfaction with her discovery, that she was ready to leave for the new destination: "distance two hundred and twelve light years, ETE[1] eight minutes and twenty-two seconds, course 38 degrees and 22 minutes x, 18 degrees 22 minutes and 8 seconds y, 76 degrees and 6 minutes z, 92 degrees and 36 seconds w, all systems active, AGRE engine on standby."

"She couldn't wait!" the Captain jangled.

"Me too, to tell the truth" added the Second whispering.

"I can see it, this place looks like a gorilla cage that hasn't been cleaned for two months" said the Captain looking around, "how come you're so hairy?"

"And you so glabrous?" echoed the Second.

"Katjusa, activate" ordered the Captain removing a tray of leftovers away from his armchair.

---

[1] Estimated Time Enroute

1 THE PROJECT

"But what is this slaughterhouse! Look at you, you have destroyed the whole nest!"

"Oh hey Molly, I was just teaching the little one how to pull down the trees."

"I can see it, this place has become a wasteland, you will have scared the game away for miles and miles."

" We'll get there in half an hour at the most."

"Yes, and then how do you bring a dead triceratops back here? Do you put it on your back?"

"I admit it would be a real debacle. Alvin, come on, let's go shopping, Mommy's hungry."

"That's good, shoo shoo!"

"I love it when you do that."

"I know you adore me Gordon but now think of Alvin who still couldn't take even a lame coelure. Now move that big body of yours away from here that I have things to do. See if I have to spend the day stacking logs. Sometimes I wish I had wings and flew away. I would really need a vacation."

"Yes, and with that four-ton silhouette you'd need an airport to land."

"And what is an airport?"

"Ah I do not know. It's a word that came to my mind."

"Listen Mr. Linguist, do you want to leave or not?"

"Not without taking a bite first."

"All right, come here, you big softie, I'm gonna plant twenty canines in your back."

Silence wrapped up the inaugural meeting of the Project Committee while the General Operations Director finished examining the plan containing the general lines of the Project itself.

"Well," said the Director when he finished his reading, "I'll start with a recommendation, especially for those who are attending a meeting like this for the first time" he said, looking at everyone slowly with a circular look, as to identify the recipients of his speech. "Everything that will be said here, will have to be clearly explained, nothing must be taken for granted or simply known, since it is right in the middle of the obvious facts, and therefore not considered worthy of mention that mistakes are usually hidden" concluded the General Operations Director, looking then at the Chairman of the Absolute Order of Space-time, who nodded gravely.

"So" continued the General Operations Director with a lighter tone, "I invite everyone to express themselves with clarity and completeness even in saying elementary things."

"But in this way this meeting could become a very large thing" commented a new member of the Committee with a low voice, as if he was meditating with himself.

The observation did not escape the Chairman of the Absolute Order of Space-time, to which in reality nothing escaped, who answered dryly "The breadth of a discussion does not have importance for this Committee."

A general gesture of assent went through the Committee.

"So, why have we failed with the current Project?" asked the Chairman of the Absolute Order of Space-time, thus starting the meeting. "I hope that the General Operations Director will be able to enlighten us on this point."

The General Operations Director swayed a little, feeling a certain sense of uneasiness because, as Director, he felt the weight of the failure of the Project on himself. He hesitated, as if to gather ideas, and then simply said, "We have put in insufficient evolutionary momentum."

"This does not necessarily lead to failure" observed one of the Committee members.

"In fact" replied the General Operations Director, taking the opportunity to explain, "So we believed in establishing the intensity of the evolutionary force in the dominant species, thinking that a slow evolution would produce an evolutionary path without discontinuity of the second species, thus leading to a line of development ..."

"Director!" interrupted him abruptly intervening the Chairman of the Absolute Order of Space-time, "Specify what it means discontinuity of second species, just to you I must remember the recommendation with which you started this meeting?"

"Yes Chairman" replied the General Operations Director, "therefore, for those who do not know, the discontinuities of second species are nothing but steps in the evolutionary line graph. Since the evolutionary line is nothing more than the sum of the improvements of the species with respect to itself, but not with respect to the environment because that it is only a matter of adaptation, if the latter has sudden evolutionary leaps, those leaps appear in the graph as steps. With a weak evolutionary force the discontinuities of the second species, i.e. the jumps, are not there or are small. However, discontinuities of the first species may appear, that is", continued the G.O.D., under the grim gaze of the CH.A.O.S., "sudden changes of slope of the graph, that is accelerations or slowdowns in the evolutionary process."

The Energy Systems Technician then intervened asking "Why did you try to avoid the discontinuities of the second species? What is so terrible about these second species discontinuities?"

The G.O.D. turned to the Social Systems Technician. "Would you please give him an answer?"

"I'll certainly do" replied the Technician, taking the floor.

"As the Director has already said, a second species discontinuity is a sudden evolutionary leap. The problem is that a leap cannot occur simultaneously on all individuals of the species. During the leap, which can last even several microcycles[2], the species is subjected to strong internal tensions because the part of the species that has suffered the leap is obviously much more evolved than the one that has not suffered it, or in other words that has been left behind. In fact, this would be the normal evolutionary course, but during a leap the differences between individuals are enormous and therefore in such a case the evolution would not simply be a race to prevail between more or less gifted individuals, but a rapid overwhelming event with a brutal character, like a total oppression or an extermination" explained the Social Systems Technician who then sadly concluded "In short, we wanted to avoid a too bloody reality, as well as find ourselves in the end with a species always prone to violence."

"In other words," added the G.O.D. disconsolate, "we were inspired by harmony."

"A commendable thought" said then the CH.A.O.S., "but one that has led us to failure. The streets of hell are paved with excellent intentions, as I am sure someone will say sooner or later, without really knowing what he is talking about" added the CH.A.O.S. in a somewhat disturbing tone, "but the Director should not be worried, I remember that I myself had endorsed that choice."

"Why are you already talking about failure?" the Ecosystem Technician intervened, "as far as I know, the species is vital, vigorous and constantly evolving, just as the Project foresaw."

"It is not the course of the Project itself that is not good" replied the Diffused Systems Technician, "it follows exactly the programmed development, its speed is the real failure. A whole cycle has already passed and we are just at the development of a language that in reality, said between us, to define it as such is little more than courtesy; a handful of handy verbs, maybe a hundred words and everything else entrusted to the emphasis of gesticulation and onomatopoeic is all they have. At this rate, it will take at least two more cycles to spread the species

---

[2] microcycle = 300 years

throughout the galaxy. In short, they are too slow" concluded the Technician.

"But wasn't speed an unimportant parameter?" opined an assistant in a low voice.

"It is not important to us but for the species it is very important!" exclaimed the Diffused Systems Technician. "In half a cycle the galaxy will collide with another galaxy and at that point the species must be ready to face the interstellar space. Jumping from one star to another, in fact, will be the only way to survive such an event, which for the cores of the two galaxies will obviously be catastrophic, and at the same time they will be able to spread from one galaxy to another. Of course, the fact is not random at all. We have chosen that galaxy among the many available, just because it was going to meet a collision. It is only in this way that galaxy after galaxy, collision after collision, the species will be able to spread throughout the universe, or at least in the local galactic cluster, which is the final goal of the Project, because regardless of the means available, no living species will ever cross the intergalactic space."

"They could always make the galactic leap at the next collision" suggested the Ecosystems Engineer.

"Certainly" replied the Diffuse Systems Engineer with critical tone, "but during the intersection, the stars of which the two galaxies are composed will have a much higher probability of impact than normal, which multiplied by the number of stars will produce a situation as of bombardment of the entire galactic volume and will disturb all the stellar trajectories. Hence the planetary orbits will all become unstable, not to mention what will happen to the two cores, which are also denser. In this situation, the species will have no other way to survive than to move continuously to avoid collisions and disasters. However, if even their planet could survive such a catastrophe, and I think it is rather unlikely, the next intersection will only occur after seventeen cycles and I do not think they will last so long, especially because they will also have to deal with the lack of energy" concluded the Diffused Systems Engineer, while the

Energy Systems Engineer nodded satisfied.

"Couldn't we delay the intersection of the two galaxies so as to give the species some more time?" proposed then the Ecosystems Engineer, to whom it seemed a great pity to throw away a work that lasted an entire cycle, that is the time necessary for the galaxy to make an entire revolution on itself.

"You can't" then intervened the Superintendent of the General Laws of the Universe and the Derivative Effects, a shady and silent figure that everyone called more briefly the Physicist, because everybody found his title, including him, a bit pompous.

"The only way to slow down a galaxy is to change the universal gravitational constant. This would produce a variation in the operation of all physical systems. For example, could someone tell me what would happen to the species if gravity would change?" asked the Physicist with a low pitch.

"I don't even want to think about it" replied the Sensory Systems Engineer, "if it decreased we would find ourselves with a species with crumbled bones, if it increased, with muscle systems too weak, a real nightmare."

"And how much would require the adaptation to this new circumstance?" asked the Physicist with a sly and satisfied smile for having frightened the Technician.

"At least ten millicycles[3]" replied the technician resolutely, "but it is not sure that the species can adapt, it also depends on the extent of variation. Of what extent are we talking about?"

The Physicist made quick calculations while everyone waited in silence. In less than one nanocycle[4] he obtained the result.

"To postpone the collision to at least two cycles, I can redefine the gravitational constant with a value four percent lower than the current one. Of course this will change all the internal motions in the galaxy and therefore also the planetary orbit that hosts the species" said the Physicist with sneaky air.

---

[3] millicycle = 300,000 years
[4] nanocycle = 0.3 years or about 4 months

"I would say a nightmare worse than any second species discontinuity!" exclaimed the Sensory Systems Engineer, while an intense nervousness spread among those who were reflecting on the devastating effects of a changed gravity.

"I would have another proposal" said the Materials Engineer, "couldn't we increase the evolutionary force of the species so that it can make a leap forward and shorten the time?"

"You can't" said the Biological Systems Engineer or, more briefly, the Biologist. "The definitive genetic sequence, which determines the entire behavior of the species including the evolutionary force, is encrypted with a fractal algorithm in order to protect the species from any manipulation, especially by themselves when they will have adequate technology. Given the irreversible nature of fractal coding, we can no longer intervene on the nature of the species, but in any case this consideration is irrelevant, we cryptograph also to exclude subsequent interventions. It is on this basis, in fact, that the species bases its confidence in the future. As you can certainly imagine, if the species realized that it is manipulated, that is controlled, it would become passive and fatalistic. Equal effect would have a manipulation by themselves, so it is also for their good that we encrypt. The genetic sequence can certainly be read, but its meaning will remain forever obscure, and it is good that it is so" was the lapidary conclusion of the Biologist.

"But, in fact, we control them!" observed the Ethics Systems Engineer.

"Certainly" replied the Biologist, "but only in the sense that we establish from the beginning their evolutionary line, so, in fact, they have to do what we want, but afterwards we never intervene. Beyond the initial implant, of which they can have no memory, we do not exist for them. They are and must be convinced that destiny is created by them."

"But if they just talk!" observed with contempt the Energy Systems Engineer.

"From talking to developing a metaphysical philosophy, it's a short step" said the Irrational Systems Technician with a mocking half smile, "in less than a millicycle they will invent an entire mystical theory about the nature of the universe, obviously all wrong. As a matter of fact, they will develop many theories and it will be the fair of the grotesque."

"Well" concluded the CH.A.O.S., "I would say that if there are no other proposals, we can exclude the rescue of the current Project."

The murmur of the Project Committee subsided.

"You will certainly realize that you are condemning to death a species now endowed with conscience. Does this choice leave you indifferent?" said the Ethics Systems Engineer in a saddened tone.

"I think I speak for everyone in saying that we are well aware of it" replied the G.O.D. quietly, "but pity is a luxury we can no longer afford. It is precisely pity that has led us to this unfortunate situation."

A general assent went through the entire Committee.

"General Operations Director" continued then the CH.A.O.S. considering the discussion closed, "is the new Project already set to become executive?"

"No Chairman" replied the G.O.D., "we have left some choices open so that this Committee can express its opinion on the matter and consequently, the genetic sequences of the new Project are still all provisional."

"What are these choices?" the CH.A.O.S. asked.

"I give the floor to the Diffused Systems Technician" said the G.O.D.

The Diffused Systems Technician consulted his notes before he set out to explain.

"First of all it is necessary to decide how to move from the old Project to the new one. There are two possibilities, of course with all the nuances between one and the other, so I will limit myself to exposing only the two extreme conditions. The first is the insertion of the new species in the environment of the previous one, so that one slowly replaces the other. The second is the elimination of the current species and only then the insertion of the new species in the environment at that point empty. In the first case we will have an almost painless transition for the species to extinguish but very difficult for the new one, because it will have to survive in an environment already dominated by someone else. In addition, the process will be very slow because it is natural that the old species will resist to what will seem to them an alien invasion. We predict that it will take fifty millicycles, which after all are not many. With the second method we will get instead the transition from one to the other in a single millicycle and with the added advantage that in the process we can also remake the whole environment. Let's not forget, in fact, that the current environment is suitable for the old species, or more correctly, the old species has adapted to the environment we have built around it, so as it is, the current environment is very little suitable for the new species for which, incidentally, we have changed all the operating parameters."

"From your exposition it seems to me that the choice is rather obvious" observed the Evolutionary Systems Technician, "so why is a decision of this Committee required?"

"Because we do not know how to implement it without producing other destructive consequences" replied the Diffused Systems Technician, "so if we do not find a solution, we will only have to implement the step in the first way, which from a practical point of view is a very simple task. In fact, it is only a matter of implanting the new genetic code on any cellular support already adapted to the environment; the seas of the planet are full of them."

"In short, introducing a virus" summarized the Evolutionary Systems Technician.

"Exactly" the technician assented.

"I can help you" intervened the Kinetic Technician, said by many the Joker because seen from afar, his specific activity seemed that of an acrobat playing with balls, even if in his case the balls were the stars and the planets.

"I can temporarily change the probability of impact in the asteroid belt in their planetary system. It will take only a nanocycle to induce in the belt such a confusion to produce a meteor shower so dense that the planet, despite its small size, cannot avoid. I believe that this will not change in any way the structure of the Universal System, so there will be no other consequences, but of course, I ask confirmation to the Physicist" concluded the Joker with an obsequious gesture.

"In fact" replied the Physicist, "I don't think there are other implications in the correction he intends to make. After all, it is only a matter of changes in statistics, or to put it simply, of introducing a temporary element of bad luck", to which he mentally added *a real trick worthy of a joker, cheater and treacherous as well as perfidious.*

"However" continued the Physicist, "you should specify the minimum mass to conclude the current Project, to verify whether it leads to significant kinematic variations in the life support of the species."

"They are becoming completely incomprehensible" said a member of the Committee whispering to a colleague next to him, both responsible for Aesthetic Systems and therefore very little used to the language that was taking over the meeting of the Project Committee.

The giggling of the two naturally did not escape the CH.A.O.S. "You two of the Aesthetic Systems, do you want to add something to our discussion?" he asked looking at them a bit sideways.

"No Your Excellency Unquestionable" replied one of the two, who had had an unseemly acquaintance with an employee of the Department of Contradictions and Paradoxes, a department in which there was an excess of humor of which he was still badly influenced, "is that here we have not understood anything."

"What do you take care of" the G.O.D. intervened, annoyed by a way of expression so little respectful towards the Chairman of the Absolute Order of Space-time.

"We paint butterflies" replied the first, "but also flowers, fruits, insects, fishes, animals and so on."

"And so on" echoed his colleague.

The G.O.D. looked at them a little bit crooked but when he realized that, on the contrary, the CH.A.O.S. was smiling amused, he took the thing more lightly and with impersonal tone began to explain in other terms the intervention of the Physicist and the Joker.

"In practice, the Kinetic Technician proposes to make fall on the planet an asteroid that in the catastrophic impact eliminates the majority of life forms, or even better, all of them. However, the Physicist pointed out that it is necessary to pay attention that the impact would not be as powerful as to change the orbit of the planet itself, because this would change the environment so radically that we should completely redo the new Project. This eventuality would require a quarter cycle, at least."

After a few moments of silence, the CH.A.O.S. took the floor again. "Well, it is decided then, the Kinetic Technician proceeds with his proposal. What other question must be submitted to this Committee?"

"The intensity of the evolutionary push" replied the G.O.D., "I give the floor to the Evolutionary Systems Technician."

"The problem is that we do not have a criterion to determine it," said the respondent immediately, "the certain thing is that it will have to be more intense than that of the current species, but we do not know how much because since we do not have a specific mathematical model, we cannot predict all the effects. After all, if we had had it, we would have used it for the current Project and we would not have found ourselves in this bad situation, it is quite obvious."

"So how did we determine the evolutionary force of the current dominant species?" asked the G.O.D.

"We have simply calculated the minimum intensity of the force necessary to have a divergence pole" replied the Evolutionary Systems Engineer promptly adding "a divergence pole is a circumstance in which the evolutionary force becomes so intense as to produce a sudden change in the evolutionary line, in short a second species discontinuity. So we kept exactly below this minimum threshold, to give them the maximum evolutionary push but without forcing them to face second species discontinuity."

"So we no longer have any margin to still keep the force's intensity under such threshold" concluded the G.O.D., "Technician of Ethical Systems" continued then the G.O.D. with an imperious tone, "briefly expose us the consequences of a more intense evolutionary force on the new species."

The called was absorbed for a while, as if to collect ideas, and then began to explain. "It is evident that the more the evolutionary force will be intense, the more the species will have a turbulent character. In fact, since second species discontinuity will appear continuously, there will be always groups of individuals who will try to overwhelm others. This, however, will be the least serious consequence; much worse will be the effect on themselves. The evolutionary force is related to the reproductive system, or rather, it is the reproductive system that determines the evolutionary force. After all, it is a very simple system: the evolutionary force is nothing more than a reluctance to reproduce by one of the two genders. This reluctance forces the other gender to continuously come up with new ways to reproduce. It is obvious that in this way the most brilliant individuals will always have descendants. This leads to the general improvement of the species, which is evolution. Therefore, in order to increase the evolutionary force you have to do nothing but increase the reluctance of a genus. But with reluctance as intense as the one we intend to give it, the species will live in a perpetual conflict between the two genera. Since the most important drive that we impose to each species is precisely the reproduction, the contrast will make them a species obsessed, unbalanced and always oriented to violence. In a word: an unbearable species. To be more precise, violent, unbearable and perpetually dissatisfied will be only one genus, the one whose reproductive drive will be frustrated, while the one in which we will insert reluctance, will live in a perpetual schizophrenic state, because on the one hand it will want to reproduce and on the other hand it will not want it at all so they will be shady, gloomy, incomprehensible and totally irrational individuals."

"A rather depressing picture" considered the G.O.D., "that's why we avoided it so far. Can we introduce a moderating force for all this horror?" asked the G.O.D., "it seems to me that in this way we would give light to real monsters."

To the question of the G.O.D. replied promptly the Ethical Systems Technician.

"Certainly, we can introduce an immaterial necessity that the Irrational Systems Technician will be able to provide us."

"In practice" replied the Irrational Systems Technician, "you would like to make them into a violent, schizoid and warmongering species, but to carve into their genetic code the thought *live in peace*, hoping that the latter will prevail or at least compensate for everything else?"

A murmur roamed through the whole Committee.

The question provoked different reactions. Who like the Joker began to sneer, who shook its head disconsolate and who discovered itself at the threshold of tears.

"In my opinion" considered the G.O.D., "a similar species would take that precept as a valid reason to make some other war. Living in a state of perennial disharmony, they will develop obsessions so twisted as to make war with the reason to make peace. An immaterial necessity will be only a third element of imbalance. They will become much more than unbalanced, they will become insane" concluded the G.O.D. with worried tone.

"Well, madness is only a matter of semantics anyhow" mumbled the Ethical Systems Technician.

"I guess that to make a species with only one genus and introduce the evolutionary push under another form is not possible" thought aloud the Energy Systems Technician who didn't understand anything about living matter. He was thinking only about fires, potentials and nuclear exchanges.

"In fact" the Biologist replied dryly, "evolution is in practice a variation of the genetic sequence, and this occurs through recombination of several sequences. This can take place only with the mating therefore a species with only one genus, not being able to reproduce but as a copy of itself, it cannot evolve, except for marginal characters. In order to evolve seriously, to a species with only one genus we would have to introduce a random factor, but this would lead to continuous mutations and in short we would find ourselves with a swarm of species with unpredictable behavior, which would hardly follow the plans of the Project. It is true that we could limit this effect with a factor acting only on the secondary traits, but in that case the variations would always be of little importance and we would come back again in the first case."

"And make three of them?" insisted the Energy Systems Engineer.

"Even worse" replied the Biologist who had already asked himself the question, "to impose an evolutionary push we would have to introduce a reluctance in at least one of the three genres and the mechanism of reproduction would then become even more complicated because in order to reproduce it would be necessary that three instead of two individuals would have to agree, and in any case this would lead to the possibility that the two genres overwhelm the reluctant one and with that we would have lost any stimulus to improvement and we would simply find ourselves with a situation of pure brute force and without evolutionary push. We have also considered the case of three genders with one reluctant and the other two smaller and weaker, so that the latter eventuality would not occur. In this case, however, being the stronger the reluctant one, it would always be able to impose its reluctance to the others, inevitably leading the species to extinction. In short, by increasing the number of genera no solutions are found, only more problems are created. The right number of genera is two and this is it" concluded the Biologist.

Silence fell again on the Project Committee.

"I think we should all meditate carefully on these issues" said the G.O.D., "we will resume this meeting when we have clear ideas on what to do.''

In silence everyone left.

1st interlude

"What's the matter with you dear, why don't you sleep?"

"Molly, something's wrong, I can feel it."

"What?"

"I don't know, it's a feeling like a catastrophe looming over our heads."

"It will be the usual tropical cyclone, this season they come one after the other."

"No no, I'm not talking about a little bad weather Molly, how long do you think we've been here?"

"Since we were born Gordon, it will be twenty seasons at least."

"I didn't mean here, here. I meant here, here."

"What are you doing, the fool?"

"Here, Molly!" cried Gordon, accompanying the word with a vague gesture.

"Ah I see, you mean here, here" Molly said, accompanying herself with an equally vague gesture.

"There, you got it."

"Then I have no idea. In my opinion we have always been here.''

"That's what George and Bogart say too, and I've talked to many others. No one has a story that tells of our ancestors or our arrival. We have neither myths nor legends; it is as if we have always been here. But I have this sinister feeling that we won't be here much longer."

"If we have always been here, we will always be here; I don't see why things should change."

"Maybe you're right Molly, things can't change."

2nd interlude

"You know what I don't understand?" said the Ethics Systems Engineer to the Evolutionary Systems Engineer, "if we have to make them warmongers, why do we make them so little shaped for violence? We have deprived them of all systems of defense and offense."

"And that's not all" replied the other, "we make them even tiny ones. The current species, in addition to being armored, is also quite large. The new species, instead, will have just one sixth of the height and in terms of weight, it will not be even a penny of the first."

"Then with more reason I ask myself, what is the point of making them so weak?"

"You see, the current species is large, heavy, almost unassailable, but it is so because we put it at the top of the food chain, so it had to have from the beginning the ability to dominate all other species, regardless of having already developed intelligence. However, despite its armored appearance, full of teeth and claws, it is a mild species, just because it is so powerful, it does not feel threatened by anyone. In fact, it has dominated for a whole cycle without having brought to extinction any species, large or small. They have very affectionate parental care and never fight each other. In short, they are a true masterpiece of harmony."

"Well?" replied the Ethics.

"Well, if we would make a species of such a kind and endow it with that contrast between males and females, they would become extinct in no time by killing themselves each other."

"Are you really sure?"

"More than sure, very sure also because we have already included similar species, just to try, and you know what happened? They all became extinct. Aggressive and also well armed? No, in order for that strategy of violence to work, it is necessary to remove all natural weapons from them, so they will not have the means to destroy themselves, at least in the initial phase of the Project. They will be a soft species with a skin that will open at the first claw so that any predator, even smaller than them or even tiny, will be able to hunt them."

"In short, we make them weak and throw them into a big hunt where they will be the main prey, a real hell" concluded Ethics.

"No not at all. An environment where they will be prey to anyone will not be the worst thing. Hell, the real one, we will put it into them with that contrast between genres, even if the old man is right in saying that when you use that word, hell I mean, you don't really know what you are talking about. You know, between you and me" continued the Evolutionary Systems Engineer, lowering his voice, "only he knows exactly what hell is and it better be so."

"Yeah" said the Ethic, "he is the hell."

3rd interlude

"All that discussion, I found it absurd" said the Energy Systems Engineer, "and then that concern for time! The time does not exist!"

"For us it does not exist, because we just are, but for those who have a life cycle with an end, time does exist" replied the Irrational Systems Technician.

"Well, for me there is only what can be quantified, this mysterious time then, how would you measure it?" asked the Energy Systems Engineer.

"As for the effects of the Project we measure it in cycles, but in fact, I understand what you mean, it is not a measure of time, it is just a count of laps. But I can tell you how they will measure it", replied the Irrational Systems Technician. "First of all they will look for something that repeats itself, a reliable and always the same event. For example, the revolution motion of the planet around their star, which I think is three nanocycles, more or less, could become their unit of time. Then they will count how many units their life will last and here they will have quantified the time."

"It can work" admitted the Energy Systems Engineer, "and how much life will they have?"

"With precision I do not know, we should ask the Biologist. I think about a hundred units."

"But it is very little! Only 300 nanocycles, in practice they can do almost nothing. Only to make that calculation during the meeting, the Physicist took ... how long did he take? Almost a nanocycle!" exclaimed the Energy Systems Engineer.

"It took even longer if I remember correctly and he was also fast with all those metric tensors. Would you know how to diagonalize a three-dimensional matrix in your mind?"

"Well, even balancing a star isn't a game and I do it all the time."

"Yes, of course" replied the Irrational Systems Technician cutting short, "however I think it was necessary to fix it so short to ensure sufficient evolution in half a cycle. They have calculated that it will take a million and a half generations, even if in my opinion they have kept it quite wide."

"We're about to make a real monstrosity. We make them weak, we crush them under the weight of a conflict between the two genders, we give them even a small amount of life and we hope that a good species will come out of all this."

"It is in the difficulties that one sees good character" replied the Irrational Systems Technician.

"Listen Wizard, spare me your pearls of wisdom, the reduction of a problem to an aphorism is not wisdom, it is incompetence. With too many difficulties you will only get a paranoid species. They will see enemies everywhere, they will be clinging to that little life of theirs and obsessed with protecting themselves, so they will become so aggressive that they will destroy whatever comes within their reach, and what's more, half of them will also be obsessed with overpowering the other half."

"Eh yap" replied the Irrational Systems Technician, "to reproduce themselves they will have to develop some qualities, the intelligence hopefully."

"Or perhaps instead of intelligence they will develop skills such as deception, betrayal and cunning, which in the end give the same result."

"It's true and I'm sure they will, but they will only be able to deceive those individuals who can't understand the difference, that is the stupid, who being stupid, won't survive much."

"You hope so. Be aware that in all the species, the stupid always tend to become the majority because stupidity is less tiring."

"This should not be the case. Their environment will be too difficult for those who will not have enough head."

"But it will happen when they overwhelm it, then the fools will take over."

"Unfortunately yes but at that point they will already be far ahead of the Project and it will not matter. But I fear that with all that pressure, they will become a species tending towards self-destruction. In fact, if I was to exist in those conditions, I would not want to exist" concluded the Irrational Systems Technician.

"Couldn't we make them already evolved? We would have saved them and their world a lot of trouble" opined the Energy Systems Engineer.

"I wish it were that simple. Unfortunately we are talking about thinking beings, and thinking beings can't help but wonder about themselves. Therefore they will have to convince themselves that they are the authors of their destiny and for this to happen, they will have to come from a past of sure natural evolution so that they can attribute it to themselves. This will produce in them an unconditional confidence in their own abilities. If we did not do so, we would only get passive beings that would spend their lives worshipping creative Gods, that is, us, expecting them to provide for the future. Believe me, an evolutionary past is the greatest gift we will give them."

"Divinity us?" said the Energy Systems Engineer sarcastically, "don't make me laugh!"

"Everyone has his own Gods my friend, who depends only on how wide his horizon is. For a newborn being, the creative Gods are their parents" said the Irrational Systems Technician in a somewhat mocking tone as he was moving away.

4th interlude

"So how do we solve this evolutionary push?" asked the Evolutionary Systems Technician to the Biologist, "we must make sure that they cannot be taken away from it and at the same time that they are not completely dominated by it."

"A difficult balance" replied the Biologist. "Normally, the balance of a species is determined by the opposition of two forces: the instinct to reproduce, because of which no vital species can limit itself, and the environment with its limited resources. However, in the new species, the evolutionary force will be too intense to find a balance with the environment, also because in order to give course to such a force, the species had to be untied from the food chain so the environment will not only not be able to limit it, but will necessarily be overwhelmed by it. The balance must therefore be intrinsic to the species itself" concluded the Biologist.

"That's right" replied the Evolutionary Systems Engineer, "and the only way to get it is that one gender will have to balance the other. How do you plan to solve the problem?"

The Biologist started to think for a while, and then he replied "since in order to obtain that intense evolutionary force, we must introduce a very strong reluctance in one genre, it follows that the other must be given an equally strong reproductive push. This will lead to balance but one of the two genres will end up being totally dominated by the reproductive instinct. You are telling me that we should avoid that very dominance, aren't you?"

"Exactly, it is exactly like that, otherwise that reality of perennial conflict that we have so clearly identified at the meeting, will become something explosive that will lead the species to self-destruction, I can assure you" replied the Evolutionary Systems Technician.

"You know, whether the species is violent or very violent, it doesn't really matter to me. The important thing is that it is vital and if it develops in the midst of a hurricane of brutality, well, for me it is a way like any other. You argue that instead it will destroy itself. Is this your conjecture or can you even prove it?" asked the Biologist.

"I can prove it" said the Evolutionary Systems Technician. "These will be thinking beings and thoughts have their own strength. If the two genders will be in biological balance, when you add the thoughts to the balance, you will realize that the balance is no longer there. Living half of them in a reality of perennial sexual dissatisfaction, their thoughts will always have a background of repressed aggressiveness, so above the biological balance will shine a constant aggressive nature that will be directed not only to the other half, but also to themselves. In conclusion, if their thoughts are left free, they will always act towards self-destruction. We have to control those thoughts and the only way to control something, you know it too, is to put an engine and a brake on it" concluded the Evolutionary Systems Engineer, "did I convince you or do I need to show you with an equation of balance?"

"You convinced me, you don't need to bring out all your algebraic formalism" said the Biologist. "You are right, in thinking beings instinct is only one of the forces at stake. We have to put an engine and a brake on their thoughts, let me think about."

The Biologist immersed himself again in silence.

"Here I am" he exclaimed after much thought, "as an engine we make them disproportionate sexual characters, which will in this way induce a fixed thought in them, and as a brake we instill a sense of guilt for having them so large. I'll take care of the former, and for the latter we'll ask the Wizard, what do you say?"

"To both the genders?"

"Yes."

"But one of them has internal sexual organs, has it not? Small or big, will make no difference."

"Right, but that genus will also have mammary organs, we'll make those protruding."

"I don't see what sex has to do with breastfeeding."

"It has a lot to do with it; after all, breast organs are always a gender character."

"Maybe, however I believe that this solution will be good for one genre, but not for the other. The sense of guilt will always act in the same direction as reluctance. If already reluctant you put also the shame in it, you will paralyze it completely" opined the Evolutionary Systems Engineer.

"Right, so to compensate for the sense of guilt that we have to give to it, we also program a sense of overestimation of itself. Those who have a sense of guilt tend to diminish themselves, so with a bit of conceit we compensate them. We certainly cannot compensate them with desire, because this would cancel the reluctance and goodbye evolutionary force. Do you think this could work?"

The Evolutionary Systems Technician thought a little bit about it. "A bit complicated but I think so, even if in this way they will come out more than twisted. Aggressive, dissatisfied and with a sense of superiority? They will be a frightening species."

"It could be but I don't think so" replied the Biologist, "and then as long as they are only primitive animals, who cares if they feel like superior beings. They will have no way to really behave as such, and then over time they will develop a balance. When they will be able to understand that the origin of their aggressiveness is just the reluctance of a genus, they will strive to cancel it and the beauty of this castle of forces dependent on each other is that when they succeed, all other factors will automatically decay. On the other hand, when this happens, they will already be much evolved and therefore the evolutionary push will no longer have much importance, for the goods of the Project".

"It seems to me that we have found a good solution" said finally the Evolutionary Systems Technician, but his tone lacked that satisfaction as when you come to an all-round solution of a problem. A little doubtfully he added: "however, to this result of discovering one's own nature should get a genus that in addition to being reluctant, we will also create totally irrational, because it is obvious that otherwise it would not persist in reluctance, which in reality in sexual species does not make any sense. As if a flower refuses to be pollinated for no known reason. How do you hope they will succeed?"

"Not alone, that's for sure" said the Biologist cheerfully, who evidently already had the answer handy.

"And who will help them?"

"It's obvious, the other kind, who else?"

"How, with persuasion?"

"Of course not, it will be impossible! How do you want irrational beings to let themselves be persuaded to abandon a behavior they consider appropriate, which is then a constraint that we have imposed on them. They will do it with the help of some technological means, a club for example."

"And what will prevent the other kind from getting a club too?"

"Oh, it will certainly do that, it will be a race to the biggest club" said the Biologist grinning, "then when they will live in perpetual headaches, they will realize that it is better to solve the problem in another way, so they will use culture."

"Bad thing the culture in similar matters" meditated the Evolutionary Systems Technician, "also because every culture always generates an opposite culture."

"True, and I'm sure this will happen too, but it is obvious that a counter-culture that will emphasize reluctance, will die by itself because every group in which the reluctant genre will prevail, will quickly extinguish, precisely because, being dominated by such an instinct, it will reproduce little or nothing."

"Right, they will be free to do as they please, but only the groups in which the aggressive genre dominates will survive, in other words, they will do as we want."

The two looked satisfied.

5th interlude

"The old man makes it easy. Proceed, he says, but it's a lot of calculations here" said the Joker.

"It seemed to me a brilliant solution" replied the Physicist, "perfidious but brilliant. I'm sure the old man liked it a lot. It must have reminded him of something when he was going crazy all over the universe, and then for him creating a little confusion is like giving birth to a new child. I'm convinced that inside he was laughing."

"Do you think he was laughing at an event that will destroy everything we've done so far?"

"And why not, not for nothing we call him that way, but let's come to the calculations. First, however, I have a question: when we will have calculated the necessary mass, how are you going to make the planet hit by an asteroid of precisely that mass?"

"Right, it will be impossible to predict what will strike what, there will be only a big bombardment" replied the brooding Joker. "Well, that's it, let's forget a unique event, let's systematically bombard with lots of small bolides until we've shaved everything to the ground, what do you say?"

"It seems to me much better and we won't have to do any orbital perturbation calculations, just the bombardment time is enough, which is soon done. Of course everything that flies will have a chance to survive, have you thought about that?"

"Right, there are also animals with wings. Bah, they won't survive long without their environment, or they will adapt quickly to the new one, which is the same for us. Let's proceed"

27

replied the Joker.

Like two old schoolmates, the Physicist and the Joker cheerfully calculated the way to generate the largest apocalypse the planet had ever suffered.

"So, let's say that every bolide, which in the end will be little more than a stone, devastates a circular area. We divide the surface of the planet by that area and we get the minimum number of bolides."

"And for the seas what do we do?" asked the Joker.

"Let's bombard those too, to be sure" the Physicist continued carelessly. "Here it is, we need half a million bolides. Now, in order to have half a million bolides that actually fall on the planet, we need to set in motion many more of them, because most of them will miss the target. So, since the bolides will disperse all over the orbital plane inside the asteroid belt, let's take the area inside the orbit of the belt and divide it by the impact section of the planet, which is then the probability of collision. We multiply the result by the number of bolides that have to hit the planet and we get the number of bolides that we have to set in motion. Here it is, eighty million. Not so many, I feared more. Now you can go ahead, it's your specialty" said the Physicist.

"Certainly" answered the Joker. "So, now the density of the asteroid belt is such that the probability of collision between two asteroids is two per billion. That is, only two out of a billion, hitting each other, leave the belt. In order to get a rain of eighty million bolides, it is enough that I remodel the probability to three per million for a picocycle[5], let's make it four per million, better to keep safe so we are sure of the result and make the old man much happier."

"We forgot one thing" added the Physicist.

"What?"

"The vacuuming effect of the planet's moon, some of those rocks will hit the moon also because as a moon is really big."

---

[5] picocycle = 0.0003 years or about 2 and a half hours

"Damn it is true! All right, I'll sort it out. Before I start, I kick it away."

"You're kidding!" exclaimed the Physicist, "maybe you missed the fact that a satellite like that is essential for life, we chose that planet precisely for its moon. First of all, that moon is the great ladle that generates the tides and continuously stirs the seas, which otherwise would soon become rotten and putrid swamps, like all still waters. Yes I know what you're thinking, there are also currents of salinity and temperature, but they are not enough by themselves to stir everything and then they don't arrive in every ravine, while the tides arrive everywhere. Then there is the vacuum cleaner effect. If there wasn't that satellite, life would never have been able to grow enough. After all, what we are doing here is making bigger something that happens anyway, and this is the ingenious subtlety of your plan: it will seem a catastrophic event but still a natural event and no one could ever classify it as our intervention. Is it something you thought about or did it just comes to you by chance?"

"Obviously I thought of it!" exclaimed the Joker irritated. "Anyway, I bow to your wisdom, so how much do I correct the calculation?"

"I would triple the number; at least two thirds of the stats will be eaten by the satellite."

"All right."

"Just out of curiosity, how long will last the event in terms of the unity of their time?" asked the Physicist.

"Oh, only a sixth of unity, it will be a very quick event" replied the Joker with a sneer.

6th interlude

"You know, the old man sometimes scares me" said the Irrational Systems Technician to the Biologist, "like with his reference to hell, which who knows what it is then."

The Biologist stared the Wizard with a slightly sinister look and then replied: "In a certain sense he is the hell. Hell for us is just a word by which we mean all our possible fears, and since everyone has their own fears, one could say that everyone has their own hell but in this sense it is only a semantic subtlety, stuff worthy of the rhetoric of the Ethical Systems Technician."

"Then what is it, a place, an idea, an experience?"

"Neither one nor the other" replied the Biologist. "Hell is to be alone, and among all of us only the old man has passed. Hell is the absence of everything. You just exist. You exist but apart from you there is nothing else, only emptiness and you who realize you exist without any purpose. Your thoughts wrap themselves in themselves, they knot endlessly and in the end you become mad. For the old man anything was preferable to that absolute emptiness, to that nothing. The worst of events, the most furious violence, the most horrendous form of matter, is far preferable for him to the nothingness in which he has been."

"I understand. So we could say that he created everything."

"One cannot really say that something is created. It's a trap that immediately generates the paradox from which one doesn't come out anymore. If you think that something is created, without realizing it you introduce the time and then, you will only wonder what was before the beginning and what will be after the end. Consequently, if the universe had a beginning and an end it would also have borders and then you will only wonder what is beyond the borders, which is clearly a paradox. So you see that as soon as you introduce time, you can only get to absurd thoughts. Time does not exist. The universe is, has always been and will always be there. But it can exist in various forms, ask the Physicist, he has a word and also a law to describe the forms with which the universe can be organized, he calls it entropy. The old man didn't create anything, he just changed entropy, that is messed up everything and it was at that moment that something started to happen. After all, everything was born from hell and everything will end up in hell. Then the old man will start all over again."

2 GENESIS

When the Project Committee met again, everything was already decided and the meeting was so much a formality that the CH.A.O.S. simply attended the work without saying a word.

"So" began the G.O.D., "first of all I will summarize the choices of the previous meeting, exposing broadly the new Project. First we decided to conclude the old Project before starting the new one. Are the genetic sequences of the new species already set?"

Immediately replied the Biologist, "Yes Director, we have five thousand new species ready."

"Aren't they a bit scant?" opined the G.O.D.

"It is true they are few, but since the parameters of the new environment are not predictable, because of the turbulent way in which the planet will be emptied and who knows what environment will come out of it, in making many of them we would have wasted a lot of work, since most of them will be extinguished immediately because we cannot adapt them at projecting stage to conditions we do not know. So we preferred to make a few but all of them with short-term, and even hereditary, forking capabilities."

"Biological Systems Engineer" set in the CH.A.O.S., "explain us what a fork is."

"Sure Chairman, I was going to do it" said the Biologist. "A fork, a word much used by our helpers programmers and sequencers of genetic codes, is the ability of a species to divide into two subspecies, in short a bifurcation, or briefly fork, of the evolutionary line. We distinguish it from a mutation because the second is a minor variation, while a fork is a substantial variation. In practice, after a fork we always have two new species with very different characteristics. Of course, an insect fork, for example, can never produce an insect and a large animal, but it can produce two very different insects that in turn will do the same, eventually obtaining a family from a prototype. Obviously, the whole family will remain linked to very similar characteristics, but in practice each one will consist of many species. The proto butterfly fork will produce diurnal and nocturnal butterflies, for cold and hot, dry and humid climates and so on. With thousands of forks, perfectly suitable species will spontaneously appear, as well as totally unsuitable species, it is obvious, but since the latter will become extinct by themselves, the environment will automatically fill up with only suitable species."

"Brilliant" commented the CH.A.O.S. after hearing the explanation.

"Thanks Chairman" replied proud the Biologist.

"Engineer, experience has taught me that the perfect solution does not exist, there are always side effects" said the G.O.D., "in this case, what are the side effects of a hereditary fork?"

The Biologist nodded and invited the Ecosystem Technician to answer, who immediately took the floor.

"In species with a cellular dimension, which reproduce at a very high rate, the hereditary fork will have the effect of an enormous proliferation. In other words, there will be a proliferation of unpredictable bacteria, i.e. diseases. This is one of the two side effects, but it is not as bad as it seems. Diseases, in fact, by eliminating weak individuals are the system to maintain life healthy."

"Certainly, and the other effect?" asked the G.O.D.

"The other effect is that in the genetic sequences will remain the parts that are no longer used, archaic excerpts that will no longer be needed, but to the careful eye will show that there has been programming or, in other words, will be proof of our existence. But I don't think they will ever find out" added the Ecosystems Engineer, "anyway the fork won't last forever, little by little the effect will be lost and it will be reduced to a mere tendency to mutation."

"Excellent" commented the G.O.D., "so we are ready for the new environment. Has the elimination of the old environment already been completed?"

"Not yet" replied the Joker, "I waited for you all to agree, even if the operation already had the backing of the old m... of the Chairman."

"I would say that the line of action is now clear" said the G.O.D. looking at the CH.A.O.S. who assented in silence, "Kinetic Technician, you can certainly proceed" he added with a cold tone, knowing that with that order he had condemned an entire world to death.

The Joker didn't get it said again. While the meeting continued, in the distant asteroid belt some rocks changed imperceptibly the course.

"Following the preliminary phase of planetary reset, we will implant the new sequences on cellular supports" continued the G.O.D., "from them will develop the new ecosystem in which the new species will be included. By the way Engineer, will the new species also be equipped with forks?"

"No" replied the Biologist firmly, "if we would give it a fork, it could happen that its programming changes, that is its behavior in line with the Project would not be guaranteed, so we thought to implant it only after the stabilization of the new planetary system."

"Sure, and in this case, how did you make sure they will fit the new ecosystem?"

"Oh, they won't have any problems" replied the Ecosystems Engineer, "versatility will be their most important feature. In fact, they will lack any kind of specialization."

"Well" replied the reassured G.O.D., "let us now move on to the question of the evolutionary push, which is then the reason why we have to redo the whole Project. We have agreed that, given its high intensity, its undesirable effects on behavior are regulated by a pair of opposing forces. The first is an oversized reproductive morphology; the second is a coercive field in mental processes. How was this field realized?" asked the G.O.D.

The Irrational Systems Technician replied.

"The two genders must have a different coercive field, which is very easy because it was enough to tie the field to the sexual sequence part, so each individual will always have the right field according to their gender. I applied the logical reduction analysis to the problem and the result is surprisingly simple. The coercive field that has to produce an excessive self-evaluation has been realized with a trick in the brain's center of the language. In practice, the word that they will think, and in time they will say more frequently, will be *me*."

A whisper of surprise ran through the meeting.

"Really an elegant solution, congratulations!" exclaimed the G.O.D.

"Thank you Director, but unfortunately the solution for guilt is not as elegant in the same way. The logical reduction analysis has not produced an equally simple result."

"Tell us this solution then" said the G.O.D. immediately frowning.

"A sense of sexual guilt in a sexualized species does not really make any sense, it is quite obvious. It is therefore clear that the thought can only be irrational and therefore not reducible to a simple concept or word, so it must be a sentence. However, while you can pre-implant a single concept in a linguistically programmable language center, anyhow it will be later pronounced, like the concept *me*, you can't do it with a sentence. Bearing this problem in mind, I was able to reduce the sense of guilt to just two words. However, they can also be used separately, producing two other unwanted and therefore to a certain extent, even pernicious thoughts. The two words are: naked, forbidden. By implanting these two concepts in the center of the language, they will appear to them in most thoughts. In one genre these two words will also be often associated with the signifier I, with the result of producing an obsession with what is an almost full meaning sentence , that is: *I naked forbidden*, to which we must add the possible permutation *I forbidden naked* whose full meaning is twofold, *I forbid naked* and *I am forbidden naked*. When instead the words will appear separate, *naked* will produce a continuous attention for nude precisely, which unfortunately will weaken the wanted coercive field, while *forbidden* will continue to suggest them to forbid something. So they will have fun imposing prohibitions of any kind without actually having a reason, so prohibitions even without meaning."

"For example?" asked the Joker.

"Well, I believe that first of all, sex will be forbidden, even though it is a fundamental activity in life. The prohibition will be so pregnant that although they will have evidence that sexuality is inherent in every species around them, they will not be able to understand it, or they will refuse to understand it. Then they will ban foods, despite being omnivorous, places, special chemicals, special behaviors such as using one hand rather than the other and so on."

"In fact, it seems to me a bit smudged solution" said the G.O.D., "but given the brilliant evidence you gave us in the first case, I'm sure it could not have been done better."

"Thank you Director" replied the Irrational Systems Technician.

"So let's continue" went on the G.O.D. "Once the new species has been planted, our intervention is over, what are the development forecasts?"

The Diffused Systems Technician intervened.

"In one hundredth of a cycle they will occupy the entire available space and at the same time they will develop languages. In the next thousandth of a cycle organized communities will appear, then an era of fights will begin that with the technological development will become wars. It will be a very critical time, especially when technology will become advanced, but it will not extend to more than a tenth of a cycle. They will live a reality of almost continuous war, which in fact they could avoid if they could understand the origin of the aggressiveness of their species, which indeed is impossible because they will always be governed by their irrational side. Finally in two tenths of a cycle they will come to the understanding of space and will be able to make interstellar journeys. At this point they will still have two tenths of a cycle to spread in space and prepare for the intergalactic jump when the intersection between the two galaxies will occur."

"Well, I would say that the Project is complete and ready to be implemented, but there is still a question to which we must find a certain answer: is it possible that the species will be able to free itself from the trace imposed by the Project?" the G.O.D. asked.

"Impossible" replied the Biologist firmly, "To free themselves they should be able to modify the programming instructions contained in their genetic code but to do so they should reverse the fractal algorithm with which we encoded it, which is impossible because of the chaotic nature of fractals. At a certain stage of development they will start playing with their code, but they will only be blind manipulations and in short they will realize that it is a road that leads nowhere and then they will abandon it, of course not before having produced a great deal of horrors. Actually the way to manipulate their code, that is the selection, will always be in front of their eyes but they will never see it because, seen how we made them, it won't be a species ruled by intelligence."

"And what will it be governed by then, according to you" asked the G.O.D.

"From irrationality."

"I would not be so sure" said the Wizard, "the unexpected always happens."

3 APOCALYPSE

"Daddy, who was there before you and Mommy?"

"There was my daddy and my mommy, and before them, their daddy and their mommy, and before them yet another daddy and another mommy, and so it has always been as long as we remember for hundreds of millions of years" replied Gordon affectionately rubbing the long neck on the rough back of his son crouched between his paws, "and it will always be so", he added.

Suddenly a bright light shone in the night sky. Gordon stretched his head to soar above the forest of tree ferns.

Or maybe not, he barely had time to think, seeing large globes of white light that in a split second and in absolute silence illuminated the whole sky.

4 CREATION

"What a big fuss! The Joker is really terrifying, I would never want to have him as an enemy" said the Biologist. "Ten microcycles have already passed and the effect of the bombardment has not yet dissipated. Look there in the sky those brown clouds, it's dust from the earth."

"On the other hand, it's very warm" said his assistant, splashing merrily on the shore.

"Let's do what we came for" said the Biologist, "throw the eggs in the water, except the marked one. Look here, there is still a lot of stuff from the previous system, there are spores everywhere and those are bird droppings. In fact, I thought I saw some movement in the air. They survived all that bombardment. Tough stuff, we did it well" he added proudly.

"Is that bad?" asked the assistant.

"I don't think so. They are species suitable for an environment that is no longer there, they will not proliferate much."

"Done" said the assistant after throwing the eggs into the sea, "what do we do now?"

"We wait" replied the Biologist.

"We wait for what?"

"Let's wait for the forks to take effect, it won't be long."

Only five microcycles had passed when, breaking large waves, the back of a giant being appeared in the sea and immediately disappeared with a big puff of steam.

"Did you see that?" said the assistant biologist excitedly, "it was a monstrous being, what was it?"

"Who knows, the results of the forks are unpredictable, but have you seen that jet of steam? It is a species that needs air.

Very well, soon it will populate the mainland too."

"In fact, now that I notice it, it seems to me that there is already a different smell. The stench of burning that was there when we arrived is no longer there, now I seem to smell like rotting."

"I believe it" replied the Biologist, "look over there at those distant lands on the horizon, don't you think they have another color?"

"Yes, they are no longer brown; they look more like dark green, vegetation?"

"Certainly, and in a little while we will see the contribution to the Project of our friends of Aesthetic Systems. I'm really curious, they insisted on not telling us anything, so as not to spoil the surprise, they said."

Only four microcycles passed before the two heard a buzz. The noise came closer, passed by them and then faded away.

"What was it?" asked the assistant.

The Biologist was radiant. "An insect. Let's follow it, which way did it go?"

"That way it seems to me."

The two moved quickly.

"Look!" said the enthusiastic Biologist.

"What is it?"

In the middle of the brown of the coast had appeared a colored speckle, orange and yellow.

"A flower" exclaimed the Biologist, "beautiful, our artists have worked well. And look there, another, and also different."

As they progressed, flowers of all species opened before them in a blaze of color. The air was filled with movement and buzzing, the scent of plant life pervaded the atmosphere. Suddenly, in the midst of the plants they saw a rapid movement that immediately disappeared.

"And what was that?" said the assistant.

"An animal. I could not tell you which species, but its presence confirms to me that we are close to the exhaustion of the fork effect. By now the whole environment is occupied, we can proceed with the last sequence."

They quickly returned to the coast, where the assistant threw the remaining egg into the sea.

"Why didn't we implant that one right away? What species is it?" asked the assistant.

"Explaining it to you is complicated, it is part of the general design of the Project."

"Oh, the inscrutable drawings of the G.O.D."

"Yap!" replied the Biologist, "now it takes a little patience, it won't be very quick. In the meantime we can do a little bit the tourists in this new environment. I am curious to see what it is filled with."

At the end of a hundred microcycles they had travelled all over the planet and had returned to their starting point which they had some difficulty in recognizing because during their absence the desolate landscape of the coast had changed into a dense arboreal vegetation full of noises and squeaks.

Suddenly, a small, hairy creature appeared hanging from a branch with one hand, looking around with curiosity.

"We're done here, we can go" said the biologist smiling when he saw it.

5 EVOLVED MEN

"Hey Jack, aren't you sick of these females? They've gotten old."

"We too have become old Josh."

"It doesn't seem to me, how much time do we have?"

"I don't know. What day is today?"

"That's just it, we always stay the same until a tiger or something else takes us away, while they seem to fall apart after nine or ten babies. What do you say, shall we go on a raid?"

"When?"

"This evening. I smelled a horde not far from here."

"Modern or primitive?"

"Primitives, we'll take them out in a second and take all the females with us."

"Primitives are real troglodytes Josh, they don't even talk."

"Yes, because you talk to the females, don't you? And what do you tell them? And then how many modern females are there around?"

"In fact, few and most are the ones we did."

"And with them, go move them! They are there all day long confabulating who knows what; they have got into their heads that fathers cannot fertilize their daughters. Imagine that! Since the dawn of time we've always done it. It's the most natural thing, as all animals do."

"That's why you want to go and raid another horde."

"You'll see, sooner or later they'll extend that ban to brothers and maybe even to cousins, but it's an absurd thing since in a horde we are all related. They could better say that they don't want to, period, and that's it. The other day my brother tried to fertilize one of them, I think a daughter of mine, who reacted like a fury and almost took his eye out. We had to club her for half an hour before she came to her senses. Troglodytes are much less tiring. They don't have their head full of nonsense because of all that talking, since they don't speak at all. With them, one club is enough to resign, in fact in some ways they are more intelligent, they know that the first club will be followed by others and in the end they will have to do it anyway, so they save themselves the trouble of being slaughtered first. Listen to me Jack, we'd better take advantage of them while there are still some around, and the children come out well with them and even if they walk on all fours, you just kick them in the ass for a couple of seasons and they straighten up like a lightning bolt."

"What is a lightning bolt?"

"I don't know, nice idea though, straight as a lightning bolt, sounds good."

"I wonder why children come out modern even with the primitives."

"You really don't understand Jack, do you? It's clear, because we put the children inside them! What matters is the father, don't you think?"

"You think so? But every now and then some hunchback comes out."

"It will be when you can't put in it right. You know, like when a running rhinoceros comes out of the blue at the very worst moment."

"It happened to me, you know? I've been suffering from spinal sciatica since that time, and I feel like I'm also a little squint."

6 FIRST DISCONTINUITY

To the meeting of the Project Committee, presided as always by the Chairman of the Absolute Order of Space-time, only the General Operations Director, the Biological Systems Engineer, the Evolutionary Systems Technician and the Diffused Systems Technician were present.

The first to speak was of course the CH.A.O.S.

"It seems that an anomalous situation has occurred in the development of the Project. We are here to evaluate this situation and therefore this meeting is restricted to the competent figures only. General Operations Director, would you like to tell us what happened?"

"Certainly Chairman, but at first I would give the floor to the Evolutionary Systems Technician to whom I ask to illustrate the content of his latest report" replied the G.O.D.

"Yes, so, a microcycle ago occurred what at first glance seems to be the first discontinuity of the second species. Obviously the fact in itself is not unexpected, but in my opinion this discontinuity is so sharp that it has more the characteristic of a fork."

"A fork in the species of Project?" asked the Biologist with a dry tone.

"Yes" insisted the Evolutionary Systems Technician.

"Impossible!" said then the Biologist.

"I thought so too" replied the Evolutionary Systems Engineer, "but a little while ago a part of the species has developed substantial improvements. The consequence is that now we have two very different subspecies, even if the morphological characteristics are not so different because otherwise there would have been no doubt to have witnessed a fork. Obviously these new improvements have produced a discontinuity. In fact, a subspecies is now migrating because it is escaping from the systematic extermination that the most evolved subspecies has implemented against them. So far, everything is going as planned, but there is more."

The Evolutionary Systems Technician took a break, arousing impatience in everyone.

"The fact is that the first subspecies has undergone two substantial improvements at the same time" continued the Technician.

The Biologist emitted a puff of annoyance. "Who ever said that a mutation cannot concern different parts of the genetic code? A mutation is a mutation, and its effect can include one or more systems. There is no reason to talk about a double mutation just because there were two different effects" concluded in a dry tone.

"I am convinced of this too" replied the Evolutionary Systems Technician calmly, "and yet I insist that we are at the presence of a double mutation. This for me is equivalent to saying that we are in front of a fork. I wonder: can a species autonomously develop a fork capacity?"

The Biologist's dry response was not long in coming: "No, it cannot. A fork is a real project, a project within a project and therefore cannot appear by chance, just as one cannot have a spontaneous apparition of life. Amino acids can be combined in a random way producing chains even very long, but from the length to the fact of having a sense it's a long way to go. It is as if one hopes to compose a book by lining up thousands of letters at random. Surely many words would be formed but not even trying for millions of cycles would be able to obtain an intelligible, coherent and error-free story, as is necessary to have a working code in all its parts. Life cannot develop by chance; it cannot be formed piece by piece, because to be vital it must have all the systems working from the very first moment. To have life there must be a project, period."

"Well said!" the CH.A.O.S. intervened with a deep and smug

tone.

The G.O.D. took the word again by addressing the Evolutionary Systems Technician. "To speak without referring to the facts only leads to useless discussions. Can you illustrate us what these two changed characteristics consist of, and tell us why you think they are two separate mutations?"

"Yes Director, it is soon said. The first is an increased development of a motor muscle, indeed, given the almost symmetrical nature of the species, of a pair of motor muscles."

"Of the adductor muscles of the hind limbs" added the Biologist, who obviously also knew about it.

"Exactly" nodded the Evolutionary Systems Technician, "this allowed them to stand upright on both hind limbs. In fact, now this subspecies has a somewhat bizarre shape. Behind it has two big bulges that protrude clearly from the longitudinal axis of their body" added the Technician, but nobody paid attention to his digression.

"And what will be the effect of this mutation?" asked the G.O.D.

"There is no need to guess because the effect has already happened" replied the Evolutionary Systems Technician. "The upright posture frees the front limbs from motor function, which can therefore be used in other ways during movement. The species had already started to use tools but only standing still and sitting. Now instead they are able to use a tool even while moving. The consequence was immediate: they rushed sticks to the hand to massacre the males of another group and appropriate their females. The other group, even if they also had sticks, could only succumb to what was a real blitzkrieg. The winning group, given the abundance of females thus obtained, had a sudden demographic expansion, obviously transmitting the new characteristic to their offspring. It seems to me therefore that this is a sure discontinuity."

"There are no doubts" assented the G.O.D., "tell us now about the other improvement."

"The same subspecies has begun to speak" said the

Evolutionary Systems Technician adding nothing else because the importance of the thing was evident in itself.

"And where would the mutation be?" asked the Biologist, "the species already emitted sounds before this discontinuity. It was inevitable that sooner or later they would agree to give meaning to each sound, which is equivalent to saying that they developed a language. So it is obvious that the individuals were already speaking."

"True" admitted the Evolutionary Systems Engineer, "but now the range of their sounds has increased enormously just out of the blue, and consequently the number of possible meanings, or words if you like. In fact, the first thing they did was to attribute themselves names and if up to this point the communication had as possible arguments only physical objects, now it also has abstract concepts, as names are. This is what I mean when I say that they have developed a real language."

"And this is a mutation for you?" asked the Biologist again.

"It seems obvious to me, something has happened to their center of language" replied the Evolutionary Systems Engineer.

"Mmh" nodded the Biologist, annoyed by the wrong deductions of the Evolutionary Systems Technician.

"Let me explain what happened" said the biologist, "the upright posture forced the species to hold its head in a completely different position. If in quadruped position the head was, so to speak, hanging from the neck, now it must necessarily be kept upright because having a not indifferent weight, it cannot recline forward otherwise it would unbalance the body and in this way they would only fall. The new posture has exercised the supporting muscles of the head that, being all the time tense, have taken on a completely different muscle strength. All the tissues of the neck have obviously been involved, including the vocal cords. With the new tension, as happens in a musical instrument, the vocal cords have increased the frequency of operation, and consequently the range of sounds they can produce. They already had the instrument to speak; they only tuned it to make it work better. In fact, the less evolved ones emit only gloomy and guttural sounds while the others have much louder voices don't they?"

The Biologist stopped but did not wait for an answer that he knew was yes. "As for the center of the language, it was already formed since the beginning of the Project, just to obtain that control over the behavior we talked about so much. Now in the new subspecies, it has simply begun to be fully functional, that's all. As for the names, they are only a first application of that programmed self concept, even if in only one of the two genres. Since now in that group the majority is female, i.e. the gender with the pre-programmed ego, with the new linguistic tool they reacted according to that program and thinking mainly about the ego, they obviously wondered how to distinguish between them. The method they adopted was to give each one a sound. In the end, the whole event was only a consequence of the Project" concluded the Biologist.

The Evolutionary Systems Technician remained a bit silent and then replied: "it must have gone just like that" he admitted. "Of course I think it's ironic that they developed a language as a result of the development of a butt".

"It could only go this way" said the Diffused Systems Technician, "after all, the most important parts of the species are those between the legs. For the effects of the general development of the Project, the most important parameter is not the spread of life itself?"

"That's right" added the Biologist, "the organs that count the most are those that we put in the most protected part of their body, i.e. at half height and could not be otherwise, it is obvious."

"Well" said then the G.O.D., "clarified that the current situation is only a discontinuity and that everything is proceeding according to the plan of the Project, is there anything else to talk about?"

Everyone remained silent.

7th interlude

"Igor, do not walk around home naked."

"Don't bother me Sveva, with all this heat I'm fine even so."

"You are indecent."

"What's wrong with me?"

"One can see all yours ... all the skin!"

"So what? We're not furry monkeys, what's wrong with that?"

"But but, and then one can see when ... yes come on, when it gets ... come on, you understand, it's not good."

"Are you being jealous? You don't want me to go around showing it?"

"Don't fool yourself; you are not the only one who has it."

"Hah! Who are you talking about?"

"Now you are the one who is being jealous. It's you guys who want us all; I can't say no otherwise I'll just get a good thrashing.”

"Well, for that matter, I'll have to beat you too. So you did it with someone else too!"

"Sure, all the times you're not here to look after us. As soon as you leave, someone new comes right away. More than anyone else the young people, it seems as if they were always ... but yes, in short ... you know what I mean, always with that thing of yours straight out like a stick."

"Mmmmmmm, I'm not overly fond of this thing Sveva, does this also apply to Ilona?"

"Of course, she is a female too, but you shouldn't complain so much, meanwhile where do you go? Don't you do the same thing somewhere else? Look, between us women, we talk to each other, eh!"

"Yes yes I know, you talk to each other even too much" replied Igor cutting short, "and when the other males arrive, what you two do?”

"And what do we do, we cover ourselves with pieces of

leather, but they come off easy. It should be ... mmmm ... forbidden, yes, forbidden to enter the other's home."

"Mmmm, I really don't like this story; I'll have to make something up. I could surround the hut with snap traps."

"Why don't you get me one of those furs like leopards wear, for example, instead of being an engineer, otherwise it will end up with us get trapped in your snap traps? Their furs are so pretty with all those little spots, and they don't come off easy, from them."

"Ah, sure not! Go skin them, not to mention catch them without being caught."

"I tie it on me and then I go around all leopard printed, what do you say?"

"Mmmmm, leopard printed eh?"

"For Ilona, you get her one of a tiger so she make the tiger printed, it is better if we are a little different."

"I do not know. But furs don't have the same shape you have, in my opinion you don't even fit in a leopard fur. Well yes, the body does, by dint of being frugivorous since when we are at the tropics, we have all become so athletic, so thin, but your legs and ass will never fit."

"Then a fur from a larger animal."

"And what, a buffalo? An elephant?"

"Come on Igor! Even a child would see that they are not my size, I am maybe a six!"

"No look, a six you were three years ago, now you are more an eight, maybe even a ten. I know why you can never find a banana in this house. Here I am! A gorilla's fur, a little plentiful, but it should suit you."

"Are you kidding me? You go put a gorilla on you! What do you want; make me regress to the age of the caves? I am a modern woman, I have a certain taste, and I can't wear the first primate you find around the forest! A gorilla, he says, and you want to send me around with a gorilla on my back? And what is it, carnival? It's true that we are at the tropics, but as far as I know we are still in Africa, not in ... I don't know, in Brazil!"

"And where would Brazil be?"

"Ah I don't know, certainly not here!"

"Then you know what? If you want a fur coat that fits you, you have to have it made to measure ... hooray!"

"What is it Igor?"

"I yelled it like that, but it's not a bad idea."

7 THE HISTORY BEGINS

"Have you heard?" said the Diffused Systems Technician to the Ethical Systems Technician.

"No, what happened?"

"They've lost their hair, come on, a meeting has been called."

The Chairman of the Absolute Order of Space-time cleared his voice to call the attention of those present who were immersed in a chaotic shouting.

"General Operations Director, initiate the meeting" said the CH.A.O.S.

"Gentlemen, the environmental conditions have changed" announced the G.O.D. with a serious voice, "so first thing first we must establish if the Project is in danger, in which case we will have to intervene. Secondly we would like to understand what has caused such an important environmental change. The Ecosystems Engineer will explain the change to those who are not yet aware of it".

The Ecosystems Technician took the floor.

"It's soon said, most of the surface of the planet has frozen" explained the Technician. "The reason for the phenomenon is that the planet has entered precession, the effect is that all species have concentrated in the equatorial belt where the climate remained warm. However, many species were suitable for a temperate climate, so in the equatorial heat they became extinct or adapted. The good news is that the Project species adapted."

"In what way?" asked the G.O.D.

"It lost its hair even if it didn't have much of it!" the angry biologist intervened, because there is nothing that makes an engineer as angry as changing a single comma of one of his projects.

"Is that all?" opined the G.O.D.

"That's all?!" echoed the Biologist, "and that's not enough for you? The hairs are very sensitive organs ready to react to the slightest movement of air. For those who have to survive in an environment where they are prey to almost everyone, it is as serious as losing their sight. And to make it even more serious, we are already observing a derived effect: they are changing the color of the skin and I am sure that this will have very important consequences" concluded the Biologist with dry tone.

"One point at a time, please" replied the G.O.D. "and then don't be so tragic, the hair loss was in the plans of the Project so it had to happen sooner or later. So let's start again: what led the planet to enter precession?"

"Uh, excuse me," said the Aesthetic Systems Engineer, "what exactly does it mean that the planet has entered precession?"

"Ah, the Painter!" exclaimed the G.O.D. "we have missed you. By the way, we all appreciated your work. In due time, we would be curious to know what you think of this novelty of color change in the species. Kinetic Technician, please explain to us what it means to enter the precession."

"It is soon said" replied the Joker. "It is an effect derived from the rotation of the planet. The axis of rotation of the planet is tilted to produce changing climatic conditions, i.e. the seasons. In fact, an always the same environment becomes monotonous, and this monotony is transferred to living species that are therefore conditioned to indolence. In addition, the seasons continuously stir the whole environment which in this way never becomes stagnant. The rotation axis had a fixed direction, because of the preservation of the moment of the momentum, so the seasons had a constant and balanced periodicity, i.e. so hot and so cold in every zone of the planet, poles excluded of course" and saying this, the Joker stopped to look at the Physicist who was listening to him carefully.

The Physicist made a gesture of confirmation and the Joker continued. "Now the axis of rotation rotates slowly like a spinning top does, just before falling. This is what is called precession. The consequence is that the planet has unbalanced seasons. When the cold seasons become longer, as it is happening now, the planet slowly cools down but then the reverse will happen and the planet will become hot again."

"In short, the environment froze and they all ran away on vacation to the tropics" commented the painter.

"We could put it like that" replied the Joker smiling.

"So why did it go into precession?" the G.O.D. resumed.

The Physicist made a nod to draw attention and give one of his obscure explanations beyond the capacity of understanding of those who knew nothing about general laws; even if he did not deliberately use incomprehensible words as often do those who try to mask a substantial ignorance.

"It happened because during the planetary reset, the resultant of the impact vectors did not pass exactly through the center of gravity of the planet" he said gloomily, sure not to be understood.

Naturally, his words were followed by a murmur of bewilderment.

The Joker, however, had understood very well to whom the criticism of the Physicist was directed, so he blurted out: "Yes, but it went through the center of the planet, we could have missed that target too and after all, that the center of gravity did not correspond exactly to the center was not possible to know."

"Given the asymmetrical distribution of continents" replied the Physicist, "it would be difficult for one to correspond exactly to the other."

"Yes, but how could I have calculated exactly the position of the center of gravity without knowing the distribution of masses on the surface of the planet, which are always moving?" the Joker replied angrily.

"You are the Kinetic Technician!" replied the mocking Physicist.

"Are you calling me incompetent?" replied the increasingly altered Joker.

Everyone was upset because when the Joker got angry there was no way to feel at ease.

"Gentlemen!" the G.O.D. intervened "can the axis of rotation be rebalanced?"

"No!" replied the Joker and the Physicist together.

"So your bickering is useless, now things are the way they are."

"Some disorder every now and then is healthy" said the CH.A.O.S. intervening surprisingly, winking at the Joker for whom he had never hidden to have a weakness. Perhaps that was why the Joker was so often so irritable, and even a little arrogant. Somehow, he felt protected by the immense power of the Chairman of the Absolute Order of Space-time.

After the bickering, the discussion resumed with a question from the Diffused Systems Technician.

"Why the effect of the precession did not appear immediately after the planetary reset but only now?"

"Yeah, why?" replied the Joker, hoping for some argument in his favor.

"I'll answer" said the Ecosystems Engineer. "The precession must have started immediately, but the planet was enveloped by an atmosphere full of residual dust from the bombardment with which we invested it, which together with the fumes of the intense volcanic activity derived, wrapped it in a consistent greenhouse effect that protected it from heat loss. When this was dispersed, the first phase of glaciation had already passed and it was necessary to wait for the next cold period for the phenomenon to occur for the first time. In the meantime the species was able to spread widely."

"Well" concluded the D.O, "as far as the precession is concerned everything seems clear to me and perhaps this story of glaciations will also have positive effects. The changes force the species to adapt and this will make it more and more versatile. Let's now come to the most important part and that is: what are the consequences for the species?"

"He always and only cares about his species" the Ecosystems

Engineer whispered to an assistant at his side, "he doesn't care about anything else. Half of the animals are extinct because of this glaciations, a real disaster for the environment and he doesn't even care about it."

"So is the G.O.D., his protégés will end up worshipping him" replied the assistant.

Feeling clearly called into question, the Evolutionary Systems Technician intervened.

"As the Biologist has already pointed out, a first consequence is already manifesting itself in the change of color of the skin that has remained glabrous. It seems that in groups closer to the equator, darker individuals are preferred in mating, with the result that the offspring inherit a gradually darker tone, while in groups further away from the equator light colors are preferred. In reality I have simplified a lot, although there is a certain order of color with respect to latitude, it would be more appropriate to say that each group prefers its own color, clearly due to the appearance of a certain aesthetic sense because the color is not functional in any way, otherwise they would all be khaki color, which in the environment where they live is the most suitable. On the contrary, I wonder why a modular system of skin pigmentation has been planned. In any case, the first consequence of hair loss is that the species will be divided into different color groups. This will naturally also have an effect on their physical appearance, since the continuous mutations will remain confined within each color group. This will cause one group to differ more and more from another not only in color, but also in appearance. In short, different races will be formed and I am also convinced, as the Biologist said, that this will have important consequences in their history. On the other hand, as far as the loss of the hair itself is concerned, as long as they remain in the equatorial areas, nothing will change at all, precisely because in such an environment the hair is almost irrelevant. For now, the only consequence has been that of a different perception of themselves, because of the irrational part we have programmed them. They started by discovering the *naked* concept , even compared to the species that have not lost their hair, and they are beginning to explore the more abstract concept of *forbidden.*"

"And how come the other species have not lost their fur?" asked the Energy Systems Technician, always prone to put his finger in the wound.

"But it's obvious" replied the Biologist promptly, "those for which the hair is functional have not lost it, because the hair is not only for keeping warm. There are those who use it for camouflage, those who use it for decoration, those who use it for defense. After all, it is a very hard molecule, even fireproof, a masterpiece of our Materials Section" added the Biologist with pride. "For this last reason even the species has not lost all its hair."

"All clear" said the G.O.D., "at this point it is appropriate to give the floor to the Irrational Systems Technician. Tell us what you think of this new glabrous skin."

"I think that with this mutation we have reached the very beginning of the true history of the species" replied the Wizard. "Only now, in fact, all the programmed systems have begun to be fully functional. From now on, the species will only be able to react according to our plans, as long as the part concerning long-term programming does not undergo mutations."

"There is no way" intervened the Biologist, "to avoid that in the species mutates just what leads to the evolutionary drive, we have made sure that the chemical system that determines it, i.e. hormones, is also essential to fix the bone structure and muscle development. So if an individual managed to free himself from the programmed evolutionary push, he would become weak and brittle bones, which will make it impossible for him to survive, let alone reproduce."

"Real slaves" commented the Wizard, "and what is worse, is that they will never know it."

"Oh, you broke our hearts with this thought of yours" interrupted him dryly the G.O.D., "existence is not substance, it is only perception so nobody is a slave until he perceive himself as such. And then have you ever thought that the slave, having no responsibility whatsoever, could also be the freest of all? Freedom is only an abstract concept that depends on how you look at it. Continue Wizard."

"Of course Director. So, the naked radical signifier, a concept that was incomprehensible as long as the hair was involved, began to appear in their thoughts as if they had invented it on the spot, helped also by the excellent exercise of learning abstraction through names."

The Wizard broke off a bit meditating and then said, how thinking out loud, "I must say that it had never occurred to me that names could be a gym for abstract thinking, it must be because of that, that the species is naming everything", then resumed his speech.

"In any case, if we had not programmed their language center, at this point the nude would not have produced any effect, indeed as a word it would not even be invented, because after all the nude is a natural state. In fact, in the future they will apply it to themselves but not to animals which in reality would be equally naked. Since we have inserted the word instead, the concept has appeared in their mind linked to the *forbidden* one, because that's how we programmed them. So they started to develop an obsession with the *naked is forbidden*, which is the only way to compose the two words."

The Wizard, who in speaking was the exact opposite of the Physicist, thus finished his acrobatic preamble and finally moved on to the considerations that everyone was waiting for.

"The prohibition of the nude has already led to the invention of the dress, which will have two effects. The first is that the reproductive drive will be frustrated, since dressing is a real mechanical obstacle to sex activity. Since every frustrated drive will only get stronger, they will quickly enter the period of violence on a large scale, that long phase that will bring them to the galactic civilization."

"Are you saying that all their wars will arise from the fact that by dressing, they will have frustrated the sexual impulse?", the

Evolutionary Systems Engineer interrupted him, "to me it doesn't seem so, after all they were still naked when in the first discontinuity they invented the bludgeoning marriage."

"Actually they weren't really naked yet, but it was fun, wasn't it?" replied the Wizard in a suddenly cheerful tone. "They will invent many more marriages, but one day or another they will discover that, for a deranged species like them, the one with bludgeons is the only one that really works.

"Also because they are not a monogamous species" added the Biologist.

"Oh no? And how come?" asked the Energy Systems Technician

"Monogamy is indicated to limit the proliferation of a species, as it is necessary to do for carnivores or predatory birds, where by monogamy we mean fidelity between two equal weights but different genres, not monogamy one to one between individuals which is obviously, totally absurd and, in fact, inapplicable. For example, the tyrannosaurs were monogamous and how faithful lovers they proved to be" replied the Biologist who perhaps intimately regretted the disappearance of the species he considered his best masterpiece, and not wrongly so, since it had been able to dominate the abyss of an entire cycle.

"Excuse me Engineer, why is it obvious that monogamy one by one is completely absurd?" asked the Energy Systems Engineer again.

"Oh, it's very simple. Each sexualized species, by balance, must have a total weight equal to the two genders, because it is not the number of individuals by gender that counts, but the biological mass itself. So, if males are bigger than females, they must be lesser in number because their total weight must be equal to the total weight of the females. In other words, as much male flesh as female flesh. Now, if there are more females than males, each male must fertilize more females, it is obvious, right?"

"Yes, this is actually obvious" the Energy Systems Engineer assented.

"This also applies on the contrary, of course. If the females are larger, they will be in lesser numbers and therefore will be fertilized in turn by several males, although we use this model more for insects, where females are often gigantic, compared to their males."

"What if males and females are the same size?"

"In that case monogamy one by one would be possible, but it is not the case of the Project. The males are larger by a factor of 1.3, an imbalance introduced to partially compensate, with greater muscle strength, the shyness of the other gender. Therefore each male must fertilize 1.3 females. If they were monogamous one by one, there would be 0.3 females without males, i.e. about thirty percent of the female population would be useless, a waste would not you think?"

"Undoubtedly" admitted the Energy Systems Technician.

"In the Project there are species that have even more spectacular proportions" continued the Biologist, excited to talk about his work, "there is one that has a weight ratio between male and female equal to seven. Obviously each male has seven females and in this sense is monogamous, to those seven females is strictly faithful. The maximum that has appeared from all forks is an aquatic mammal with a ratio of thirty-seven, the male is a real monster while the females are ..."

"We are rambling" interrupted him the G.O.D.

"Yes" replied the Biologist, truncating his digression, "I am about to conclusion. The Project species has not been programmed to monogamy, not even to that 1.3 because it will have to proliferate far beyond the environmental possibilities, otherwise it will never become the galactic species. It is just the excessive proliferation that will force them to look for resources on other worlds."

At the end of the dissertation, the General Operations Director tried to resume the thread of the speech asking: "Wizard, please answer the question of the Evolutionary Systems Technician."

"The question about clothes, of course" the Wizard resumed

then, "I didn't mean that clothes alone will start the violence, I meant that they will emphasize it a lot. We all know it; the reason for their endemic aggressiveness is the reluctance of their females. Just look at how calm is a male who has just copulated, while one who does not see even a shadow of a female is always a formidable warrior, considering also the tempting prospect, in case of victory, of a nice rape on the opposing females. It is paradoxical that if they adopted rape as a habit, the species would live in peace" concluded the Wizard, almost unable not to digress.

"A relative peace" added the G.O.D., "well, that's as far as the first effect is concerned, and what do you tell us about the second effect?"

"Ah yes" replied the Wizard, "I had forgotten about it. The second and more positive effect of the invention of the clothes will be to have a handy tool to occupy areas with a cold climate. This will greatly improve the proliferation of the species."

"It seems to me an accurate analysis" said the G.O.D.

"There is, however, some undesired effect" murmured the Wizard.

"Please, Wizard, don't be reticent."

"So, this is an effect that I already mentioned in the Project phase. Those two words will also appear in their thoughts independently. But if *naked* will stick only to the sexual drive, reinforcing it, which will be even better for us, the *forbidden* will produce prohibitions as in themselves, in short a long series of taboos."

"And what importance will they have?" asked the G.O.D., "they will be only some of the many meaningless laws that they will give themselves in the course of their history."

"I don't think so. Unlike the laws, the taboos will be totally irrational and above all much more stringent, so they will be reasons for tension, confrontation and wars."

"Irrelevant" cut short the Diffused Systems Technician. "Wars will pervade much of their history, whether or not there is a valid reason for them. On the contrary, I will say more: there are never valid reasons to make war. In reality, the reasons for war are just excuses to vent repressed aggressiveness, because there is always another way to solve problems, beyond violence."

"Well, it seems to me that the discussion is over" said the G.O.D. "then Aesthetic Systems Technician, what do you think of this our coloring them?"

"Oh, you did not color them. The modular pigmentation is the work of my department. Unfortunately we did not succeed with all the variants. The blues and greens will be missing because the relative pigments were all poisonous."

"What? Did you make changes without saying anything? And have you not thought about the consequences?" yelled the G.O.D. surprised.

"There would have been far worse consequences if they were all the same. After all, it will be precisely that touch of exoticism that will distinguish them, to keep them vital in their sad reality of war. However, we didn't warn anybody because you are all too scientific and you don't want to hear about art."

"Let's hope so. When will be the forecast of the next discontinuity?" asked finally the G.O.D. again calm.

"Ten millicycles" replied the Evolutionary Systems Technician.

"So goodbye in ten millicycles" concluded the G.O.D. with a cheerful voice.

It was a pity that almost at the end of that period, when the species sensed the existence of creators and began to worship them, none of them noticed because they had all gone on vacation.

8th interlude

"How is it Paco? Cold outside?"

"Don't even talk me about, a chill comes down from the Pyrenees, I don't know when they'll defrost, we've been waiting here for years to pass. What are you doing Pepe?"

"Oh, studies of expressive anatomy, see these are buffaloes and this is a deer and this is you."

"You think? Am I like that? With a black outline?"

"But no, black is artistic. Art Paco, it is art."

"And what about that sort of big ape there?"

"That's one of the intellectual tribe, those who put the dead underground."

"Ah yes, I don't like that story Pepe, I don't like it at all. And then they always talk about strange things."

"But they are harmless."

"Well, harmless not so much, I think they will do a lot of damage in the long run."

"Like what?"

"How long has it been since you haven't talked to your women Pepe?"

"Ah, I don't know, I don't remember. Talking to women is tiring Paco, every two words, one is in quotes. And then in the long run they are so cloying, they have no cultural interest. They either talk about children, or about setting up home, or about themselves."

"Well, you should then, because they talk a lot with those intellectuals, and they're messing with their heads."

"And what do they say?"

"They stand around a fire and talk for hours. They discuss what happens after we're dead, where we come from, why we are here, who created us, blah blah blah blah blah, things like that."

"And they talk for hours about such simple things? The Great Factor has created us, we are here waiting for the Pyrenees to defreeze to pass over to the North, we come from the South and when we die we become hard as wood, end of story. Pass me that color Paco. In fact, you know what I think about that business of burying the dead?"

"What."

"I think that as long as we were dying only because of a saber tiger or a lion, nothing was ever left of our bodies and so we never thought about it. Since we came to the North, a lot of us die for the cold instead of the wolves and the body that remains there all stiff disturbs, because it reminds you that you can end up in the same way, so those there thought to do like dogs and bury the remains. It does not seem to me a proof of great intelligence and even less of evolution; on the contrary, in my opinion it is a regression to an animal."

"You're a man of common sense Pepe, but who knows why, women like to be there philosophizing all day long."

"And after they have philosophized what they do?"

"Oh well, what do you want them to do, they're still males too. When they have knocked them out with their chatter, they do all of them, but strangely enough, the women don't oppose to them as they do with us."

"Mmmm, I guess they're not as stupid as they look."

"We'll have to do something before we run out of females."

"Sure Paco, we'll have to do something. As soon as I'm done here, we'll talk about it with the others. Pass me that clay color please."

"And what would be the clay color?"

"Here you see! The artists will always remain misunderstood, in every time!"

"So let's stop all this bitching and talk about serious things."

"Okay, here is a shin."

"Thanks … mmm … also well cooked. I meant let's talk about this female thing."

"Oh yes, look, I can't stand it anymore. Mine keeps talking about how good that one is, how smart the other one is, a singsong I won't tell you."

"And what do you say to her."

"At the beginning I gave her a beating, but as soon as I stopped she was even more petulant than before. In the end I let it go. Now I'm simply going off on my own."

"Mine instead says nothing but every time she goes out to go to them she wears a flower on her head, or whatever she finds because with this climate, flowers you don't find often. Usually she wears a bone, but the principle is the same."

"What is a principle?"

"The intention."

"And what is the intention?"

"All right, never mind, in short, it bothers me."

"What's bothering you?"

"That she dresses up good for them, no?"

"Well, I don't see anything wrong with that."

"Neither do I, if she always did that, but instead she's troglodyte with me. Absolute mutism, which is also fine with me, but as soon as I touch her, she begins to cry. And as if that wasn't enough, lately she has got into the habit of rolling in dung to become a real turnoff for me. But then, when she has to go to them, she washes herself and sprinkles with grease to perfume herself."

"Yes, mine do that too."

"One day I heard one, I think it was one of your Paco, confabulating with another about the possibility of moving."

"Bah, that would suit me, they've become unbearable. Mouths to feed and that's it."

"Look, in case they leave, they take everything with them. You don't think they will leave you the tent, the harpoons, the flints and all the kitchen equipment, do you? They will leave you with just your underwear, you'll see!"

"We'll see if they can."

"Uh-huh, they put you in front of them screaming and screaming until you can't take it anymore. They will succeed, they will!"

"Hey guys, you don't want us to invent divorce before the marriage, do you?"

"Sure not, what do you propose Pepe?"

"Well, for now we are many more. Before things get bad, it will be better to kick them away."

"Easy for women to follow them."

"Right, then we must prevent them from following the

others."

"And how, you put a rope around their neck?"

"Yes, and doing so you end up with a snarling, mangy wolf in the house."

"We must eliminate the possibility of choice. It's either us or nothing, don't you think?"

"Right Pepe, and how do we do it?"

"We take them out, we are more."

"Well, but they are not so bad, someone is also nice. It seems to me a bit drastic solution."

"That's what I was afraid of, they've started to mess into your head too. As far as you know, the mating with them is fertile?"

"In my opinion, it is. Mine is pregnant but I assure you that I had nothing to do with it."

"Is someone here responsible for his pregnant woman?"

"No, no, no" was the choral answer.

"Okay, then the mating works, that means danger."

Pepe's conclusion was followed by an uncontrollable chattering.

"Ohei, cut the crap, then we agree? Do we take them out?"

"We all agree."

"And what do we say to the females? Be sure that they will feel bad about it."

"We give them a good collective beating, so they learn to behave themselves. You'll see that in a little while they will lose the desire to play the fool, and to be sure to put an end to this story, we have to impregnate them all, so there is no trace of those there, okay?"

"Ok Pepe."

8 CULTURAL REVOLUTIONS

"Here we are again" said the Chairman of the Absolute Order of Space-time, in opening the meeting of the Project Committee. "General Operations Director, tell us where things stand."

"Yes Chairman. So, this rather long period, which for the species has been an abyss of two million and three hundred thousand units of their time, has passed without any unforeseen events. It was a necessary period to consolidate its behavior, after the tumultuous upheavals of the first periods of the Project. From now on they will no longer be able to change much, conditioned as they are by habits that have lasted one hundred thousand generations. Now they are exactly as we wanted to be: dynamic and in constant technological progress. Of course, they are also pervaded by unspeakable violence, as we expected. According to what I am told, no later than a tenth of a millicycle ago, they gave a brilliant proof of this. Evolutionary Systems Technician, can you tell us about that event?"

"Certainly Director" replied the technician, "as the evolutionary equation assumed, a little while ago the species has suffered a discontinuity that has divided them into some subspecies. One of the newborn was a species led to abstract speculation, demonstrated by the circumstance of having invented the bizarre use of burying the dead. It seems that this new speculative quality suggested to them that violence was not the only way to deal with the unexpected. Despite a more consistent muscle development of their relatives, they began to preach non-violence. This minority of gurus, let's call them that, with long hair and a strong physique, began to exert a certain fascination on females, who are creatures very prone and suggestible to speculation about life and everything in general, as we know. The males at first let them do it, and then when the females started to put flowers in their hair, they realized they were facing a big problem. As pragmatic people as they are, they faced the situation with the only effective method to stem a cultural influence: they killed them all."

"What is the consequence of this event?" the G.O.D. asked.

"Actually none and maybe that's the point. The species has such a deep-rooted behavior that it refuses to accept any change, like this one that was in progress, so it will never evolve again."

"In short, no more discontinuity, i.e. the end of evolutionary leaps" concluded the Biologist.

"Worrying" said the G.O.D., "in any case, as it is, is it evolved enough to reach the galactic diffusion?"

"Yes, but..." the Evolutionary Systems Technician replied.

"That's enough, what matters is that they enlive the galaxy" the G.O.D. cut short while the CH.A.O.S. nodded satisfied.

"So what is the current situation? I would like a report from those responsible for the various areas" the G.O.D. said.

The Biologist spoke first.

"After the last ice age, the species has settled on almost all continents. Each territory has its own breed, distinguished by a color and as an effect derived also from different somatic traits, which have developed because inter-color mating is not well accepted. The environment, pervaded by aggressive diseases, has kept the species healthy; another great success of my Department" concluded the Biologist with his usual pride.

"A blow to the enthusiasm" said the G.O.D., "before we congratulate ourselves it is better to hear everyone. Who is speaking now?"

"Me" said the Diffused Systems Technician. "I don't know if there has been a drawing in the present arrangement of the emerged lands, but it doesn't seem to me a brilliant geography. Sooner or later the species will also colonize the empty continents, but the delay will produce a different evolutionary state between those who have already conquered a territory and those who have yet to do so, because every society to become organized must always pass through the same number of stages: primitive, nomadic and finally agricultural. I foresee therefore strong tensions between these last continents and all the rest of the planet."

"I don't see what to worry about" said the G.O.D., "the backwardness of the new continents will be resolved with a beautiful war of conquest or extermination or the two things together."

"Yes" assented the Technician with impersonal tone.

"I would like to answer the doubt that has just been exposed" said the Ecosystem Technician taking the floor. "There was no plan in the current geography of the continents simply because there was no reason for it. That said, the environment is fully functional. The species has begun to devastate the territories where it has settled. We expect more and more devastation as the population increases, until it overwhelms the entire ecology and finds in a bloodless planet the powerful motivation to interstellar jump in search of new worlds to plunder. So, all is for the best."

Finally the Wizard spoke.

"It seemed to me that the colleague of the Evolutionary Systems was sorry for the extermination of that hippy branch of the species. Actually, come to think of it, that branch would have become extinct anyway. In fact, given the nature of the species, any group that will keeps going along with its females, will only go towards extinction. Such types of cultural revolutions will still happen, as female dominated groups, but they will always become extinct without any external intervention, because in them the reproduction will be completely insufficient. Their reaction of extermination was therefore only an outburst, the course of events would not have changed if they had acted otherwise, as on the other hand it must necessarily be; for the purposes of the historical course, their actions are irrelevant. In any case, as far as I am concerned, the programming worked as expected: females are egocentric and unreasonable, males are obtuse and aggressive. The societies in which they have organized themselves are all based on taboos for no reason. The great novelty is that they have developed theories about the existence and nature of their world, needless to say, wrong. But they have intuited the existence of someone who created them, so that now we are the object of worship, someone more someone less."

"Ha-ha-ha." With a great laugh the Joker suddenly appeared.

"Ha ha ha, the slaves who adore their masters, ha ha ha ha, we were really wicked, maybe we shouldn't criticize them so much. They are violent, they are bad, blah blah blah blah, what about us?"

"Oh here's the Kinetic Technician" exclaimed the G.O.D., "where were you, to plot something with the Physicist?"

"Plot? Plot, me!?" replied the Joker resentfully, "even though when there is the crisis, I am asked for the prompt solution" he mumbled to himself with a sharp voice.

9th interlude

"Someone more someone less, you said" said the Biologist to the Wizard, "I am curious to know; what is this worship of theirs?"

"Oh, it's a complicated matter" replied the Wizard, "they actually adore themselves and it's only right that they do. After all, unconditional self-confidence is an essential condition of the Project. But let us come to worship: in essence, everything they cannot control, they consider to be a manifestation of superior beings, that is, divinities, to whom they attribute exceptional powers."

"And why do you say that they adore themselves, and where do we get into all this?"

"They worship divinities, but unconsciously they worship themselves, because they have attributed to the divinities forms and behaviors equal to their own. For example, they have aggressive, dissolute, vindictive and even sensual deities. The latter, of course, exclusive invention of the male gender. Those invented by the other gender are instead ethereal and abstract, with totally indefinite functions, except for the gender that is always, firmly feminine. As you can see, they are the mirror of themselves."

"Give me a concrete example Wizard."

"The males have invented a deity whose only quality is the exuberant appearance of female features. In short, an erotic pin-up."

"Go figure! And the fact of having a great ass and a great breast is for them a divine quality? It's incredible that they don't come to understand that they have similar thoughts because they are sexually frustrated."

"They cannot understand it, we prevented them with those two words that govern their thoughts, and in this the Joker is right to say that we were wicked. They are convinced that the females are coy only because of a cultural attitude. They don't think *they are* like that, they think *they just behave* like that. Of course the females also think the same about themselves. They are firmly convinced that they are not coy, they believe instead that they are the males who are always too much excited."

"So where do we get in?" insisted the Biologist.

"We get in because many of their deities actually correspond to our fields of expertise. So, without knowing it, they are really worshipping us, don't you find that funny?"

"Oh yeah? Me too?"

"No no, you are still far away to become a deity, the nature of life is still incomprehensible to them but they have sensed the existence of the old man, and also of the General Operations Director."

"Really amazing, and who else has become Gods?"

"The Energy Systems Engineer, they call him the fire god."
"Uh-huh, they're not that far off the mark, at least at the level of their knowledge."

"Yes yes, and also the Joker, they call him the god of the misdeeds."

"This is even more hilarious!" exclaimed the Biologist.

"Yeah, finally hear this one that is the most bizarre: they invented the god of time."

"Of time! But it's like inventing a deity for movement!"

"Yeah, it's really meaningless, isn't it? I told you they would make a big blunder."

"And then if they think that way, they will never reach the interstellar jump" added the Biologist. "This time thing is really worrying. In fact, now that you have told me, the more I think about it, the more alarmed I get. Perhaps it would be appropriate to call a meeting of the Project Committee. The Project will fail if they do not abandon that idea soon."

"Trust my friend. So far the Plan has worked well; after all, the equation of progress has only one solution."

"Yes, but it has a lot of parameters" said the Biologist gloomily, "anyway we always have plan B."

"By the way, how's it going with them?"

"They are my pride, my masterpiece. Every now and then I go to look at them and I am always enchanted by them."

"But where are they?"

"On the same planet, of course, elsewhere they could have stood out, and in any case an entire ecosystem would have had to be built around them to make them survive and therefore they would have been immediately discovered."

"And the species didn't notice?"

"Not at all. First of all because they are convinced that they are the only intelligent species so even if they met them, they would not recognize them as such. And second, because they are an aquatic species and therefore by the species they would be assimilated more like fish and finally because when one has free hand in the laboratories of genetic design, has ample opportunity to shuffle the cards a little, so I have made sure that the species tends to stay away from where the species B is allocated."

"And how did you do it?"

"You should be proud of me Wizard, I programmed an irrational impulse that keeps them away from a pole, the very one where the B species lives."

"But aren't the poles a bit cold?"

"They are very much so, although this has not prevented the species from going to live on the ice of the other pole. Think how effective that conditioning was; they occupied a pole made only of ice while they completely neglected the other pole which has an entire continent in addition to ice and they did not even dwell on why. Rather obtuse, don't you think? Anyway the B species, despite being warm-blooded, lives in the sea like many other warm-blooded animals so the temperature outside the water is a secondary issue for them."

10th interlude

"Wizard, in the end it seems that you are the one who is most informed about how the Project is going" said the Physicist.

"So it seems, but I had nothing to do with it. It's the species that is irrational in itself, so I can easily understand their way of thinking."

"So tell me about this time of theirs."

"Let's say that time appeared in their minds as soon as they became aware of death, that is when that branch of theirs began to bury the dead, a habit that has been adopted by all the others. As long as they died without having the way to grow old, once they became adults, life was always the same for them. I believe that in their language the word death did not even exist. Existed maybe the words predated, ate, killed, and disappeared, but not dead. Then with progress, they learned to survive predators and then, managing to grow old and die on their own, death became a real event. That is why I say that it is death that qualifies life, and that is why not dying, we are not alive. Time is a measure of the amount of life."

"I understand" nodded the Physicist. "However, if they do not abandon that idea of time, they will never get to the interstellar jump."

"In fact, we may have to intervene soon. Where are we with the point of intersection between the two galaxies?"

"There are still three hundred and fifty millicycles to go" replied the Physicist.

"Well, then there's nothing to worry about."

"Not for now" added the Physicist, "by the way Wizard, what do you know about the contingency plan?"

"Never heard of it" replied the Wizard with cautious expression.

"Contingency plan, Plan B, Wizard. I overheard the Biologist talking about it."

"Let's hope the G.O.D. doesn't hear it too, I don't think he'd take it well."

"Then you know something about it."

"Let's say that some of us don't like that old man's obsession with completing the Project by any means. Too much cruelty, too much violence."

"So someone is thinking of an alternative project, a plan B" concluded the Physicist.

"Yes," replied the Wizard reticently.

"What is it?"

"An alternative species."

"And what would be the intentions of this alternative project? A coup d'état, a revolt?"

"None of this, you can't go against the CH.A.O.S, its power is too great by far. It is an alternative in case the species turns out to be inadequate, an alternative to failure."

"A sleight of hand, in short. If the species fails, you are ready to pull out another one. And with this conspiracy, you really won't act against the species of the Project?"

"Do you perhaps doubt our good faith? And then we do not conspire, we prepare only an alternative plan."

"When the interests are twofold, it is difficult to understand which side one is on" said the Physicist gloomily, "and in that case, whatever side one is on, for the other is necessarily a traitor, so you see that even in good faith ..."

9 DIVINE INTERVENTION

"Dead end!" exclaimed the Chairman of the Absolute Order of Space-time at the beginning of the Project Committee Meeting, "we must find a way out. General Operations Director."

"Yes Chairman" replied the G.O.D., "Physicist, nobody better than you can illustrate the current situation. We would also all be grateful if you would be a little clearer than usual."

"It's difficult to be clear without a common knowledge base" replied the Physicist sourly, "in any case the situation is this: they believe they live in a three-dimensional space, so it is clear that they will never reach the interstellar journey, also because their belief can no longer change."

"It's obvious to you but not to all of us" replied the G.O.D., "please be clearer, and also tell us why they cannot change their minds about the nature of space."

"Mmm, as for changing their minds, the Wizard can explain it better. For the question of space, I will try to simplify the explanation with a three-dimensional model, which is how they see space. Think of a very small being that can only walk."

"An ant" suggested the Biologist.

"That's right, an ant. Put it on a very large sphere. Since it is big, to the ant that sphere will look like a plane, that is, a space with only two dimensions. Instead the plane is actually a sphere that is a curved surface in a three-dimensional space. What is technically called a two-dimensional variety immersed in a three-dimensional space. The ant, however, cannot see the third dimension so it believes it is not there. So it will never understand that the shortest path between two points is not an arc of a circle, that it will believe a straight line in its space, but the chord of the arc that penetrates inside the sphere cutting its volume. So, the ant will never see the short paths from one point to another. The species does the same thing, it believes that space has three dimensions because its senses say so, and the other dimensions it has called them time without investigating further. So they will never come to understand that the space they see is not a three-dimensional variety, but an immersed three-dimensional variety. It is not very intelligent."

"Intelligence is not a primary characteristic of the species" cut short the G.O.D, "Technician of Irrational Systems, why the Physicist claims that they can no longer change their minds?"

"It is soon said. In a group of individuals with a certain common idea, if one changes his way of thinking, he is seen by the others only as an eccentric. Or crazy, if the new idea is much different. As a result, each individual tends to think like the others and this makes an idea stable. The larger is the group, the more stable is the idea. Ideas change, of course, but as the population grows, they change with increasing difficulty, until they can no longer change."

"Clear" said the G.O.D. "so we will have to intervene."

"We must suggest to them how the space is really made" proposed the Ecosystem Technician.

"This is not what is needed" replied the Wizard, "sooner or later one of them will be able to understand it, if it has not already happened. The problem is to make sure that it is believed by all the others."

"To do this there is only one way" suggested the Diffused Systems Technician, "to raise the prestige of someone who then will be believed, whatever he says."

"Smart!" exclaimed the Joker, "and how do you plan to raise the prestige of those who will actually make the discovery?"

"We tell him that too" replied promptly the Diffused Systems Technician.

"Yes, but in this way, our existence will be clearly revealed, thus frustrating their evolutionary past" objected the Evolutionary Systems Technician.

"Then choose someone who will pretend that the findings are his own" said the head of the Department of Contradictions and Paradoxes, who everyone called the Lawyer, exceptionally present at the meeting.

"A female!" exclaimed the Biologist.

"That's right" said the Wizard, "they seem to be made for the purpose."

"Ha ha ha, your ironic sense has no end" said the Joker, "in other words you would like to ensure that those among them are the most irrational, are those who make the most important scientific discovery in their history."

"So we have a solution" concluded the G.O.D. without paying attention to the Joker, "what do we tell them?"

"The gravitational engine, an application that later on will also be necessary for the interstellar space" proposed the Energy Systems Technician.

"Good idea" exclaimed the G.O.D., "Wizard, you take care of the matter, nobody knows how to deal better with the irrational nature of the subject."

10 TECHNOLOGICAL PROGRESSES

"You know, I dreamt about a strange machine" Rose told Mildred, her colleague and friend from the Materials Engineering Department.

"Ah yes, and what was the use?" Mildred asked.

"It was a machine to produce gravitons."

"Hullallà, science fiction stuff, did you dream about it several times or was it only when you dined onions and peppers?"

"Don't mock, I know it's nonsense, what do you think I don't know Newton? But in the dream it really seemed to work. I'd like to build it, at least to show you what I dreamed."

"Yes, why not!" replied the other one, amused "after all it could be fun to do some DIY, as long as it will be a small gadget. If you've dreamt of something like a two miles linear accelerator, you can forget it. Go ask Livermore."

"No no, it's an object no bigger than a blender, in my opinion it was really a blender."

"Then it's okay, and if it doesn't work, we can always use it to chop the vegetables."

The construction of the machine did not take long; after all it was just an electric engine with a speed regulator and an eccentric weight on the axis.

"So Rose, now explain to me how this thing is supposed to work. It looks just like a sander to me; just add sandpaper to it and the comparison would be perfect."

"In fact, it seems exactly that, but this one has to spin, or rather vibrate, at great speed. Now I'll explain what came into my mind."

"Yes, come on, explain it to me, I'm really curious to know

something about this whacky idea of yours" said Mildred.

"So how do we produce an electromagnetic wave?" Rose then asked.

"It's simple, we make electrons vibrate in an antenna" Mildred answered confidently.

"To us it seems simple, but it is not simple at all. Think how long it took to discover it. Anyway, we make them to vibrate and as a result the electromagnetic wave is formed, right?"

"Right."

"And if we adjust the vibration speed of the electrons, we adjust the frequency and also the amplitude of the electromagnetic wave, in other words we have the control, we can modulate it, right?"

"That's right, too."

"Then it occurred to me that if electrons generate an electric field and when they vibrate they generate the electromagnetic wave, or a photon beam if you like, a mass that generates a gravitational field, if we make it vibrate it generates a gravitational wave, that is gravitons, don't you think?"

"It does not seem the same thing to me, in the electromagnetic wave there is an effective transport of energy, in the gravitational field there is only a potential."

"Better still, if there is no energy transport, the gravitational wave will not be subject to the speed limitations of restricted relativity, it will be an almost instantaneous wave, indeed, without almost! In practice it will not be simply a wave, but a stationary wave."

"You're really crazy, if this is the case then all blenders, off axis motors, even swings, should generate a gravitational wave?"

"Eh no, that's just what came into my mind, I don't know how, in a dream. The gravitational wave is quantized as the photoelectric effect, so it is formed only with a vibration higher than a certain frequency, which is very high."

"Oh yes? How much high?" Mildred asked with an air of sudden interest.

"Eh no, the formula is mine, if it works it would be a great discovery, and it's mine, only mine."

"Don't you trust me? I'm your best friend!" said Mildred, almost offended, "and then you didn't discover it, you just dreamed it, maybe the wizard Merlin suggested it to you in a dream."

"In case it was Morgan le Fay, you know I never dream about men."

"Neither do I. I would never dream of a man, with all those hairs and all those hands" Mildred added.

"In the meantime let's try to see if it works" cut Rose short, "the frequency also depends on the mass that vibrates. For this weight of only one gram the calculation provides five hundred thousand revolutions per minute."

"Five hundred thousand?! Are you stupid? Who has ever made an engine run so fast?!?"

"That's exactly why the effect has never been discovered, can this engine reach that speed?"

"In theory yes, it is an engine of an aeronautical gyroscope, guaranteed for two hundred thousand revolutions and you know that everything that has to do with aeronautics has very conservative margins of guarantee, although in this case the guarantee refers to the engine perfectly balanced, not with an eccentric on the axis. So I cannot tell you if it will be able to spin so fast. And then when you asked me to get you a very high speed engine, I didn't think it was that high. Anyway, even if it does get there, I think it will be better to be out of this room at that moment."

"Okay, then let's add extensions to the power line" Rose said.

When everything was ready, the engine with its eccentric was fixed to a clamp on a workbench in Rose's cellar. From the engine came out three wires that passed under the door and ended in the basement hallway where Rose and Mildred had crouch on the ground, with the engine control in Mildred's hand.

"So shall we try it?" said Mildred.

"Let's try it."

"How do I make the engine run, clockwise or

counterclockwise?"

"Boh, indifferent I think."

Mildred closed the switch and began to increase the frequency of the engine supply current. From behind the door came a hum that, as the engine accelerated, became a louder and louder whistle until it became so loud that it went out of the audible field and the cellar fell into silence.

"Where are we, is it spinning?" asked Rose anxiously.

"Yes, we are at a hundred and sixty thousand revolutions per minute, it seems to be holding up."

"Continue."

"I'm doing it, but the higher the speed, the longer the time it takes for the engine to speed up, it takes patience."

The two followed anxiously the digital rev counter on which the numbers were scrolling rapidly.

"But how did you come up with such a bizarre idea" said Mildred while maneuvering the speed control, "in my opinion it's also dangerous, you'll see that at some point that engine take off like a rocket, or the eccentric detaches and set off like a shotgun blast, or it gets so hot that it sets your cellar on fire or ..."

"Stop being a jinx" cut Rose short, "you'll see that there is no danger, the engine is very small and this door is made of oak, and also very thick" assured Rose.

The figures increased in absolute silence.

"We are beyond the resonance frequencies of any object" said Mildred, "which is why you can't hear anything, it spins so fast that nothing can vibrate so quickly anymore.''

Two hundred fifty thousand, three hundred thousand, four hundred fifty thousand.

At the threshold of the five hundred thousand rpm they heard a crash that instinctively made them lower their heads, but from behind the door came no sign of some catastrophic event.

"Look, the current consumption has been reduced to zero and the engine is stopping, some winding must have broken or the cable must have come loose. I'm not surprised, with a speed like that."

Little by little, inside the cellar the engine slowed down until it returned to the audible threshold. The two of them heard again the high-pitched whistle of the engine, which gradually decreased in tone, then the vibration again and finally they heard nothing more.

"Let's go inside and see what happened" said Rose.

When they opened the door, an unexpected spectacle appeared in the half-light in front of them.

The engine, still attached to the vice, was floating in mid-air with the whole table, along with all the junk the cellar was full of. Some of it had even ended up against the ceiling.

"Holy cow, you did it!" exclaimed Mildred.

"What! What has succeeded me!" said Rose who did not understand.

"Don't you see? We have filled the cellar with gravity in reverse; everything flies like in The Wizard Apprentice! It's the antigravity, we generated the antigravitons. Are you sure that the wizard Merlin, or rather Morgan le Fay, didn't teach you this?"

"Oops, that wasn't what I expected. I thought only artificial gravity would come out of it" Rose said.

"I'm sure you can do that too. In my opinion it has something to do with the sense of rotation. Since it is a wave, it will have a phase. Do you bet that if we reverse the direction of rotation of the engine, we create an opposite phase wave? Come on, let's do the experiment again" said Mildred suddenly enthusiastic.

"And how? The machine is flying through the air, it will never stand still while we start it."

"You can't find your way out of a paper bag, Rose. We tie it to this column. Take that rope that twists like a worm in the air."

"Wait Mildred, why aren't we floating?"

"Because the engine is stopped, it's obvious" replied Mildred.

"But all the objects are still weightless, even if the engine is stopped."

"Oh yes, taken by enthusiasm, I hadn't thought about it. How can they stand there in the air without an energy that supports them?"

The two stopped as if enchanted to look at the objects floating as if by magic in the air.

After a while Rose recovered and said: "You know what I think? I think that the engine has generated a gravitational wave that has inverted the mass of the objects, making it become negative, like a spin reorientation of the electrons, so to speak, and the result is that now the mass is negative, and furthermore the result is also permanent."

"Never knew that the mass had spin, but evidently it must have something very similar. However, if the wave is stationary, as you said, the result can only be permanent" observed Mildred.

"Right, but it wasn't strong enough to go through walls, that's why only the objects fly in here. I'm sure if I take a piece of plaster off the wall, it goes up in the air."

"Give it a try."

"I'll try."

Rose scraped a little bit the damp wall of the cellar from which a splinter of material immediately came off.

"Look, it's going up like a balloon!"

"Great, let's go drop it" said Mildred on the way back down the hall.

"And now clockwise!" she announced as Rose barred the door behind her.

"Look, I turned it clockwise before."

"So the other way around, don't be a pain in the ass. Are you always so fussy?"

The experiment repeated the second time produced just the effect that Mildred had imagined, canceling the previous anti-gravitational wave and in the cellar everything fell to the ground with a crash.

"Wow!" exclaimed Mildred when they noticed the effect, "Nobel Prize stuff, this will revolutionize all the theories about gravity!"

"But what a Nobel and Nobel!" exclaimed Rose, who suddenly became practical, "this thing I patent and I become rich. Just thinking about it for a few seconds, a lot of practical applications have already come to my mind: transportation without wheels, airplanes without wings, going into space without rockets... Basically you can fly anything and once in the air, it stays there, you don't even need an engine anymore! We could even set up a factory of flying carpets, if we fancy do it!"

A few days later, when the excitement for the discovery dissolved, the two began to explore and evaluate the possible implications of the discovery.

"It will be a revolution even more profound than the one introduced with electricity" considered Rose.

"Yes, practically everything will have to be rebuilt, and many things will have to be undone as well. The roads for example" added Mildred.

"Architecture will become something else entirely."

"No more earthquakes can bring down a building. On the contrary, you could make buildings that are not even leaning on the ground, but only anchored to the ground."

"No ship will ever sink again."

"If that's what it's for, you won't even need ports anymore."

"And what about airports then, think how useful a runway can be for a plane that can take off vertically like an elevator."

"A greener world, there will only be a bit of road signs scattered here and there. No more strips of asphalt tearing up the territory."

"Greener perhaps yes, but on the other hand it could become a more dangerous world" Rose concluded by putting an end to their daydreaming.

"More accidents you say? Do you think that without driving on a road there will be more accidents?"

"No, it is true that without a road the cars will no longer have landmarks, but it is also true that the traffic will disperse over a much larger area, or rather over a larger volume, so it will become rarer and eventually I think one thing might compensate for the other. Now that I think about it, we will have to invent a new highway code, or rather an air code. Anyway, I was thinking about something else."

"What?" asked Mildred.

"Have you considered that the stationary wave makes a permanent conversion of the mass, a bit like the magnetization for iron?"

"Yes, so what?"

"Think of a vehicle to start the wave. Then think of a standing wave that expands just a little beyond the vehicle's mass and converts a few rocks in the ground into negative mass" said Rose dryly.

"Holy cow!" exclaimed Mildred.

"Here it is. After a while, the environment would fill up with flying objects, like gravitational garbage, and then I want to see you moving without the protection of a solid sheet of iron like a tank."

"It will be necessary to invent gravitational scavengers, people who go around restoring mass to everything that flies, like gravitational vacuum cleaners."

"Exactly, but it would be better if from the very beginning we found a way to confine the stationary wave, don't you think?"

"You're right, we have to think about this, just as it is, the gravity oscillator is a danger."

"As well as, after all, practically all the inventions just made. Perhaps only the blue cheese as a discovery has never been dangerous, but I have doubts about that too. Maybe, as far as we know, the first version contained a poisonous mold" opined Rose.

"True" admitted Mildred.

"Damn, while I was talking, I came up with the solution" exclaimed Rose.

"Have you thought of a way to shield the wave?" Mildred asked.

"Shielding it is not an option! How can you shield a wave that by nature penetrates anything with mass! With what, with vacuum? It is a field, not a vibration; it propagates even in the vacuum. No no, it occurred to me instead that an object flies when its mass is negative, but it's not necessary that all its mass is negative, it's enough that the algebraic sum of its masses... oh gosh, a few days ago you couldn't even think about this expression, do you hear it? Algebraic sum of the masses, what do you think?"

"In fact it sounds very strange and if you had told me this a week ago I would have laughed in your face, but now..."

"Well then, where was I? Ah yes, it is enough that the algebraic sum of the masses of which it is made is negative and the whole object flies, or rather , is rejected by the Earth, in short it flies. But the object could very well be made of a very massive nucleus, like lead for example, and a light shell, like aluminum. It is the power of the wave, which is the mass of the eccentric on the engine, which determines its penetration into the matter. We saw it in the cellar, the cellar didn't fly away."

"Right! Then it would be enough to do some tests to see how many grams the eccentric needs to demass ... Wow! I've created a new verb, to demass, how does it sound to you?"

"Appropriate I would say" replied Rose.

"Isn't it? Then it just suffice to demass a block of lead heavier than the box that contains it, and since what it's important is the total mass, the box goes up in the air while still having positive mass."

At that point in the discussion the reasoning was clear to both, and the conclusions came to both at the same time.

"... so a gravitational engine could be a block of lead with inside a cavity where there is the engine with adjustable power but with a maximum limit, which is to demass all the lead ..."

"...at that point it is sufficient that the block of lead has a natural mass superior to that of the object to be lifted and..."

"...and the object flies without demassing anything around it..."

"...and you can also adjust how much it flies."

The two of them looked at each other for a few moments in silence.

"Looks like we got it" concluded Rose.

"Looks like we got it" Mildred assented, and then added, "of course we have to do some rehearsals.''

"Of course, but I'm sure it will go as we planned."

"A true revolution!" exclaimed Mildred all happy.

"Yes, but we will not live to see it. Even at the time of the discovery of electricity, it took two hundred years before people stopped going to sleep with the candle in their hands."

"But is it in your blood?" said Mildred with angry air.

"What?"

"The party pooper syndrome."

"If I don't tell you my thoughts, who do you want me to tell them to?"

"You're right, sorry. I just feel so excited about the whole thing!"

"It's good that you are close to me in this" whispered Rose.

"My help is precious to you, eh?"

"That's not all" added Rose more and more quietly and shyly taking Mildred's hand.

Mildred let it go, then a little embarrassed by that unexpected gesture she said: "Anyway I think we will live long enough to see the antigravity applied. Surely we won't live long enough to see the world become a space civilization, and sooner or later it will become one, but I'm sure we will see some major changes in the next few years."

"We'll see" concluded Rose, that was the one of the two most prone to pessimism.

Finding someone who believed them was not at all easy and, in fact, they did not find anyone, as had always happened to all the inventors of history. At first Rose went in search of interviews with the great chiefs of the automotive industry, but not being willing to reveal to officials and secretaries the content of the interview she asked for, what she got was just a long series of rejections. After spending two years from one office to another and from one industry to another, Rose gave up.

"There's nothing to do, if you're not already somebody, nobody listens to you as much as you might have something important to say" she complained to Mildred.

"It had to come. I didn't say anything while you were going here and there because you could really have had a fluke, but it almost always happened like that, Rose. Look at the steam engine, for example. It was discovered three times, the last of which was the work of a certain Newcomen you may have never heard of, until Watt, who was from a family with powerful connections, rediscovered it, or rather proposed it again with a few improvements, and who knows if it was really from his sack, and eventually patented it. And going back in time, how many supported the heliocentric theory before Kopernik? And what about Maxwell, when he discovered the existence of electromagnetic waves and was accused of eccentric with ideas of no practical use, how about that!"

"Yap" nodded depressed Rose.

"I could go on for hours with these examples, Rose. The truth is that it has very rarely happened that the genius has been recognized. The only thing that is always recognized is your social position and your friendships. If you have those you can do everything, you can say the worst nonsense and you will be believed. If you don't have them, if you are a miss or a mister nobody, you can also be the genius of your century, or maybe even of history, and in my opinion this is what you are Rose, but nobody listens to you."

"But this thing is too big to let it go, and thanks for the genius but I don't feel like one" exclaimed Rose with anger.

"I agree with you, it's too big. So what do you propose to do?"

"Let me think about it for a few days, okay?"

"Okay, Rose."

After a few days Rose had come to a conclusion.

"So here's what I thought I'd do" he said to Mildred, "let's install the engine on my car and drive around in midair like it was nothing. Someone will see us and maybe think of a trick, but sooner or later someone else will think it would be nice to have that trick too. We set up a small workshop and we produce the engines ourselves. We did it once, we can do it again. As soon as we have earned the money to register the patent, we register it and we wait. You'll see that somebody wakes up sooner or later."

"It seems to me that it could work" replied Mildred pensive, "and after all we risk almost nothing. Of course if we want to send people around in midair we also have to give them a way to slow down" opined Mildred who had a mind more oriented than Rose to mechanics, then she suggested, "for example you could install two motors, each spinning in the opposite direction to the other, so just adjust the two eccentric masses to obtain gravity or anti-gravity."

"Had you already thought about it?" said Rose suspiciously.

"Oh yes!" replied Mildred candidly, "I've been thinking about all the possible applications and how to put them into practice while you were walking around the offices for months."

"Okay, to be honest I've been thinking about it for a long time too, about the brake I think it would be even better to solve the problem with two engines both antigravity, one in front and one behind and adjustable power. So when the car will have the rear anti-gravity engine more powerful, it will be as if it were on a slide and will accelerate forward, and when the two powers will be reversed it will be as if it were uphill and will slow down. In short, like a helicopter."

"It's an even better idea, Rose" admitted Mildred.

"Thank you Mildred."

"And in that way the effect of two stationary waves, which in other ways are not adjustable, will be adjustable so you can control the speed and height of the movement. You really are a genius Rose" concluded Mildred.

The first engines of the workshop, which the two called Anti-Gravity Rose Engine Garage, began to run on the streets of the region installed in the cars of some of their friends.

Soon the rumor spread around, especially in the countryside because the cars with the anti-gravity engine were not bound to the roads and the movements all became very simple. In fact, beyond the roads that it was no longer necessary to follow, with their cars you could overcome any obstacle with a stroke of the pedal. And then they consumed very little, with a normal car battery you could run the electric engine for hours and hours because after all the real power to keep the car in mid-air was provided by the Earth's gravity.

In less than three years there were more than a thousand rigged cars on the road in the region and Rose and Mildred's workshop worked full time to meet all requests.

Finally someone important in the automotive industry noticed the invention. As first thing it happened that that someone got one of those engines, making to buy it from an intermediary. Then he tried to appropriate the idea by passing it off as his own, but when he went to apply for the patent, he discovered that the patent had already been registered. He then sent an official to AGRE Garage with a ridiculous proposal for the purchase of the rights to the engine, but he only got a big rejection. Soon the proposals multiplied and over time became more and more important.

"Listen to this Rose, it says - Very precious doctor etc. etc. etc.... please take into consideration our offer which we believe to be adequate because blah blah blah blah blah...of eight million American dollars...mmmm, that's not bad..."

"Fuck them" said Rose.

"Wait for it to continue."

"Fuck them"

"But do you want to hear it or what?"

"Fuck them!"

"Ah ah, I love you when you do that. Well, I'll read it out loud anyway" said Mildred sneering, "it says - to which we add the royalties on all the products derived from your new technology blah blah blah blah ... at the rate of four percent ...".

"Fuck them all!" said Rose, who in the meantime had stuck his head in a hood.

"They're getting bigger and bigger" considered Mildred all sweaty for the hot summer heat, as she walked around the workshop in her grease dirty underwear, throwing the eight million dollars rolled up in some corner.

"Fuck it, there is no price for the happiness I have here in doing this thing with you" said Rose in a muffled voice.

"I adore you when you say that" Mildred replied, "and I, too, would like to be nowhere else but here."

In the same period the two began to receive letters from the Physics Departments of the universities of the region and then from increasingly distant universities, who asked for their willingness to give a lecture at their research laboratories to illustrate the theory behind the invention, because after tests and trials, it had finally become clear that antigravity was not at all a trick of a provincial magician.

Rose and Mildred, well remembering the two years they had spent begging for interviews, did not even bother to answer, but rather, as a reaction, they hired helpers.

Their workshop grew and soon became a small industry which, as production increased, caused the number of other automotive industries and those related to them to fall in equal proportion, a phenomenon that was almost imperceptible at first but which over time became more and more an unstoppable avalanche.

In that period they also had to hire in a hurry an efficient security service, in the form of large and well-armed men because some chiefs of industry, or perhaps all of them, thought well to stem their economic damage with the simple solution of eliminating the competition, an expression that in that case they tried to apply literally.

When their commercial power was big enough, they set up a workshop for the production of airplanes, unlike the cars for which they only produced the engines, which completely subverted the principle of flight, because with their device, an aircraft did not need wings to fly and paradoxically, the technical progress seemed a return to airships.

From airplane, the workshop soon became air-space and at that point, the two began to buy the factories of competing industries from which they had been ignored until a short time before and which, linked to a technology now obsolete, were going to become relics of the past, while all the chiefs of industry questioned by Rose during those two years of research, had the opportunity to meditate for a long time on the meaning of the phrase '*Hell knows no fury equal to that of a woman refused*'.

In little more than twenty years the Anti Gravity Rose Engine Garage, became meanwhile AGRE Corp., became the most powerful industrial company in the world, and Rose together with Mildred, whom Rose, for the wise choice to cancel any kind of competition, had made take the position of president as well as her permanent lover to better strengthen their bond, became the most heard voices on Earth.

In reality it happened that from time to time they would say something stupid but given their position, this was always taken for an absolute truth that no one would think of discussing, as always happens when the powerful speak and although they are also human, they always believe they have all the answers.

11th interlude

"So, are we ready to tell them the nature of the space?" asked the General Operations Director.

"Actually I already did it but they didn't even notice it" replied the Wizard.

"Mmmm" nodded the General Operations Director, "and why didn't they notice? Maybe you got the wrong way?"

"Well, sure I couldn't make appear a burning tree with a voice inside it that recited technical information, it would look grotesque, don't you think?"

"Yeah, grotesque, but funny" admitted the pensive G.O.D., "then how did you do it?"

"I communicated it through one of their widely used methods of spreading ideas, a movie they call it, but so far no one has noticed it."

"And what would a movie be?" asked the G.O.D. intrigued.

"Moving images together with sounds" explained the Wizard briefly.

"I understand. And does everyone look at it?"

"In millions if the movie is good, otherwise almost none."

"Then evidently, the movie you used wasn't very good."

"On the contrary, it was one of the greatest successes of that form of communication of theirs; the fact is that they didn't really notice the message."

"What a pity" mumbled the G.O.D.

"So what do we do, wait a little longer to see if they can find out?" asked the Wizard.

"Waiting still seems a risk to me. Now that we have the right agent, it is better to use it. As we well know, it won't last long and if by chance it will die without making the discovery, we wouldn't get anything, even if by a fluke we have two agents, but I think they are the same age and therefore they will die more or less together. And then I was also told that they do not dedicate themselves to space at all. So it is better to do it now. Let them make that discovery" concluded the G.O.D.

"You're right, we might as well do it now, even if in reality we are a bit ahead of the Project's plans."

"It's obvious that we are a bit ahead, with that push we gave them! Better so, they will have many more millicycles to prepare for the intersection."

"Do you think they will notice?" asked the Wizard.

"Notice what, the intersection? I hope so, the gravitational wave of the galactic collision will be like a hurricane that will be announced at least fifty millicles earlier" replied confidently the G.O.D.

"So shall I proceed?" asked the Wizard in the end.

"Proceed, Wizard."

11 GALACTIC ERA

"Rose?"

"Shut up and let me sleep" Rose replied in her drowsiness.

"Rose!" repeated Mildred by slapping her ass.

"What is it? Let me sleep."

"Rose, I've got an idea too."

"Okay, you tell me tomorrow, now let me sleep."

"Rose, they were right!" exclaimed Mildred as she leapt to sit on the bed.

"They? They who? You're really annoying!" Rose replied, hiding her head under the pillow.

"Those of Star Trek, Rose! They were right... IT CAN BE DONE!!" exclaimed Mildred, screaming and jumping up on the bed with an exalted look.

"What can be done?" Rose asked at that point awake.

"The time warp[6], Rose! It is not a nonsense! It can be done!!" The two looked at each other fixedly.

"You dreamed him too" said Rose with an inquisitive look, pointing a finger at her.

"Hah! I knew you couldn't have had that intuition on your own!" replied Mildred, also pointing a finger at Rose.

"And ... ?" said Rose stiff, while waiting.

"And nothing, it's our stuff" Mildred simply replied, in the tone of whom considered the subject closed and by sitting down again.

The two smiled at each other as accomplices.

"What was he like in your dream?" asked Rose at that point, curious.

---

[6] Time distortion

"I felt like I was immersed in the Rocky Horror Show. They sang it for real, and they even danced it."

"Cool!" considered Rose with a hint of sarcasm.

"What was he like with you?" Mildred asked.

"Cold, I felt very cold, I will never forget it. It was all very cold, as if I had been transported to a pole, and then I heard a voice repeating a formula, and repeating it, repeating it. But since we are awake, explain it to me."

"It's like in the song Rose, time means nothing, it makes no sense. We are blind and we don't know it!"

"And what is there instead of time?"

"That's also in the song Rose, that one there, that man who says it's just one step to the left, and hands on your hips. Do you remember him?"

"To be honest I don't remember it at all" admitted Rose.

"Well, then you really should see it again. Anyway that sentence says it all, you don't need to do anything else, it's just a matter of knowing how to move. Now I understand that after all we are like ants attached to a flat surface and we do not see the space around us. Come down from the bed, I'll show you how to detach yourself from that plane, or at least I think so."

Rose now fully awake got out of bed and stood next to her friend.

"Okay, give me your hand. Oh God what a sensation! He told me like it was a dance lesson!" Mildred added as if speaking to herself.

"But who was he?" asked Rose.

"Who was with you?"

"If there's one thing I hate about you, it's that you always answer with a question" said Rose, annoyed.

"Yes, but you love so many other things about me" Mildred cut short, "so who was he?"

"I don't know, I only heard a voice, but did you really see him?" answered Rose.

"Yes, I really thought he was the wizard Merlin, only in more modern clothes, but not so much after all. So look at me, you have to move your leg exactly as I do, understand?"

"Yes."

"Ready?"

"Yes."

For a moment the two disappeared from the known space.

"Damn, I almost broke my leg" exclaimed Rose.

"I took a blow to the back. Luckily it was only a short step, maybe if we did it longer we would fall from ten feet high, instead of falling only two feet" complained Mildred.

"We were reckless" said Rose.

"Yes, sorry it's my fault, taken by the enthusiasm I didn't think about the consequences. But who would have thought that we would have found ourselves in the middle of the countryside half-naked to walk home, luckily it's nighttime."

"Half naked will be you, I'm really naked" Rose complained. "That's what you get to go to sleep with nothing" Mildred reproached her.

"Yap, because you don't like me naked in bed, do you?" replied Rose resented.

"Of course it's really amazing, with one step we did two miles" considered Mildred without paying attention to her friend's complaint.

"Like the Puss in Boots, and it's cold too, to tell the truth" continued to complain Rose.

"If I had something on, besides underwear, I would gladly give it to you. In fact, if you think it will make you feel better, I'll give it to you. Here they are" said Mildred, taking off her panties and pulling them on her friend. "I have to find a way to control that step with precision" she said, continuing her meditations undaunted.

"And also understand the relationship between direction and distance, and I don't want your panties" added Rose in discontent, clutching her arms to her cold body while she walked jumping on her toes.

For a few days Mildred worked hard in the workshop where

the AGRE Garage was born, which the two had kept in the name of the good times they had spent there, and also to have a space of their own where they could try the various improvements to the AGRE engine that they continued to churn out.

When she finished with her project, Mildred called Rose to show her the new creation.

"What do you think?" she asked proudly.

"It looks like a refrigerator with legs" said Rose dry.

"It's just a refrigerator, or at least it was originally, to which I added legs" Mildred said enthusiastically.

"And what should it be for?" Rose asked.

"Now I will explain. I used a refrigerator for several reasons. The first is that it is a box ready to contain us even if a little tight, but it doesn't bother us. The second is that it is isolated so it protects us from the cold. The third is that it is made of metal so it resists the most unexpected conditions and the last one because it is easy to open and close it and the closure is watertight."

"All very good reasons, depending on the purpose that for now is not evident, then?"

"I replaced the refrigeration compressor with one of our AGRE engines so you can stay in mid-air without falling down."

"I'm beginning to guess where you want to go" Rose said with new interest.

"Exactly. The legs are mechanical limbs of those used for assembly lines, controlled by stepper motors in turn controlled by a PLC. For this experiment a computer was useless, much more complicated and much more delicate. The PLC instead is industrial stuff made to withstand even extreme conditions."

"So it can walk" concluded Rose.

"What's more, it can make any movement, even what we did a few nights ago."

"My leg still hurts" murmured Rose.

"The PLC control panel is inside the refrigerator" continued Mildred in her explanation without paying attention to her friend's complaint.

"So you can adjust the movement of the legs from inside."

"Yes, I've already programmed it with the same movement we did the other day."

"I understand. You want to do the same thing again but inside the refrigerator" concluded Rose.

"That's just to begin. Before leaving, we light up the AGRE until we have almost zero mass, so wherever we end up, at most we fall like a feather."

"What if we end up *inside* something, instead of on top of something?"

"I don't think that's possible. Just as it is not possible to put a foot inside the rock in our space, I don't think it is possible to do it in that other space. After all, matter also exists in that extended space; it will occupy a volume, won't it?"

"I think so."

"So the space must be such that if you can make a movement it means that there is space to do it, or at least I am convinced that this is the case" concluded Mildred sure.

"All right, in the meantime let's admit that it is so. What is your plan?" asked Rose.

"For now my plan is to make a small movement and see if with mechanical legs we can go back to the same place. Being mechanical, I can make the legs do the exact reverse movement."

"What if we can't?"

"Well, we came back the other night, didn't we?"

"Yes but on foot. What are you going to do with that thing? And if instead of two miles we then make a hundred miles?"

"Aside from the fact that it can walk, I admit it would be embarrassing if someone saw us walking at night followed by a refrigerator."

"We could always argue it's Uncle Bob" said Rose sarcastic.

"Yes, terminator" Mildred mocked.

"It is better that one goes and the other stays here with a van. In case she doesn't make it back, with just a ring with the cell phone, the other one goes to retrieve her, including the refrigerator" proposed Rose.

"Okay, I'll go" said Mildred.

"What if something happens to you?"

"Nothing happened last time."

"How is your back?" said Rose again sarcastic.

"You are right. First I program the PLC to come back on its own after three seconds, or two seconds, and I put a GPS beacon inside it in case it doesn't come back, so we can recover it. For now, let's do this."

"Much better this way. Of course we wait until nightfall" Rose assented.

The experiment was successful. The refrigerator returned perfectly intact from its journey, even if with a slight inaccuracy in the position of the return and with a few seconds delay, because finishing in mid-air, before returning it had to wait to be on the ground again and the return movement was therefore not the exact one to make the same reverse route. The second experiment was just as successful when Mildred entered the refrigerator. For the third experiment, Mildred installed a rudimentary periscope in the refrigerator to see where it ended, even if the GPS gave her the exact coordinates.

Encouraged by the successes, they programmed the PLC to make continuous jumps even in their absence, to accumulate data and try to understand the relationship between the entity of the movement and the final point of the jump, but from the results it seemed that there was no rule.

"It all seems random Mildred, just change an angle by a nothing and you end up in a completely different place, without there being a relationship between the two things" complained Rose.

"It's more complicated than expected" Mildred meditated, "maybe space is like this as long as we are close to the Earth's surface, maybe in real space it's simpler" she said doubtful.

"Look at this, it's as if the space is pleated" Rose said, drawing Mildred's attention to some data, "with this corner

Uncle Bob ends up close, with half a degree more he ends up far away, with another half degree more he ends up close, and on and on. There is no order."

"We should do this experiment in space" concluded Mildred, "and in any case we'd better move where our little games can't be noticed. Sooner or later a refrigerator that appears and disappears will be noticed. So far nothing has happened because we send it at night, but it's all blind travel and sooner or later Uncle Bob will end up appearing over a nice country party."

"You are right and then going into space is not a problem, since we produce the capsules to go there, the problem is then to make those movements. It's not like there's a ground that you can put your legs on" observed Rose.

"But it's the movement itself that counts, not the fact that you do it with your legs, don't you think?"

"Definitely true."

"So I replace the legs with gyroscopes and move it with the inertial method" concluded Mildred.

"Ah, you and your gyros! I feel like I'm going back to when you first came to my house with that airplane gyroscope."

"Things have changed a lot since then, haven't they?"

"Yes, and for the best. Especially because all this has brought me you" said Rose in a sweet voice.

"So you make me blush, you know I'm a mechanic, not a romantic" murmured Mildred.

The experiments in space did not give better results. It seemed as if there was no connection between the initial movement and the final destination. Sometimes a certain order appeared in the data, but then it happened that an angle in the middle of two others, did not lead at all to a destination in the middle of the two reached before. In addition there was also the space itself, where the GPS system did not work and therefore for each jump they got very uncertain positions. However, the repeated experiments, during which the device always managed to return to the starting point, increased their confidence in the strange device that had eventually turned from a refrigerator into a camping caravan well reinforced and isolated to withstand the vacuum and cold of space.

"Rose, if we want to make progress, we must make substantial improvements. We're not making any progress anymore, we're still collecting data, but as far as understanding it, we grope in the dark" Mildred said one day.

"You're right" replied Rose.

"We should find someone who can make precise measurements in space and maybe help us with data processing."

"I agree Mildred, we need an astronomer" concluded Rose.

"Exactly."

"What exactly would be my assignment?" asked the young man sitting in front of the two bigwigs of AGRE Corp., a shy astronomer discovered by Rose through his old university acquaintances, who at that moment was feeling a little in awe of the fame and power of the two women and still wondering what they wanted from him.

When they explained what their proposal consisted of, he immediately felt uncomfortable and even a little scared, because he had never considered going into space. For him, space was something to look through telescopes or examine with numbers on computer terminals or even better, on squared sheets of paper.

He was tied to the vision that until then one had of space, namely that of a place for a chosen few with superlative intelligence and perfect physique, without either quality being actually indispensable, as demonstrated by the first launches in which the crew was a primate, and instructed by space agencies for half of their lives to perform impossible tasks. A place where any move outside the procedure would have resulted in the immediate cessation of life, and he still could not believe, because he had never experienced it, that with the AGRE engine, space had become just a big sky where you could go with the same difficulty as taking a commercial flight.

After all, he thought, an astronomer is more like a scholar

who spends his life in a library than an experimental scientist and he had never even wanted to go to the great observatories on top of the mountains so as not to suffer the discomfort of high altitude.

"But in practice, will it be necessary to remain in space?" he asked with mistrust.

"No way" Mildred answered animatedly, "we don't stay in space either, not a chance! No one stays there, it's so uncomfortable! And then it's not even beautiful, and it's no use anyway. With our capsules we go up and down like an elevator. We are only talking about fifty miles; it takes just over an hour, including all the maneuvers, which are quite simple and almost completely automated. The reckless people make the journey at sixty miles per hour, that is, in forty minutes. Would you define a reckless person as someone who travels on the road at sixty? Anyway, you would be just a passenger. We go up in the morning, do our experiments, you detect the positions of the stars and in the afternoon we come back down. Every day you will be home for dinner."

"And why can't we take these measures here from the ground then? The stars can also be seen here" opined the astronomer.

"We can't tell you this for now" replied Rose, "we are planning a series of experiments on a new project of our company and industrial secrecy, competition, political interests, blah blah blah blah... in short, the usual things, you understand me, don't you?" she said, while saying a list of clichés to break the subject.

"All right, all right, let me think about it for a few days" said the astronomer at the end.

"No, you have to decide right now" Mildred replied dryly.

The astronomer, still full of doubts, looked at her suspiciously and replied: "Then I agree to accompany you into space for once, just to see how it works. If it seems to me a simple thing, if I do not panic, malaise or other such amenities, I will accept your offer. Otherwise I don't want to know anything more than what you have already told me and that's the end of the story."

The two looked at each other and Rose said, "All right, let's go."

"Now?"

"Yes, now, do you have two hours free?"

"Yes, but..." the astronomer hesitated.

"Come on, it's something that needs to be faced as soon as possible" Mildred reassured him, heading towards the studio door where they had received him, "we have a capsule ready out here in the garden. Did you think we had to climb to the top of a Thor Delta or maybe a Saturn IV rocket on a launch pad?"

Considering that the astronomer knew very well that the impressiveness of the rockets of the first space age was due only to the need for propulsion, but that the actual space capsule where the astronauts were housed was little more than an aluminum can twice the size of a man, he no longer opposed the proposal of the two women. But one thing is the logical reasoning, another is the irrational impulse and the astronomer faced the entry into the capsule with the face of one who is climbing the scaffold. But then, to his surprise, he didn't notice at all the transfer into space because AGRE Corp had become so expert in modulating the power of its gravity engines that in the capsules one couldn't feel any more acceleration than one would in a broken-down condo elevator, and when after half an hour sitting comfortably in an armchair like an airplane, the astronomer asked when they would leave, he received as a reply that they were already halfway through the trip.

"So?" Mildred asked the astronomer when they had arrived at the planned altitude.

"But shouldn't we float without gravity?" asked the astronomer. "And to the two people who discovered the way to create artificial gravity you ask this question?" Rose said laughing and tapping her hand on his shoulder, "I thought you were smarter."

"You're right, excuse me. It's just that I'm still tied to the image of space in pioneering explorations, you know when you saw astronauts in complicated spacesuits floating in cramped spaceships."

"Oh yeah, here instead you sit comfortably in sweater and pants and do not float at all, quite different no?" considered Rose.

"You can say it out loud, very different. If it's really all like that, then I think I'll take the job" concluded the astronomer.

"Great" exclaimed Mildred, "then for today we go home and tomorrow morning we start" she said, maneuvering the controls of the capsule, which began to descend slowly like the cabin of an elevator, without having to face the high speeds that had always caused the enormous difficulties of re-entry into the atmosphere.

"In the end, the difficulty of space flight is all in the re-entry into the atmosphere" Mildred explained to the astronomer, "but if you fly through it at sixty miles per hour, like an old cart, nothing happens except a bit of static charge accumulation, like when you fly into a thunderstorm, then when you're inside the atmosphere you can go up to two hundred. Of course if there is bad weather you shake a little bit, but there is no danger."

"How many times have you already done it?" asked the astronomer.

"I don't know, we've been going up and down almost every day for a few months now, working days only, of course. On Sunday we stay in the garden to water the flowers. Well, I water the flowers, Rose tries to water me. Rose do you remember how many times we did it?"

"No," replied Rose like a voiceover while she was flipping through a magazine, "this dress would look really good on you, Mildred" she added.

"Let me see."

"This one, what do you think?"

"Rose, you want me like a doll, I have told you many times that I am a mechanic."

The astronomer looked at the two astonished by such

carelessness in facing what until a short time before had been the central adventure of the life of a chosen few.

The work was not what he had imagined, and when the astronomer discovered that what was being asked to him was the exact opposite of everything he had always done in life, namely discovering his own position with respect to the stars, instead of discovering the position of the stars with respect to his own position, he became demoralized. Then he also wondered how they were able to move thousands of kilometers into space in a very short time and without perceiving anything. As time went by, however, the position calculation that initially required him a day of sweat and scratching, he managed to do it in less than half an hour and the work seemed less hard, even if it kept that something mysterious.

"So let's see. Do you have a girlfriend David?" Mildred asked the astronomer one day while he was busy doing his stellar position surveys.

"Girls don't look at astronomers" replied the astronomer without raising his eyes from his calculations.

"Don't tell me that you also think that women only look at the rich, the powerful and blah blah blah blah blah? Are you another man full of clichés?"

"I don't think anything, but in fact I've always been alone, like all my colleagues, so I can scientifically say that girls don't look at an astronomer."

"Well, I look at you" said Mildred carelessly, swinging her leg over the other.

"I'm beginning to glimpse an order" said the astronomer without paying attention to what Mildred had said, not even when a sandal flew over his worktop, "all the data seem messed up if you think they are arranged on a flat surface, but as soon as you put them on a wave surface, everything becomes orderly.

"A wave surface?"

"Yes, since nothing matched, I tried to consider the data as if they had been taken from a ship in the middle of the ocean, in short on a moving surface and with waves. But everything works only if I take data with one of the three coordinates set. In short, considering only the movement in section, or if you prefer, a movement along a plane."

"What about a movement in all three dimensions?"

"Oh yeah, in 3D you say. Linear algebra, it's linear algebra only. A metric tensor, you need a metric tensor, a three-index matrix."

"Can you find it David?" asked Mildred.

"Not yet, because I have few data, after all we are talking about three by three by three, that's twenty-seven unknown equations to find by interpolation of experimental points, but I will get there step by step. That's for sure."

"When do you think we will get this so-called metric tensor?"

"A few days now, I have practice in the calculations and if someone could help me with the interpolation of the data, even less so."

"I'll help you" said Mildred.

When they obtained the matrix that according to the experimental data described the space around them, they realized that among the twenty-seven equations there were repetitions and that in reality there were only sixteen independent equations.

"Damn!" exclaimed the astronomer when he noticed it, "an immersed variety!"

"That is?" asked Rose, fasting since the time of the university of differential analysis.

"In practice, the sixteen equations are a four by four matrix, i.e. functions in a space of four coordinates that identify three-dimensional surfaces. But in a four-dimensional space surfaces are only surfaces, while in a three-dimensional space those same surfaces are volumes."

"In short, we live in these volumes."

"That's right."

"But the matrix places the volume in a four-coordinate space" observed Mildred.

"That's right."

"And the four-coordinate space is flat?" Mildred asked.

"Yes, it is probable."

"And are three-dimensional surfaces flat?" asked Mildred, who was already guessing.

"No, that's exactly the point. They are waves, indeed they are like folded sheets...damn it!"

"What?"

"Now I understand how you can move us thousands of miles in an instant, I thought you had developed a particularly powerful propulsion but no, you have found a way to go through the folds!" exclaimed the astronomer.

Rose and Mildred looked at each other and in their eyes there was a storm of emotions: surprise, exaltation, excitement, satisfaction, complicity. The latter above all, with which through that silent look they had decided instantly not to tell to the astronomer that they were surprised by the discovery even more than him.

"Let's try" said Rose resolute, "can we calculate a distance between two points with that metric tensor?"

"It's obvious, that's why it's called metric tensor" replied the astronomer, "just diagonalize the matrix and multiply the elements on the diagonal so found."

"Can we do the opposite? That is to say, given the four coordinates on a point on the immersed surface, calculate the distance from a fixed point?"

"Obviously yes. You put the desired coordinates instead of x,y,x,w in the matrix and then you diagonalize it and on the diagonal you find the distance."

"Can you also do half and half?" Rose finally asked?

"That is?" asked the astronomer

"That is to set a distance and only two or three of the four coordinates" added Rose.

"Calculation more difficult because there is not always a solution, i.e. the point does not always belong to the surface described by the tensor, but theoretically it is not excluded."

"Okay, let's try it" said Rose resolute. "three light years, Alpha Centauri direction."

"Trivial destination" whispered the astronomer, mentally correcting Alpha with Proxima, "it's going to take me a while".

Two hours later, the calculation produced the result in the form of three coordinates.

Rose did not hesitate for a moment to enter the three coordinates into his gyroscope control computer, a computer that still appeared to the astronomer as a mysterious machine whose purpose he had been leaved out and that he believed was only the AGRE engine control system.

"One thing is for sure" declared Mildred before starting the program, "however it goes, we'll be back" and she pressed *execute* under the loving gaze of Rose and the frightened one of the astronomer who had understood what was about to happen.

A few seconds later Mildred said, "David?"

"We are close to Proxima Centauri" said the astronomer as he looked at the external images transmitted by the cameras while admitting to himself "less trivial than I thought."

"Okay, let's go back" said Mildred.

The astronomer had just enough time to take two pictures that Mildred had already activated the reverse motion program and the images of the space familiar to them reappeared on the monitors.

"David, we have to talk" Rose said.

"I think so too" said the astronomer who had understood everything by then.

"Of course you will understand that we can no longer let you go" said Rose in a dry tone.

"I imagined that too" assented the astronomer stiffening himself.

"Normally, in matters such as these, it is considered a valid solution to make the uncomfortable person disappears, but ...".

"... but we too have been subject to such a policy in the past and we promised ourselves never to use it" continued Mildred.

"Case in point, our Mildred here has fallen in love with you David. For that circumstance, and for the love I have for Mildred, I would accept as a solution to our problem ..."

"...that I become part of your...how would you define it, society? Family?" continued the astronomer who had understood where Rose was going with it.

"After all, Mildred is also a beautiful woman, don't you think?" added Rose.

"Surely she is" assented the astronomer a bit blushing and smiling shyly at Mildred who looked at him with an inquisitive look.

"...and then, fame, honors ..." added Rose.

"I don't want any fame, honors neither" said the astronomer dryly.

"So what do you want?" asked Rose.

"She is enough for me" he said quietly, pointing at Mildred with a nod.

12 ROUGH MEN OF SPACE

The great battle fleet dominated the Arm of Perseus with the power of its huge AGRE cannons.

Despite the technological progress of two hundred thousand years had led man to populate the entire galaxy, the weapons were still the same ones used at the dawn of its history: throwing a 100-ton bullet at the enemy using the gravitational wave of the AGRE engine or dropping a heavy club of hard wood on his head was not so different.

There had been an interval in which men had used the energy of fire, explosions and other bizarre things to fight each other, demonstrating in that field a fantasy unparalleled in any other application of their science, but with the advent of the AGRE engine they had returned to the simplicity and the guaranteed result of the blows on the head, albeit on a completely different scale.

Certainly from a mass that was thrown against you, you could always defend yourself with that same gravitational wave that had set it in motion and for this reason the battles had become an art of amplitude and phase modulation of the AGRE wave that made the bullets swirl between the spaceships like billiard balls, and the officers in charge of armaments were actually real musicians who composed complex symphonies on the keyboard of the AGRE modulator. Battles that at the first mistake ended with a silent impact in the vacuum of space.

There had also been a time when men had let women participate in the war, in which they had proved to be just as skillful as the men were, but then they abandoned that habit because of the unpleasant inconveniences that always happened among mixed crews who spent long time in space, and had returned to their much more efficient crews of only aggressive men and spaceships covered with naked women's photos, permeated by the chauvinism that made the crew a close-knit group of tenacious fighters rather than a pack of angry roosters who were constantly fighting over the inevitable strife caused by the presence of women.

It took several millennia of disasters in space to understand that the ancient superstition that women bring bad luck in navigation was not at all a superstition but a simple common sense statement.

"What has always impressed me is that throughout the galaxy we have never found the slightest trace of life" the Admiral told the ship's chaplain as he watched the fleet's movement on the monitors, sitting pensively in his armchair in the middle of the command room. "Not even one bacterium that is one. It is almost worse than having found life hostile or perhaps so strange as to terrify us. After all, I think I would have preferred to face any horror rather than this absolute void. It's terrible!"

The chaplain answered with one of his standard doctrinal formulas. "It is in God's plan that we are alone. Because we are made in His image, He created the universe for us."

"Bah, priest, always with your dogmatic formulas. Have you personally never wondered why life has only appeared on Earth? We found organic matter everywhere."

"It is in the designs of God..."

"Yes all right, that's enough" cut the Admiral short, "Commander, what are those tracks on the left monitor?" the Admiral yelled then.

"They look like marauders Admiral, perhaps from the Arm of Orion who are coming out of the variety" replied the Commander of the ship.

"They are many."

"And it seems they haven't all came out yet. The tracks are growing as fast as we can see."

"I don't like it; we don't have the maneuverability to sustain a clash with that swarm of wasps. That's for hunters, not for heavy ships like us. Commander, plot a course for the outer rim."

"Navigation officer, time and route to the Unicorn Ring, nearest position" ordered the Commander.

The officer entered the request in the computer that in a few seconds calculated the parameters of the new metric tensor.

"New route set and transmitted to all other ships, ready to activate propulsion" announced the officer.

"Activate" ordered the Admiral.

The female voice of the central computer of the great flagship announced the maneuver with a persuasive tone of a pornstar: "Distance eight thousand five hundred and three light years, transit time forty-five minutes, course 48 degrees x, 36 degrees and 12 minutes, 2 degrees z, 78 degrees 11 minutes and 2 seconds w, entry into the variety in four seconds, three, two, one, AGRE active, thrust, entry into the variety carried out, ETE[7] forty-four minutes and fifty-eight seconds."

"Perfect, too bad you can't give us a blowjob in the meantime" said the Admiral with a sneer, "you know Chaplain, it took us tens of thousands of years to realize that the only really indispensable thing women do are children. We were saved from the disaster of self-destruction only when we separated; they in the brothels, we sailing through space. That's what I call them, the planets I mean, because there are almost only women on them. And being always in space, if you want to go with a woman the only way is to pay. So in essence, even if they are planetary in size, they are still brothels. Of course they protest, but fortunately we no longer listen to them. The only one who did something really good was the one who invented the AGRE, and also her friend, to tell the truth, the one who discovered the existence of variety. They were two exceptional women."

The chaplain gave a half smile without saying anything.

"But how the hell is it possible that an engine was invented by a woman?" jangled the Admiral, then resuming the initial speech added: "After all, we have done nothing but transfer our

---

[7] Estimated Time Enroute

112

way of life on a much larger scale. Since we were twenty billion and we began to expand into space, what have we done that is so different? Now we are three hundred billion, but we do exactly what we were doing on Earth: exploitation of resources and war between us. There, plowed fields, here whole planets. There, continents against continents, here, arms against arms. Now not anymore, but it's only recently that we stopped. And then it's ironic that the galaxy has five arms, just as many as there are continents."

"Six to be exact" replied the chaplain.

"Bah, don't be a fussy priest, we've never occupied one and that's strange too. We have colonized many icy worlds, yet we have always left Antarctica alone, as if there was something that kept us away."

"Yes, Admiral," replied the chaplain.

"Man has always looked to the stars, it is something like carved into our genetic code, but in reality it has never been necessary. Why are we so unreasonably pushed towards the stars? What we did here, we could do by staying on Earth. We have not discovered anything, since the time of the Upper Paleolithic we have not evolved, in fact, in many ways we have gone back. Not that I'm sorry, with the business of women for example, we went back to the caves, but since they don't interfere with our business anymore, everything is much better. Do you know that the only time in history when the war was almost continuous was when men were listening to them? A strange correlation, don't you think? At that time the dominant philosophy was called gender equality, which like most philosophies has proved to be wrong. Don't you priest think there is a pattern behind all this?"

"God's designs follow mysterious paths" found nothing else to say the chaplain with a false smile.

The persuasive voice of the central computer interrupted the Admiral's verbal avalanche.

"Metric Tensor diagonalized, exit from the variety in four seconds, three, two, one, final position Unicorn ring, outer rim,

ATE[8] forty-four minutes and fifty-seven seconds, unidentified contact at alpha 89 degrees and 26 minutes, theta 48 degrees and 12 minutes and 15 seconds" said the computer with a languid and sensual tone as if it had announced the start of an upcoming strip show.

In the command room of the spaceship, all hell broke loose. "Commander!" cried the Admiral, barely audible above the sirens and alarms. "What the fuck does unidentified contact mean?"

"I don't know Admiral, as far as I know it never happened."

"I know too that it never happened, cowboy Commander! What the fuck did that bitch mean?"

"We are checking Admiral, it seems that in the position indicated by the central computer there is a spaceship."

"And who are they?" the Admiral shouted again.

"We are trying to establish a communication, they are transmitting but their signals are completely different from ours, we do not even know if they are voice or video signal" replied the Commander.

"Finally non-human life?" exclaimed the Admiral, returning to a less colorful language and suddenly excited about the discovery.

The seductive voice of the central computer was heard over the confusion in the control room. "Microwave band carrier at 2.4 giga-hertz, modulated signal with constant frequency detected at 500 kilo-Hertz, synchronization subsignal 30 Hertz, video picture identified, audio side subband identified, distance 40 kilo-Hertz modulation 22 kilo-Hertz" announced with a provocative tone that originally, the Admiral thought, had certainly belonged to a female with big lips and big tits, and now seemed also pervaded by an insolent complacency for herself.

"It sounds like an intelligible signal and also contains our own audio frequencies, Admiral" said the Commander.

"So they are human. It will be some eccentric adventurer,

---

[8] Actual Time Enroute

maybe from the nucleus, finished off course" concluded the Admiral. "No alien contact, the absolute void, as always" he added disconsolate, falling back in his chair.

"Open the transmission" he ordered then listlessly.

When the video panel appeared on the big screen on the bridge, the whole crew was amazed.

"Good morning men" said from the speakers a sweet and sensual voice that seemed to come out of an erotic dream.

"Shut up that computer" snarled the admiral in amazement as he fixed the image on the screen.

"It wasn't the computer that spoke" said the Commander, also with his eyes fixed on the screen, as he was gawking.

"They speak our language!" said the Admiral.

"So it seems" replied the Commander.

"But are they aliens or are they not?"

"I don't know" replied the Commander, while a big smile appeared on his face.

12th interlude

"And so there was a contact" said the Diffused Systems Technician.

"Well, they have already had many contacts, only they have never noticed them, or have not recognized them as such" replied the Biologist.

"What? How?"

"On the planet. They have been seen many times on the original planet, but you know, the species has always believed to be the only intelligent form of life" said the Biologist.

"Because we made them believe it" replied the Diffused Systems Technician.

"It's not true!" the Wizard intervened vehemently, "this is not true at all. The only thing we did was to give them confidence in themselves, we did nothing to make them believe that they are unique. We didn't even make them believe that they are in the divine image, these are all things that were invented by them. They have lived together for millennia but in order to reject the evidence of not being the only intelligent species, and consequently of not being in the divine image, they have relegated them to legends. Figments of the fantasy, they have called all the events in which they have seen them. That's why it was useless to populate so many worlds" added the Wizard. "If we had done so, the species would have simply rejected the existence of others. No intelligent species can accept another intelligent species, too much antagonism, so to solve the conflict it ends up denying its existence and even if it found it in front of it, it would classify it as not intelligent, or as bizarre of nature."

"Whatever! Where did they come out from and how did they get into the halo? I do not remember that they were present in the plans of the Project" asked the Diffused Systems Technician.

"How they got there you have to ask the Joker, I think" replied the Biologist, "where they came from I'll tell you: they are a fork of an aquatic species."

"A fork?" said incredulously the Diffused Systems Technician, "but wasn't it said that the fork could not be used for an intelligent species?"

"Not at all. As far as I am concerned, the rule was only valid for the Project species because it had to remain bound to its programming. Some of us simply interpreted the directives in our own way" replied the Biologist.

"You did, didn't you?" said the Diffused Systems Technician.

"You know, not everyone liked that idea of filling the universe with the war so dear to the CH.A.O.S."

"Then there was a conspiracy!" exclaimed the Diffused Systems Engineer. "At this point I am curious; tell me something about this new species."

"It's not really new, we call it species B. As I said, they are a fork of an aquatic species. They are mammals like their ancestors but unlike them, they have arms and hands to manipulate objects. In fact, they are very similar to the species. Let's say they are half one and half the other. We used just part of the species project to program the fork, even if in this way they have inherited some useless aspects for an aquatic species, such as hair, and instead they lack the distinct hydrodynamics of their ancestors. They are a compromise but being both mammals, the fork grafting was very simple. Of course we have removed all the tension."

"That is?" asked the Diffused Systems Technician.

"You should know" replied the Biologist, "the genitals are the disappearing genitals of the aquatic species so they are not governed by their continuous presence, then we have equipped both genera of mammary organs, which it was very easy since in embryo they all have them. Of course we have greatly expanded them because in water the weaning of offspring lasts much longer. In this way we have obtained a species where there is no tension between the two genera because the role is perfectly balanced. In fact, at first sight it is impossible to distinguish between the two genera. Obviously, no programming in the center of the language so neither of the two genres is bashful and therefore they are not even aggressive and even less self-centered."

"But so you have taken away any evolutionary momentum" said the Diffused Systems Engineer.

"Yes, so what?" replied the Biologist, "since there was no need to give them an evolutionary past, they appeared from the fork already evolved. They prospered until we revealed ourselves to them. They know very well about us, since they live right below our access point to the planet."

"And what do they say?"

"Nothing, they are grateful to us, but they do not consider us gods for this. For them we are more like fathers."

"Rightly" added the Wizard.

"And the halo?" asked again the Diffused Systems Technician.

"How they got there I don't know, but of course I'm very happy about it. They spared us a problem, but we would have been ready to transfer them at the moment of the intersection. Evidently they must have immediately understood that the galaxy would be entirely occupied by the species, so they headed straight to the galactic halo. After all it is a space even larger and that will be very little devastated during the intersection, given its low density" replied the Biologist. "An intelligent choice, but on the other hand it was to be expected, intelligence is measured mainly with the ability not to enter into conflict with all the others, and they, in fact, have never entered into conflict with anyone."

"You already knew about all this here" said the Diffused Systems Technician.

"We and someone else" replied the Wizard.

"Who?"

"The Joker and the Physicist."

"What about the G.O.D.?"

"Up to the intersection he must not know anything, then it will not matter" said the Biologist.

"What if he finds out?"

"Well, the G.O.D. doesn't care directly about what happens in space, he never has."

13 MYTHOLOGY

"Fuck, they're mermaids!" exclaimed the Navigation Officer, then added in a whisper "how about that, in the Unicorn Ring, we meet the mermaids!"

"And they're all naked too" added the Commander, and then in a low voice, "and also great beauties. Look at the huge tits they all have."

"Thank you men" replied smiling one of the mermaids from the screen, "but we are not all females, some of us don't have pussy" she added with a sly smile.

"It doesn't look like it" the Navigation Officer considered in a whisper, "to me that crack under the belly looks like a real pussy and they all have it."

"And anyway, they all have tits, and what tits! I've never seen such tools" the Route Officer at his side suggested to him in a low voice, "as far as I'm concerned, they are all females and I don't want to know anything else."

The Admiral, recovered from the surprise, stood up before speaking.

"I am Admiral Berg, commander of the Perseus Arm fleet."

"Nice to meet you Admiral Berg" replied another mermaid floating on the screen as if she were swimming upside down in a swimming pool, "we are the People of the Halo, but there are no grades between us, only duties."

"Do you live in the Halo?" asked the Admiral.

"Yes Admiral, but we are not born there, we are from Earth too" said another mermaid, leaving everyone stunned.

"That's why they speak our language!" exclaimed the Admiral punching his other hand.

"No Admiral, we left Earth thousands of generations ago

and our language, like yours, has changed a lot since then. But some of us have stayed there, to maintain contact and to see what you were doing, so we can express ourselves as you do."

"You have been watching us" said the Admiral in a sharp tone.

"Yes Admiral, as a species you have always had a dangerous nature, but we cannot complain about that. We, like our ancestors, have always had a good relationship with you" said a mermaid with a sweet voice.

"Who are your ancestors?"

"You know them as dolphins."

"I should have imagined it" said the Commander to himself, "the only species that has never had enemies, not even us, which says it all."

"Can we meet directly?" asked the Admiral.

"No Admiral, our environments are not compatible. Your ship is like a gas bubble, ours is like a swimming pool, so we would not even have the space to accommodate you. Everything here is flooded, as it could be one of your spaceships that fell into the sea."

"Are you going around in space with a ship full of water? You will have a very low maneuverability, not to mention what can happen in case of a breach" said the Admiral.

"Of course we also have a lot of air. We breathe like you but our natural environment is water. Outside we get dehydrated right away, apart from the fact that we would move with difficulty. And then we have a totally different logistics and even if we wanted to, we would have no way of accommodating you. We don't have kitchens because what we eat swims with us and we don't even have what you call bathrooms, we just filter the water. As for the leaks instead, we are much more resistant than it seems. If we have a leak, the water that escapes solidifies immediately in contact with the cold of the space and the ice can be very hard so the leak closes immediately by itself. We could even build a whole ship just out of ice and it would work great, just think what a comet looks like. The problem would be just to get it out or into a warm atmosphere. But do you really believe that with gravitational propulsion, the mass of a ship is important?"

"No, of course" admitted the Admiral.

"Admiral, may I?" asked the Commander.

"Please" replied the Admiral.

"Many millennia ago, there were stories of sailors, people who sailed our oceans, who told of encounters with beings equal to you, whom they called mermaids."

"Yes, Commander, every once in a while someone approached you."

"For us it has always been about mythology, do you understand this word, mythology?"

"I understand it, Commander" replied the mermaid.

"And it was also a mythology of horror, it was said that the mermaids killed the sailors" added the Commander.

"As far as we know, no one among us has ever hurt any man, the meetings took place only out of curiosity" a mermaid answered quietly. "After all it was easy to avoid you, since the Earth is mostly ocean. Perhaps the accidents happened because some of you were so disturbed by the encounter, that you suffered psychic damage, and as for the females, we never met them. I guess because they never went to sea" concluded the mermaid with a large smile.

"Why haven't we found you before?" asked the Admiral, "we have been wandering the galaxy for millennia and no one has ever found life except us and the one we brought with us."

"Rarely do we push ourselves inside the halo and we never go over the edge. We thought it was more prudent to stay out of your space" was the mermaids' response.

"And now? Why did you suddenly appear?" asked the Admiral without realizing that he had begun to unconsciously use female conjugation.

"To tell the truth it is you who have suddenly appeared" replied a mermaid.

"Yeah, that's also true" admitted the Admiral.

"Anyway this is not the first time we have met, but as it happened on your oceans, no one will ever believe the narrative you could make of it" added the mermaid.

"That was in the past when people were superstitious, now it's very different" Admiral Berg said then.

"You think so? Try then and you will see how it will end. When they will have called you crazy countless times, in the end you will stop telling it, as all the men who have seen us have always done."

"This time is different!" exclaimed the Admiral, "my entire fleet has seen you and then we have the recordings."

"Do you believe that, Admiral? And what is a fleet compared to the galactic population? You will always be a small minority, and for the recordings they will say that it is only cinematic tricks. They will accuse you of having invented them, that it is not possible that an alien life speaks exactly your language, and moreover with voices like those of your females. Fantasy births, collective hallucinations that are the result of unconscious desires, also considering the size of our breasts, of male crews that have been out in space for too long, will say your females, who are more than half of the population. Do you really believe Admiral that you will be believed or rather that your career will be permanently ruined?"

The Admiral stood still thoughtfully. It didn't take him long to realize that the mermaid had every reason.

"You know us well eh?" he said bitterly.

"We have been watching you for a long time" replied a mermaid, floating in a graceful somersault, with long hair swaying in the water like veils.

"But we could always come to the halo to look for you and thus prove your existence" insisted the Admiral.

"Go ahead Admiral. The density of the halo is one thousandth of that of the galactic arms, and extended over a quadruple volume, do you really think you can find us without precise coordinates?" replied with a sweet and sympatethic voice a mermaid with long blond hair, full of pretty floral tattoos.

"Admiral, we understand well your desire not to feel lonely, we feel in your every word. Be settle for what you have discovered by now and leave things as they are. Take a good look at us; half of you would oppose us in the fiercest way. Even if we only appeared in your fairy tales, your females have always seen us as competitors, even if there is no cross fertility between us. And you males have always fallen for us in an equally unreasonable way, even males that you cannot distinguish from females" said another mermaid.

"Are there any males among you?" the Admiral asked incredulously.

"It's obvious, half of us are, otherwise how could we exist? We are still a mammalian species, can't you see that we have breasts?" said a mermaid making her breast sway with her hands, which floated in the water with a hypnotic movement that hardly dampened.

"Ghhh, I can see it!" whispered the Navigation Officer through his teeth.

"So there can never be coexistence between our species?" asked the Admiral finally.

"We were created to live divided" replied a mermaid.

"We were created she said!" the chaplain intervened animatedly, "did you hear it Admiral? God is behind all this!"

"Who is God?" asked a mermaid.

"He who created us in his image and who created you too, because at least half of you are like us, but the other half also belongs to a creature of God."

"Oh, maybe he's talking about the G.O.D." suggested another mermaid at the first one, "strange assonance, it has almost the same sound."

"I understand," said then the first mermaid, "no man, it is not the G.O.D. who created us."

"And what do you know about" replied the chaplain with an abruptly inquisitive tone, "you are only half a woman and half a fish."

The mermaid made a half smile and turned to the Admiral

and said: "Do you understand Admiral?"

"Yes, I understand" replied the Admiral, lowering his face, "now I know what I have to do."

He raised his head and in an imperious tone ordered: "Commander, close the communication, new route for the third sextant, take us to Macralok, the troop needs to relax."

"Good idea Admiral, the biggest brothel in the Arm. Navigation Officer, new route" yelled the commander.

"Computer, do you mind if I call you Katjusa in that porn star voice?" said the Admiral.

"The reference is unknown to me, to annoy me is not in the parameters of my functioning" replied the mellifluous voice of the central computer.

"Who is Katjusa?" asked the Commander.

"A name that reminds me of an event in the past, a woman of course. How they know how to mince you, nobody knows. So Katjusa, listen to what you have to do: you have to erase every record of the ship from the moment we entered the variety. When we met that fleet of hooligans, we turned around and went straight to Macralok."

"To proceed with the deletion of the navigation files it is necessary to provide level five authorization" replied the computer in a honeyed voice as if she was proposing a nice blowjob to him, while she was taking an alphanumeric keypad out of the Admiral's armrest.

The Admiral typed in a long code.

"Authorization acquired and exact, the memory has been erased, would you like to extend your order to the computers of other ships?" asked the computer with a thin voice like a sex kitten.

"Of course."

"Order executed" replied the computer immediately, "new course acquired, distance three thousand two hundred and two light years, ETE two hours, sixteen minutes and forty-eight seconds, course 237 degrees and 22 minutes x, 18 degrees and 5 minutes y, 3 degrees and one minutes z, 137 degrees and 15 seconds w, standby for the destination."

"Chaplain" said the Admiral, "whatever you will tell, we will deny everything, do you realize that?"

"I realize that Admiral."

"And another thing, I didn't like your last outing, but you never did, did you?"

"It is so Admiral."

"Activate" ordered the Admiral with a growl.

14 EDGE ADVENTURE

"Did it ever occur to you that we are basically nothing more than a big garbage truck?" said Captain Boriwen of the Tiger to his Second mate.

"Well, in short, it seems to me a somewhat trivial way to define our activity of training land" replied the boatswain Da Silva.

"Don't bullshit Da Silva, earth-training is a word invented by space adventure writers before we really went into space and before we really understood something about space. And those writers didn't know a damn thing about stars and planets. Of course, they had never been in space, so they could only count on their imagination. Earth-formation is impossible Da Silva! Think about it, the planets are as they are because they have reached a stable equilibrium and any change we could make, would be a temporary change until the planet returns to its equilibrium condition, which is undoing all the changes we would have made to it. In short, in modifying planets we would have faced a useless trouble. The only way to earth-form a planet would be to change its orbit if it is too hot or too cold, but this is something we still do not know how to do. Imagine that, to move an entire planet! That's indeed science fiction."

"So what do you call what we do?" asked the Second mate.

"Pollution, pollution plain and simple Da Silva, nothing else. Let's put it bluntly, all we do is find a class T planet around a class G star, which fortunately there are so many of them, both T planets and G stars I mean, and we dump a whole bunch of organic garbage on it. We let it settle for a few centuries and here is a new ecosystem ready to host us. That's it. This is what we really do."

"So somehow we modify its ecosystem" insisted the Second.

"But not even that. Before filling it with garbage you can't even talk about ecosystem, or at least vital ecosystem. All we find are planets with water and organic matter, but as for life, even elementary life, no trace of it has ever been found. Organic acids, aromatic complexes, amino acids, hydrocarbons in abundance is all that we have found, in short, only turbid and smelly broths in which we have never found trace of a single protein, or at least we have never found it so far. At that point we infect them with all kinds of bacteria and those do thrive in those primordial broths. Bacteria, algae, microorganisms, plankton, spores, seeds, larvae; we throw down everything without standing there watching what is better and what is worse, because the system finds its balance anyway. Only then can we talk about ecosystem."

"Then we could at least say that we create an ecosystem, right?" insisted the Second.

"But not even that, you are too poetic Da Silva. As for life, we don't create anything; we spread only the system we come from. In fact, all we do is pollute. You know, we transport all this crap to form worlds, I mean our hold is a real cesspool, but in reality we could just go down to the planets, you and me, and shit on it and we will get the same result. Do you have any idea how many bacteria are in our shit? Not to mention spores, seeds, mold, a real crap, that's why it's called shit."

"And you, Captain, are instead a true noble soul" replied the Second annoyed by the captain's language, "I would rather say that we are only sowing on fertile soil. We are like farmers, only our harvest takes a few centuries to ripen, but since we have been sowing on hundreds of planets for centuries, every year we have new ones. The good farmer, while reaping, sow" concluded the Second in the conviction that he had said something wise.

"Yes yes, continue with the poetry, you. So, do we have a new course?" the captain cut him off.

"I'm reading the results of the long-range sensors but nothing so far. By now we've reached the edge, further on there is almost nothing and the halo is too rarefied for it to be worthwhile to go looking for a planet."

"All right, when you find something, call me; I'm going to my cabin to take a nap."

"Sure thing, captain" replied the Second.

The Tiger's deep space telescopes incessantly photographed the surrounding space while the on-board computer compared the photo sequences in search of the slightest fluctuations in the position of the stars that revealed the presence of planetary systems. At the same time spectrographs analyzed the absorption bands in the color of the stars to reconstruct their chemical composition, which like a fingerprint, identified the stars of the various classes, looking for those of class G.

By crossing this data, the computer was able to discover the existence of suitable planets within a radius of hundreds of light years, even though most of them were only gaseous planets. From a distance, however, there was no way to know what was what and the choice on which systems to explore, fell from the computer to the crew, in this case to the captain, who chose with the only possible method, which is random.

It was in this circumstance that was demonstrated the importance of the luck factor, which had always been essential in any exploratory mission. As had always been since the dawn of history. The great explorers, who received honors, were in fact exactly the same as those who, before them, in the same exploration, had died, passing for loser, but in reality, the only different thing they had had was bad luck.

In the middle of an Arm, the process of searching for planets lasted a few weeks because of the high number of stars and lasted less and less while approaching the galactic nucleus, but there at the edges of the galaxy, there were very few stars and in most cases, spaceships such as the Tiger stand in space for months without finding anything.

The captain's nap became a sound sleep, then a prolonged absence and for a few days there was no more news of the captain. The Second, in the meantime, had camped on the command bridge of the huge spaceship, transforming it in a short time into a campground, also because in addition to him and the captain, the Tiger housed only the onboard computer, which since the time of Admiral Berg, everyone called Katjusa.

More than ten days had passed when the onboard computer finally announced with its persuasive voice that she had identified a possible target.

"Planetary system identified at alpha 312 degrees 12 minutes and 47 seconds, theta minus 8 degrees and 26 seconds, distance two hundred and twelve light years, stellar mass index 0.98, planetary mass index 0.04".

The Second stretched out long before reacting to the news. "Hey, Cap" he said on the intercom, "Katjusa found something."

"How much stuff?"

"Only one system, we are not even spoiled of choice."

"Okay, tell her to calculate a course while I get there."

When the captain arrived on the bridge, Katjusa announced in a voice in which it seemed to sense a bit of petulant satisfaction with her discovery, that she was ready to leave for the new destination: "two hundred and twelve light years away, ETE eight minutes twenty-two seconds, course 38 degrees and 22 minutes x, 18 degrees 22 minutes and 8 seconds y, 76 degrees and 6 minutes z, 92 degrees and 36 seconds w, all systems active, compartments sealed and watertight, AGRE engine in standby."

"She couldn't wait" the captain jangled.

"Me too, to tell the truth" added the Second whispering.

"I can see it, this place looks like a gorilla cage that hasn't been cleaned for two months" said the captain looking around, "how come you're so hairy?"

"And you so glabrous?" echoed the Second.

"Katjusa, activate" ordered the captain removing a tray of leftovers from his armchair.

The Tiger appeared at the edge of a planetary system, where telescopes immediately took measurements of where they were and what kind of planets they were. The voice of the computer was heard after a few moments.

"Metric sensor diagonalized, ATE eight minutes and two seconds, twelve planets identified, two S-class, three super S-class, two T-class, five D-class. Periods in standard galactic years, zero point eight, one point fifteen, one point fifteen, one point..."

"Halt!" shouted the captain, "what are you saying Katjusa, that two planets have the same period?"

"Yes, Captain, two planets in opposition occupy the same orbit" replied the computer with a soft and submissive tone.

"She makes me horny when she's so obedient, are they by any chance the two Class T's?"

"Yes, Captain" replied the computer with a whisper, as if it were a declaration of love.

"Lucky son of a bitch!" exclaimed the captain.

"Really a great fortune" added the Second, "a single planetary system and moreover with two Class T planets, it's our lucky day!" commented the Second.

"You can say it out loud, all right Katjusa, let's get to the closer."

In contrast to the silence of the AGRE engine, the hum of the gyroscopes of the inertial propulsion made itself distinctly heard and the heavy spaceship, full of its organic load of primordial life that, in fact, was as the captain claimed very similar to the contents of a rotting pond, set course for the planet.

"We will follow the standard procedure as usual: we put ourselves into orbit, do optical and radar analysis, map the planet and then send down our load of crap. I'm really curious to know if this planet is just like the other one" said the captain.

The Kobayashi Tiger did not take long to enter a low orbit around the planet, where the sensors began their analysis.

Not a minute passed by, when Katjusa's voice was heard again.

"Planet eighty-eight percent watery, presence of biological mass, approximate estimate of composition by weight, seventy-four percent clupea philcardus, eleven percent palaemon serratus, other species in varying proportions" she said with the voice that would had a waitress dressed as a bunny in a nightclub, that had summarized the menu of the day to some wealthy customers, expecting a hefty tip.

"What?" the Second and the Captain exclaimed together.

"Translate Katjusa, what would a cloopee philcactus" growled the captain.

"Clupea philcardus Captain" Katjusa replied in an increasingly persuasive voice, "sardines, the planet is full of sardines."

"But, the hell ..., I can't believe this is happening to me. At first I really believed that we had had a damn luck to find two planets, but not this way!" exclaimed the captain, furious.

He thought about it a bit before adding "It is obvious that these worlds have already been colonized. Da Silva, how did we get to a planet already handled? Isn't the computer looking for the unknown ones?"

"In fact it is so, Captain, in the databases there is no trace of this planet. I've just checked" replied the Second, furiously tapping on his keyboards.

"Are you sure?"

"Sure, Katjusa confirms it too, you can believe her."

"So where did those sardines and the others come from, what were they? Those peelimooon sierrajeez..."

"Palaemon serratus, captain, shrimps ..." Katjusa intervened with an increasingly sweet and whispered voice.

"...those prawns and who knows what else? But then how many of them are there?" continued the captain, shouting without stopping.

"A lot Captain, really a lot" replied the Second who was scanning the planet through a telescope with a polarizing filter to see underwater, "you can see shoals everywhere."

"At this point we have to go down and find out what's going on. Here is a mystery like a bureaucratic mess of the Arm's administration that forgot about this planet or who knows what else. I've always said that bureaucrats don't do shit, they're just ride chairs while we're out here to solve the problems of their mess. In fact you know what I say?" continued the Captain, more and more upset, "first let's go and see if the other planet is full of these shitty sardines too."

When the spaceship was in orbit around the other planet, which was on the other side of the star around which the twin planets revolved, the telescopes began a new analysis.

"Planet eighty-six percent water, presence of biological mass, approximate estimate of composition by weight, seventy-five percent scomber scombrus, twelve percent palaemon serratus, other species in varying proportions" Katjusa said in an unusually monotonous tone that contributed to increase the irritation of the Captain.

"Translate" he growled.

"Mackerel" was the laconic response of a Katjusa with an almost offended tone, for which one could have guessed even a rolling of her eyes if the computer had had them.

"And we have completed the mixed fried fish!" concluded Da Silva sneering.

The captain took on a desperate expression; put his hands in his hair and screaming "I must think" he walked away from the bridge.

It was almost an hour before the captain returned, angrier than before, and with his face full of furious scratches.

"There's nothing else to do but go down and see" he said in an annoyed tone, trying to calm down, "it is expressly forbidden to pollute a planet that already has life forms, although I have no idea who wrote such a rule, since we have never found any planets with life. Do we have equipment for aquatic exploration?"

"Oh yes, we have a little bit of everything here, I think there are also two fishing rods somewhere."

"Fuck you Da Silva" exclaimed the Captain.

"Heh heh heh" sneered the Second, more and more amused. "We descend to an emerged land near a shore and from there we begin. Katjusa, keep the ship on standby until we get back, don't take any action, is that clear?"

"Clear Captain" replied Katjusa with a sweet and gentle voice again.

"Let's go Da Silva."

The exploration module, which from the outside looked like a huge tank, leaned gently on the shore of a sea just moved by a warm breeze. The two mates sure of an environment harmless to them because of the presence of terrestrial fish fauna, came out of the tank without any protection other than that of their clothes and immediately realized that even those were too much.

"It's very hot here" observed the Second, "if it weren't for this bare land, it would seem to be on a tropical beach, look what a beautiful blue sea."

They stripped themselves of all their clothes and without even thinking about, as naked men as they were, headed for the shore of earthy sand, where they entered with their feet into the sea, regardless of procedures and precautions.

"Even the sea is nice and warm, really enjoyable you have to admit it" said the Captain returned quiet.

"Sun and sea, naked on a beach, a real dream" added the Second. While they were considering whether to go further into the water for a swim before beginning their investigations, a head with long blonde hair emerged from the water. The head was followed by shoulders and finally a half-bust with two breasts that would leave any man open-mouthed.

"Hello men" said the figure while behind her appeared two other identical figures.

"Wow" exclaimed the Second, "where did you come out from?"

"We would have to ask that question to you" answered one of them.

"Right" the Captain assented, "we are the crew of the spaceship Tiger of Orion's Arm on an exploratory mission. I am Captain Boriwen and he is my second officer Da Silva. And who are you and where do you come from?"

"Then welcome, we are the people of the sea and we come

133

from nowhere, we live here."

"But it's not possible!" the Captain blurted out, "all human beings come from somewhere, on the planets we get there only by spaceships. Nobody, in quotes, *lives here*, except those of the planet of origin of all of us, which is not this one."

"But we are not human beings" replied another.

The Captain and the second looked at each other in astonishment.

"Excuse me, but to us you look like women, and beautiful to tell the truth and you speak our language so you must be human beings" insisted the Captain.

"That's because you didn't see our bottom" replied one, and as if to add a demonstration to her reply, she quickly approached the shallow water of the shore, where she stretched out along its entire length and it was at that point that the two men saw what it was all about.

"Mermaids!" exclaimed the Second.

In the meantime, the other two mermaids, who had also approached and stretched out in the shallow water, invited the two men to lie down with them. The two didn't need to be told twice, given the gentle manners of the mermaids, added to their bursting beauty, at least as far as the body had human form.

"This tail of yours has a charm" said the Second to the mermaid lying next to him.

"Do you like it?" replied the mermaid, shaking it as if wagging a tail, producing abundant splashes of water.

"Yes, it has its own charm, so long and elegant, it gives you a spindly line, you will be at least nine feet long. You all look to me like you came out of a fairy tale; do you know that in our legends there were beings like you?"

"They were not beings like us, they were just us" replied the mermaid.

"Really? Didn't you say that you live here?"

"Indeed we do, we have lived here for a long time, but we also come from your own planet. We moved here many generations ago" replied the mermaid.

"And you have brought the fish with you, that's why the sea is full of sardines, isn't it?" concluded the Second.

"Clever boy, otherwise what were we eating? There was nothing here but the sea, and it was a bit dirty to tell the truth. At first it smelled awful. I wonder why everything in the galaxy stinks so much of sulfur" said the mermaid curling her nose, "in short, we had to take everything with us. Anyway there are mackerels here; it's on the other planet that there are sardines."

"What?" intervened the Captain who was listening to the conversation, while wondering if it was appropriate to try to touch the mermaid next to him. "So there are mermaids like you on the other planet too?"

"Of course, we are two families with different tastes, those who like light fish, those who like dark fish" replied the mermaid with a smile and then added, "but every now and then we exchange, just for the sake of variety."

"So you also have spaceships?"

"Yap."

"And if you have spaceships, you will have a technology, an industry, workshops" the Captain continued in the interrogation.

"Obviously."

"And where are they? We have seen nothing."

"Underwater" replied the mermaid next to him, "we prefer to go unnoticed, anyhow you can touch me Captain, I see that you have had this desire for a while."

The Captain made a gesture of surprise, as one caught in the act just before stealing, and then hesitant put his hand on the belly of the mermaid who looked at him smiling.

To the touch he felt a very different skin from human skin and it was that feeling that gave him the measure of how much the mermaids were a really different species. A shiny and oily skin, but touching it did not give him a feeling of disgust. Rather it was like caressing human skin sprinkled with abundant tanning oil, and to that thought, the feeling gave him an intense pleasure. Then the Captain gathered up the courage and caressed that smooth skin down to under a breast. The mermaid continued to smile. His hand went up again, and he fingered the big breast that looked like something out of an erotic comic book.

For a desire that could not be explained, to which perhaps contributed the blue and warm sea, the gentle breeze, the nakedness of his body, the captain approached the nipple with his lips and tried to suck. Sweet, almost sugary milk immediately came out of the nipple. This also caught him by surprise and in a sudden impulse said to his Second "you have to try" before letting go completely, attached to that breast, lulled by the waves, in the arms of the mermaid who began to sing a gentle and sweet song.

The sun of the planet was now almost at sunset when the two of them came back from that day on the beach, during which, slowly, the mermaids made them experience all the pleasures that their imagination was able to imagine and on a couple of occasions they went even beyond that. In the end the mermaids announced that they would leave them alone for the night, but that they would return at dawn.

The two, left alone, lit a fire on the shore and like two companions on vacation in the tropics they began to feast with some supplies from their tank, meditating aloud on the events of the day.

"What do you think?"

"I don't know, they're exactly like in the legends, they are really a dream."

"But in the legends, I think I remember that they used to kill the sailors."

"Is that so?"

"Yes"

"So what?"

"Yeah, so what?"

"Exactly."

Long moments of silence followed.

"Listen, what you want in life?" asked the Captain to the Second, breaking the silence.

"Me?"

"Yes you."

"Until this morning I knew, now not anymore, I think."

"So what is life to you?" insisted the Captain.

"Mmmmm. Futility, agitation for little, problems. But one thing is for sure, most of the time: dissatisfaction" replied the Second.

"I have lived more today than in the rest of my life" considered the Captain as having changed the subject.

"True. I totally agree" concluded the Second.

Still long moments of silence.

"How old are you?" the Second asked the Captain.

"Forty."

"If you are lucky you live sixty more. A day and a half like this day, in proportion" considered the Second.

"Yap" the Captain assented.

Again a long silence.

"So if we were to stay here another two days..." said the Second like out of the blue.

"I was thinking that too" the Captain interrupted him without letting him finish.

"Then we agree."

"Absolutely."

The night came and the two slept like never before, lying naked on a beach, without danger, without discomfort, without harassment of noise and insects. The morning found them sitting on the sand at the edge of the backwash, with a resolute gaze waiting for the return of the mermaids, who did not make them wait long.

"Good morning" they said in a chorus as they emerged from the water, and with a big smile came to lie down beside them.

"We have to solve a problem, right?" a mermaid told the Captain immediately.

"There, you see?" the Captain then said to the Second, "now I understand where this magic that surrounds them comes from. With you, we always understand each other, on all levels and for everything" he added, turning to the mermaids. "Yes, we have a problem to solve."

"And the problem is: what do we do with your spaceship?" said the quiet mermaid, smiling.

"I don't know how come you understand everything so well. Even if, to tell the truth, we haven't even talked to each other about this, but I know that my Second thinks the same as me, don't you Da Silva?"

"Yes Captain, we want to stay here forever so we have to make the spaceship disappear."

"As I thought" concluded the captain.

"It's not intuition, Captain, it's experience. Since our people have memory of it, when men meet us they don't want to leave us anymore. It has always been so."

"I believe it, seeing how beautiful you are, but above all, how kind and open to any desire you are."

"Thank you Captain, however, our look does not have much to do with it. Even among you there are some great beauties that you are inclined to desire, but your species always behaves so harshly, so... unhappy."

"So it is clear that as soon as you see us, you fall in love, that's why we were sure you would want to stay" concluded another mermaid.

Making a spaceship disappear is a more complicated business than it seems. The two mates realized it as soon as they begun discussing a strategy with the mermaids. Empty space is a place where nothing can be destroyed. The mermaids pointed it out to them, when they proposed to solve the problem with a bang.

"From an explosion always come out fragments that in space will then follow a straight motion, even for centuries or millennia. Therefore, all it takes is for someone to find two fragments and measure their speed vector, then extending the two vectors backwards where they met to find the exact point where their trajectories originated, i.e. the place of the explosion. So sooner or later someone will come, you can be sure of that."

"But why you don't want to be found? I mean, not that I mind, because here two of us are enough" asked the Captain.

"And in any case, if we get bored of each other, we can always be one on one planet and one on the other" added the Second.

"I don't think it will happen" replied the Captain, "as far as I'm concerned, I'm fine on my own here but I know that happiness needs sharing otherwise it soon becomes frustrating, and then every now and then I'll need the company of my fellow man, if only to exchange a few thoughts. For this purpose two of us are enough, three already would make this planet seem a bit crowded to me."

"We prefer to remain hidden" replied a mermaid, "and the reason is already in the words you have just said to each other."

"By the way, do you have names?" asked the Second.

"No, real names like yours we don't have. In the water we draw the attention of someone with a modulated whistle. Everyone has their own whistle, well that's a name, but you would have difficulty repeating it so feel free to give us a name as you like."

"Oh how nice, then I guess I'll call you like the tattoos you have on your skin, for example I'll call you Flower" said the Second to the nearest mermaid, who was beginning to consider her as his companion.

"Oh thank you Da Silva," replied the mermaid, "it's also pretty."

"We could blow up the spaceship on a very low orbit, so the fragments will fall back on the planet and nothing will be found" suggested the Second, resuming the discussion.

"But can't you just leave it in orbit for as long as you are here?" asked the mermaid who had called Flower.

"Heh heh heh, no way. Katjusa remained on the spaceship, and despite her mellifluous and sweet voice, she is more of a pain in the ass than you can imagine. At the slightest suspicion of something wrong, in a microsecond she sends out a warning call on all communication bands with a built-in position" said the captain.

"Who is this Katjusa?" asked a mermaid.

"The onboard computer, she runs the whole damn thing."

"But then if it is a computer, just turn it off" opined another mermaid.

"What a naivety! It's not that easy, she doesn't have the on-off switch" replied the Captain.

"There will be a power source on the spaceship, turn that off" insisted the mermaid.

"Yes, and for each one we turn off there is a backup system that Katjusa controls, and anyway at the first attempt to cut her power in a microsecond she sends a distress signal and secret goodbye."

"Take away her way to communicate, she will have an antenna" suggested another mermaid.

"Unfortunately we don't have just one, you know, in case one breaks up. The spaceship is basically like a hedgehog full of spikes, which would be the antennae. As we detach one of them, she realizes it and in a microsecond she sends..."

"... a distress signal, I've got it" the mermaid interrupted him. "Then wouldn't it be possible to convince her not to send out any alarms?"

"And how do you plan to convince her? By showing her your tits like you did with us? She's a computer, honey! She follows very precise programs" replied the Captain.

"Modify the programs then."

"It's a way, but it takes time because she has a lot of mission management programs and all with failure alarms, so as soon as we modify one, Katjusa notices and ..."

"...sends a distress signal in a microsecond", the mermaids chanted in chorus, concluding with a laugh.

"It would take a computer virus" the Second thought aloud. "Right, a virus!" exclaimed the Captain, "but where do we find one? Do you have computers?" he asked the mermaids.

"Of course we do."

"Then you'll also have computer viruses."

"No Captain, we can't help you in this because we don't do anything to harm, and not by moral rule, we simply find it useless. We are the exact opposite of you that the first thing that comes to your mind to solve a problem is the destructive solution. For example, if we had thought like you, we would have killed you immediately to keep our secret, because there are only two of you. But in doing so, we would only have gotten others to follow you. In fact, as you are explaining, your spaceship not seeing you coming back would have sent the alarm and who would have arrived here, would have arrived also very angry and well armed. Do you see Captain? To the damage always follows a damage, to the destruction always follows another destruction" concluded the mermaid.

"But you could have also destroyed the spaceship."

"And how, captain? We have no offensive systems, we have never built a weapon in our entire history, we are not like you who are always armed to the teeth."

"So you didn't kill us just to keep others from coming?"

"No Captain, see? You still think in a negative way. We have not killed you because it is not a solution for us, regardless of the results that would be obtained. You are here and therefore we must accept you. And with a guest it is always better to have a good relationship, even if he has not been invited."

"Then you don't really like us."

"Well, we are two different species, we can't start a family and make many beautiful children together, that's for sure, but you have your qualities that we like enough" said the mermaid slyly.

"For example?" asked the Second intervening in the discussion after having reluctantly abandoned Flower's breasts to which he had meanwhile attached himself.

"For example your sexual organ so ... so much. It's not bad" said one mermaid while the others smiled and nodded.

When they heard that statement, the two exchanged a look of mutual understanding and as males, they suddenly felt like they had gained two pounds of proudness. As a consequence, the discussion was suspended for a couple of hours. Then, with a snap of his tongue, the Captain resumed the argument.

"All right, I get it, you don't have a virus. But do you see that now it would have been useful?"

"Oh yes, at the moment, destroying always solves, but there is always also a non-destructive solution, it's just a matter of finding it" his mermaid answered him.

"Easier said than done!" exclaimed the Second with a listless tone like that of one who is directing his attention in a completely different direction, then returning with his gaze on Flower who was smiling at him.

"It is about convincing Katjusa not to say anything, everything else is academic" the Captain then cut short. "With all the security systems it is equipped with, that spaceship could go around the space even alone, it would lack only the fantasy of where to go, but to travel a way back, the fantasy is not necessary."

"Excuse me, your computer still does not know about our existence, so what should it say? Just never let it knows" opined a mermaid.

"Maybe she knows. After all, as she has found the presence of fish, she may have already found you too."

"But if she found us, how would she classify us?" insisted the mermaid.

"Right. As a species you are not known to us. I would say that Katjusa has classified you as belonging to the most related family in her database, dolphins maybe?" said the Captain.

"Surely, we live exactly like them."

"Good. I would say that we have a solution" concluded then the mermaid. "Go back to your spaceship and tell the computer that here besides the fish there are only dolphins and the computer will believe you. Then go back to where you came from and nobody will ever know about your discovery. You have the coordinates and in a second moment you can always return with a less indiscreet spaceship."

The two of them thought about it a little bit and the more they thought the more it seemed to them that the solution suggested by the mermaids was the only one possible, and there

142

and then they forgot that Katjusa's telescopes followed and recorded their every action.

So they decided to spend a few more days on the planet, before returning the spaceship to its arsenal.

They were carefree days, during which they collected memories for a lifetime, and in the end, completely changed in the most hidden corners of their souls, they resolved to leave.

Indissolubly bound by those memories, by mutual agreement they bid farewell to the exploration company and as professional navigators as they were, with makeshift means in the form of an old space cart with a computer with a metallic and nasal voice that spoke only infinitives verbs and a marked defect in the pronunciation of the 'v', they returned to the twin planets of the mermaids.

What they found, however, were only abundant sardines and mackerels and by mutual agreement, they decided that their life had had more than a man could ever hope for, and that living further without the mermaids would be a pointless nuisance. After saying goodbye with a long hug, they solved their sorrow for the loss of the mermaids with the method applied by their species since time immemorial, i.e. destruction and with a smile on their lips they shot each other.

15 THE GALACTIC WARFARE

Everyone was present at the new Project Committee meeting, with noise in proportion.

"Fifty millicycles have passed since the last meeting" began the Chairman of the Absolute Order of Space-time with an initial thundering voice that became lower and lower as the assembly fell silent, "because apparently there were no more deviations from the Project. However, the situation has changed; General Operations Director begins the meeting."

"Yes Chairman" replied the G.O.D. "So, I will summarize the situation briefly. This rather extended interval of the Project was characterized by the absence of unforeseen events. However, now this statement is no longer true but first of all it will be better to examine together what is happening. Social Systems Technician, tell us all."

The Social Systems Technician took the floor.

"The situation can be summed up in just two words: total war" said the technician then rummaging through the pile of documents he had brought to the meeting while everyone waited patiently.

"Here it is!" he announced triumphantly after finding what he was looking for. "A map of the galaxy. It's a flat cartography, that is, only three dimensions, because it is in it that the species moves. I have made copies that you can pass through."

He delivered to his neighbor an object that could have been well described by a man as a glass lens in which sand was immersed, distributed in such a way as to reproduce the shape of the galaxy: a large central ball with a disk formed by long spiral ribbons around it.

"As you can see" began to explain the Social Systems

Engineer, "the galactic core has one color, the spiral arms have another. They are the two zones of influence of the species. They are divided because the species is divided into two groups, that of the nucleus and that of the arms. The two groups are conducting a war that involves the whole galaxy. Apparently the population of the nucleus is trying to expand into the arms while the one of the arms is trying to prevent the invasion of its territories, but without trying to invade the nucleus in turn. In short it seems an action of containment of expansionist aims of the nucleus."

The Energy Systems Technician immediately intervened.

"War is an endemic state of this species, so where is the novelty? What distinguishes this war from any other war in their history?"

The Evolutionary Systems Technician promptly answered the question.

"It is true that there has always been war, but in the last sixteen microcycles the species had reached an almost total peace, due to the cultural change we had foreseen at the design stage. They did not understand their nature but they accepted the fact that the two genders are better off living divided and since the new social structure has spread all over, all wars have ceased, reducing themselves to just a few brawls, which is inevitable for a similar species. So this war so vast, indeed total, should not have happened anymore."

"I do not agree" said the Wizard, "no cultural conquest can ever overwhelm an endemic drive. It can mask it, even cancel it, but only for a limited interval, sooner or later its nature will always reveal itself."

"It's true" replied the Evolutionary Systems Technician, "but here we are dealing with events that are too fast. The restoration of the habit of war should have happened gradually, with the normal modes of territorial warfare or rivalry between some groups and then spread gradually. Here instead we are dealing with a hostility that suddenly ignited throughout the galactic volume. As if everyone, indiscriminately, had entered the clash."

"Both genders?" the Joker asked in a skeptical tone.

"Of course not" replied the Social Systems Engineer, "only males. The females have remained on the planets; they do not even have the means to get away from them."

"Some kind of jail" said the Joker.

"Well it's not really like that and anyway it depends on how you look at it" replied the Social Systems Technician. "In fact the males live on their own in space, without sharing in any way the life of the females beyond the necessary reproductive activity. So it is difficult to say who is confined and where. Are the females confined to the planets, or the males confined in space? In reality we know very well that males are little more than puppets operated by females who control them through the emission of pheromones. Therefore it is more appropriate to say that the females stay quiet on the planets while the males have been pushed into space. Of course the males are convinced that they have left, but what animal life would prefer the cold and emptiness of space to a warm planet! In the end, the males have learned that the only way to be free is to keep well away from their females, as happens with all sexual species."

"In short, they have completely renounced the feelings" concluded the Irrational Systems Technician.

"Something had to be given up" considered the Biologist intervening in the discussion, "but, in fact, they have become a sad, very sad species. If there had not been this crisis, soon we would have had to worry about their state of sadness and the consequent lack of desire to procreate. However, the new facts have swept this concern away. In fact, it seems to me that they have thrown themselves enthusiastically into this new war effort."

"It seems to me too" added the Evolutionary Systems Technician, "and the question is: why? Which new factor has intervened?"

"Ehm" mumbled the Diffused Systems Technician to draw attention. "During your long discussion I had the opportunity to meditate deeply on this problem of war" he said in a somewhat mocking tone. "A total war can only happen because of a general change of circumstances, be they physical or cultural. Do you think that a sudden cultural change in the whole species is likely or possible?"

"I exclude it" replied the Evolutionary Systems Engineer promptly, "cultural diffusion is governed by a finite speed equation."

"Then all that remains is a physical change. Do the Physicist or the Kinetic Technician have something to say about it?" concluded the Evolutionary Systems Technician.

"Now that you ask me" replied the Physicist with his usual grumpy tone, "there has indeed been a change of circumstance, but it is very slight."

The silence fell.

"And..." said the G.O.D. after a while.

"Do you want to know what it is?" mumbled the Physicist.

"If it doesn't bother you too much" said the G.O.D. in an impatient voice.

"I'm surprised that the Diffused Systems Technician didn't notice it, the phenomenon has already started by a millicycle, the Joker knows it as well" replied the Physicist.

"Oh yes, I know that too" intervened the Joker, "and since I see that he does not speak willingly ..."

"I don't speak because usually nobody understands what I say" the Physicist interrupted him, "do you really want me to tell you? Well, it is soon done: the nucleus is undergoing a homeomorphism due to the approach of the intersection."

"What did he say?" asked the Aesthetic Technician to his colleague by his side.

"See?" grumbled the Physicist and withdrew himself in mutism.

"He said that the galactic nucleus is deforming because it is beginning to feel the gravitational pull of the approaching galaxy" explained the Joker, "and before you start asking questions, it is better that I explain the phenomenon in its entirety. In their approach, the two galaxies feel the gravitational pull on each other. These forces are still very weak because there are still almost one hundred and fifty microcycles missing at the intersection. However, since the galaxies are more similar to gaseous bodies than to rigid bodies, they have started to deform. Instead of two spheres, now the two nuclei have a slightly egg-shaped, while the phenomenon is still invisible in the arms that by their nature are more variable in shape. The deformation of the galactic nucleus is the cause of perturbation of the motion of the stars that compose it, and since these stars are very close to each other, it is likely that collisions have begun to occur."

"Wow!" exclaimed the Biologist, "there must be quite a mess down there."

"Not yet" replied the Joker, "but there will be soon. Perhaps the part of the species that populates the galactic nucleus has noticed and started to move, but for now the phenomenon is still very subtle. Anyway, this is the only physical change that has occurred."

The Diffused Systems Technician intervened, who was taken aback and had immediately studied carefully the galactic cartography provided by the Evolutionary Systems Technician.

"As you can see from the map, the occupied area in the nucleus is only the peripheral area of the outer surface. In fact the actual nucleus is unreachable due to the excessive density of energy that fills it, so the species has colonized only the planets on the surface. So here is my hypothesis about what is happening to the nucleus: the stars of the outer part have changed their orbits. From the point of view of a planet, the change in the orbit of its star is a gigantic phenomenon from which it is impossible to come out unscathed, so the species has moved. Inward, however, they cannot escape because it is not inhabitable, so they must escape outward, that is, to the arms. And here the conflict arises: the arms are already occupied."

"Hence the war" concluded the Evolutionary Systems Technician.

"A logical conclusion ..." said the Wizard.

"Thank you" replied the Diffused Systems Technician.

"...but hurried" added the Wizard.

"Why?"

With patience, the Wizard began to explain his thesis.

"First, I believe that fifty millicycles of space navigation were enough to teach them that separate territories in three-dimensional space are not as separate in real space. It is true that the species reasons in a three-dimensional way, not to say two-dimensional because most of them never raise their eyes from the ground, but their strategists and navigators have long abandoned that habit. To escape from the core they could easily jump the arms and move directly to the periphery, or the halo, it's just a matter of taking the right route. That's something they know how to do, but they haven't done it. Secondly, they have not come any closer to occupying all the planets available in the arms, so a territorial clash is not possible. We are talking about three hundred billion individuals, which for a galaxy, even if compared to the arms alone, is not at all a large amount."

"So, what would be your conclusion?" the G.O.D. asked.

"The conflict is cultural, although it has just been said that a sudden cultural change is not possible" concluded the Wizard. "By this I do not intend in any way to deny the validity of the equations of diffusion of ideas, but those equations exclude a cultural change in the short term, not in the long term. In my opinion, therefore, the cultural change had already been going on for a long time, we just didn't notice it. The instability of the core only provided the spark for the bursting of the contrast, provided that this instability had some part in all this and is not merely a coincidence."

"And what would this cultural change be?" asked then the Evolutionary Systems Technician.

"Hard to say, the species has not been observed for almost thirty millicles so we have no data. Who knows what happened, but surely the two populations, nucleus and arm have been divided, the map in this regard leaves no doubt. In conclusion, since the species is one and one only, the division is necessarily cultural. Now, what has always been the engine of their aggressiveness?"

"Sexual repression" replied the Evolutionary Systems Engineer.

"In thirty millicycles, is it possible that the species has evolved freeing itself from such innate behavior?" the Wizard urged.

"Impossible" replied the Biologist, "the first long phase of the Project has deeply rooted in them that behavior. Even if they had started such an evolution, thirty millicles are not enough for it to be completed on all the individuals of the species, or at least a large part, considering that they are also a large number and even scattered throughout the galaxy."

"So the motivation for war has always remained the same as they had since the dawn of their history" concluded the Wizard.

"Do you therefore maintain that it is to be excluded any other reason for the species to go down in war?" asked at the end the G.O.D.

"Yes, Director, the species has indeed progressed and now they know how to find a way to avoid fighting. The only case in which they are absolutely unable to agree is when sexual motivation is involved. In that case they stop thinking and become emotional. Moreover, in this case the only serious reason would be the territorial one which, as we have seen, is not actually there."

"In short they are making war for their females" concluded the Joker, "as always."

"For now, nothing tells us that this is the case" replied the Wizard, "but we are unaware of their current social structure. Some unforeseen change must have taken place."

"A sudden change in their social structure?" exclaimed the Social Systems Engineer, "do you have any idea of the stupidity you are saying? How can a change in the short term appear in three hundred billion individuals?"

"Gentlemen, we are discussing without data. Remaining in the field of hypotheses we will only fight and indeed, it seems to me that your interventions are already pervaded by a somewhat polemical tone. The meeting is suspended waiting for new data" cut short the G.O.D. "The Evolutionary, Diffused and Social Systems Technicians will organize a quick exploration, we will meet again in a millicycle."

In silence everyone left the Meeting.

13th interlude

"Maybe we should have told him about the halo."

"He will find out for himself."

"And when he does, he's gonna be very angry."

"But in the meantime we will have gained some microcycles, by now we are close to the intersection and each microcycle makes it more and more difficult to go back."

"Let's hope so."

"So shall we do this exploration?"

"Oh yes, let's go spy a bit, you know just for fun, because we already know what there would be to discover. As always the Wizard is right, as usual there are females involved."

16 THE DOMAIN OF THE GNA

"You know, the galaxy had become almost boring without some war here and there" said the Superplexor to his Fleet Maneuverers, "with these great maneuvers we've animated it a bit, but for some years now we've been at a standstill and space has become boring again."

"It's like a game of tic tac toe" said the 36th Fleet Maneuverer.

"Tic tic tic what?" asked the Superplexor.

"A very old game, Plexor, the two opponents had balls and crosses in nine squares, the winner was the one who could place three in a row, but there was no way to do it if the two players did not make a mistake, so it always ended up even."

"Mmmm, an interesting comparison, it looks just like our situation."

"Yes Plexor, so far no one has made mistakes, but sooner or later it will happen. If I didn't have the evidence, I would find it impossible that in forty-eight years no vessel has ever made it past the blockade."

"Space has become an exact science" replied the Superplexor, "since maneuvers have passed under the control of computers, there is no way to escape unnoticed. After all, the routes are only eigenvalues of a matrix determined by the metric of space, and therefore they are calculable by everyone, to the millimeter."

"But space changes, Plexor" observed a Maneuverer.

"Yes but very slowly. However, it is not certain that no one has ever got over the Arms blockade. Maybe someone has succeeded, only that he never came back to report it."

"True, but the distinction is irrelevant because the result is the same" observed a Maneuverer.

"But why the hell this blockade exists?" asked another Maneuverer. But the question was rhetorical and nobody expected an answer.

The blockade of the Arms had begun subtly, imperceptibly, two centuries earlier. In the Nucleus no one knew the reason; in fact, initially they had not even noticed it for the simple fact that no nucleus ship undertook routes beyond the first third of each Arm.

It was a time when people traveled for trade, a little for tourism and very little for culture. The two areas of the galaxy both had planets of every kind, from arid to aquatic, from idyllic tropical to permanently frozen, and no one had a valid reason to travel outside its own space. Only a few eccentrics who wanted to see a different sky above them did so.

Little by little, however, the nucleus crews realized that if they wanted to go further out into the galaxy, they would encounter more and more difficulties.

The administrations of Arm's planets opposed a bureaucratic resistance that at about half distance from the outer edge became an almost solid wall. Formally the space was viable by everyone and in any direction, but in practice, the vessels of the nucleus were confined by such resistance.

Unapproved flight plans, take-off authorizations postponed indefinitely, congested routes, non-compliant equipment on board, staff not equipped with all the prescribed vaccinations, unexpected quarantine of the port of destination; any excuse was good to refuse them external routes.

They even went so far as to argue that on a planet on the edge one could not go because it was completely on strike, exhuming a concept that belonged to prehistory.

At the beginning the pilots of the nucleus did not pay much attention to all those excuses because in reality they had no need to go to the edge; in the galaxy the resources were spread everywhere and there was nothing in the Arms that could not be found also in the Nucleus and vice versa, so in front of the difficulties posed by the Arms, they gave up with a shrug of their shoulders and it ended there.

That passive resistance gradually formed a boundary in a galaxy that had been united until then. The two populations began to live a separate life and gradually became two different populations, divided by a clear border.

It was a cultural boundary of which no one had ever formally admitted its existence, but, in fact, it had become nonviable. Then one day someone from the Nucleus attempted a direct route to the edge without asking permission to the Arms. He never returned.

An accident (perhaps), isolated that nobody noticed. Over time, however, others tried, getting the same result and the databases of the spaceport computers accumulated one record after another of open and then never closed routes with the strange correlation that they were all facing beyond the Unicorn Ring or in the direction of the halo for an equivalent radius.

As the number of lost vessels increased with time, the phenomenon was eventually noticed and someone reported to the GNA, the Galactic Navigation Authority, which in turn made a report to the Economic Chairman of the Nucleus, who, after a due pause, to allow the minimum layer of dust to be deposited on the report to make the practice doable, forwarded it to the Congress of the Planets of the Nucleus. The Congress took it into consideration only twenty years later, which in terms of government procedures meant almost immediately, during a session with eighty-two percent absences, a perfectly normal percentage in the habits and customs of that time of peace and prosperity without problems.

The Congress unanimously approved a motion to be transmitted to the Parliament of the Federation of Galactic Arms, which replayed that it would investigate the phenomenon at the competent structures and transmitted it to the Arms section of the GNA, where, thirty-five years after its writing, the report was lost.

The procedure was repeated several times with the same

result and after more than three centuries of losses and cover-ups, it was finally clear to the Nucleus that the Arms did not want to let them travel to the edge.

The long cultural separation had meanwhile clearly divided Arms and Nucleus. Different languages, fashions and arts, but above all they had differentiated in the character of the people. The Arms population was, who knows why, more adventurous, with an almost pirate behavior that sometimes even crossed the line. The core population was more phlegmatic, more dedicated to the exercises of intellect, without having managed to produce anything really important in that field. In short, some of them were cheerful but rude people, bordering on the unbearable, while the others were stiffed, sad and bored intellectuals, whose heaviness was also completely unbearable, and in the end, human beings were still those who had always been in their history: always and invariably unbearable (except for a small minority to which ninety-eight percent of the population thought they belonged).

Also for this division, in addition to a certain arrogant haughtiness that tended to consider the Nucleus as the most advanced center of civilization and the Arms of the galaxy as the equivalent of a backward and somewhat ignorant country territory, the men of the Nucleus were slow to realize the embargo that the Arms had silently tightened around them and that perhaps it was not even intentional.

In the end they reacted with an explicit request for explanations, but they forwarded it through diplomatic channels that ensured the certainty of the answer without content. Response whose preamble always began with a "Not that we ..." from which it could be deduced already at that point that continuing the reading of the next two hundred pages would have been completely useless.

From the diplomatic channels the problem was dealt with direct meetings of high government officials (ministers, admirals and presidents of various degrees) in successful social gatherings held on the most beautiful planets of the galaxy and for which platoons of young superlative women were hired, with the wage inversely proportional to the amount of clothing, usually reduced to the pure formality of its existence (for which the galactic fashion provided for three triangles of semi-transparent fabric, two of which equilateral and one isosceles, the latter dangerously close to being reduced to a thin straight line, which adhered to the skin by electrostatic force only), whose task was to settle the differences of the powerful through appropriate erotic maneuvers, and in which only the personal affairs of those present were successfully concluded, while government issues were drowned by the attentions, almost always oral, of the escorts who, as the time went by, became younger and younger.

Then they moved on to semi-private informal talks, which allowed the powerful to deal with even those delicate personal affairs that could not be discussed in public.

Finally, after a century and a half from the beginning of the embargo, or at least from the date when it began to be discussed, the formal request to suspend the embargo was finally made.

At the same time, information secret services had been reconstituted, which had fallen into disuse after millennia of peace, but the scarce habit of intrigue only managed to recruit young men who, taking advantage of their privileged position, cheerfully infiltrated the planets of the other side wherever they found an access point, that is, a brothel.

And it was no surprise that they made the most important discoveries there, because one of the few sure rules of human behavior is that especially in bed the human being, and specifically the man, is of weak intellect. The news, however, were not taken seriously, given the frivolous source of them, and for other years nothing happened.

In the meantime, at the formal request for suspension of the embargo, the Federation of Arms opposed the request for proof of the existence of the embargo. Both central governments therefore set up commissions of inquiry that could only work on the reports of the agents posted in the opposing brothels and for this reason they did not reach any certain conclusion.

Finally the military moved with requests for routes to the edge. The unfulfilled requests became ultimatums that remained dead letter and finally the procedure lasted centuries, produced a resounding reaction for the galactic civilization, which materialized in a joint declaration of all the planets of the Nucleus of non-recognition of competence of the GNA of Arms, which, in the obscure bureaucratic language of the galactic administration, meant war, even if this word never appeared in any dispatch of the period.

The Nucleus then attached itself to the embargo, even if its existence was always denied, to move its spaceships against the Arms, but it was only a formal reason.

Miraculously, the only reason that the secret services had been able to find for that embargo was also the real reason, but the discovery was of no use because no one believed it to be so.

It was said that the population of Arms had found a new way to live in the halo. It was said that the traffic of men to and from the halo had been constantly increasing and that from the halo, the men did not want to return.

It was rumored that there lived a branch of the human species that had detached itself from time immemorial, where it had evolved according to unattainable canons of beauty, and that it was made up only of women, who, consequently, suffered from an endemic lack of men and therefore were all very, very, very benevolent towards any male, being him handsome or ugly. And it was quite obvious what effect such rumors could have on the fantasy of men in perpetual conflict with their women.

Of course it was all brothel talk, reported by women who carry a grudge against low-paying customers and therefore considered stingy, which is the worst thing a woman can think of about a man, and the reason why she knows how to unleash an endless string of mischiefs, injuries and malicious insinuations. So all the information was to be taken with caution but, in fact, the embargo existed and, in fact, no one had ever clarified the reason. And the fact that the men of the Arms were always more vital than the men of the Nucleus and that, vice versa, the

157

women of the Arms showed with those chatters that they had become more and more curmudgeonly over time, made the men of the Nucleus start asking themselves questions.

"What if it were true?" opined someone.

"Behind every fantasy there is always a bit of truth" the wise men, always experts in clichés, used to say.

"True or not, we have to find out the reason for this embargo" used to announce the governors, who were the only males in human history to have never suffered from the endemic lack of all males since the Upper Paleolithic, when they made the mistake of tolerating that ridiculous hippy revolution, revived since then on the occasion of every cultural revolution.

But as is well known, the human being is insatiable and always wants something more than what he already owns, so even those roosters who spent their lives moving from one orgy to another at the expense of the gigantic galactic public administration, wondered if it was true that a larger territory of conquest was really available beyond the Arms.

In the end, the Nucleus governors wondered if the Arms governors had not tightened the embargo just to prevent them from entering the new territory, because that would be the way they, like everyone else, would behave if they were in their place.

Since everyone tends to attribute to the others their own way of acting, in the end they were convinced, without of course admitting it, that the Arms governors had spread an impenetrable veil on the halo in order not to divide with the Nucleus the new ground of conquest, and in this conviction they asked and obtained a universal conference between Arms and Nucleus that was called "Universal Peace Conference" and was held on a planet called "Earthly Paradise", without this name having anything intentionally ironic, or sarcastic.

Centuries later historians would have identified that very conference as the summit meeting during which the powerful of the period, in the best tradition of the powerful, declared war through an exchange of compliments, sentences and mutual courtesies.

"Dear SuperPlexor, what a pleasure to see you again!" exclaimed the President of the Arms Federation.

"Mr. President! I see you in great shape" said the canute Superplexor, chief of staff of the Confederation of Planets of the Nucleus.

"You too Superplexor, you look like a young man."

"Eh, time goes by Mr. President, even if it doesn't seem so, you should have seen me when I was your age."

"But you are still young Superplexor, and then the important thing is to be young inside" replied the President with a greasy air.

"Yes, but if I were twenty years younger..." replied the Superplexor with a false smile.

"Unfortunately, youth comes only once. They must have been good times for you" the President considered then.

"They were indeed, but now things are no longer what they used to be Mr. President. By the way, what a beautiful place you have here!" exclaimed the Superplexor at the end, concluding the exchange of pleasantries.

"Oh well, yes it is quite suggestive, isn't it? But we had to work a lot on it, once it was all countryside here" replied the President with a modest air and making a wide gesture with one arm.

"Suggestive is putting it mildly. Sun, sea, white beaches, blue skies, all this lush green not to mention the service staff, but are they all like that?" he asked then pointing to a girl who wandered around the beach practically naked, carrying a tray full of cocktails with umbrellas.

"Of course, we select them on purpose, Superplexor. You sure understand, when you have to make important decisions, it is better to be surrounded by beauty so that you can be serene, don't you think?"

"Ab-so-lu-tely! Wise words dear President, wise words. Pity that I am now an old man! Ah, if I was twenty years younger" repeated the Superplexor, as if to return to the safe ground of the platitudes.

"Don't even say it Superplexor, you still have a lot to give!" exclaimed the President, discovering two round arches of teeth.

"You say?" replied doubtful the Superplexor to whom the adulations of the President were beginning to kick in.

"But certainly, you must have more confidence in you charm, I'll show you" said the President nodding to one of the young naked women who were wandering around the beach, ready for anyone would have her called.

The girl approached them and the President said: "Darling, I'd like you to meet the Nucleus Superplexor, would you be so kind as to show him what your duties are?"

"With great pleasure, Sir" the girl answered with a big smile and two big blue eyes, barred like those of a doll.

She got down on her knees in front of the Superplexor and started pulling his pants off.

"But what do you do! This is not the place!" exclaimed the Superplexor with great surprise, taking a step back.

"You don't have to worry about SuperPlexor" reassured the President, "there is no one on this planet other than the delegation of the conference, who happens to be all men. And the people on duty are all like the one in front of you, and they all have a job like the one you has just seen."

"Really? Interesting, really interesting" said the Superplexor still a little embarrassed, "you really know how to enjoy life here in the Arms."

"You only live once, dear Superplexor."

"It's really true dear President, if I were twenty years younger, I would have made this young girl dance on one leg!"

"However, if the situation embarrasses you, allow me to take my leave. I leave you to the loving care of this beautiful young lady" said the President as to get away and then added "but do you see Superplexor that you are still young? Look what happened between your legs!" concluded the President as he walked away.

The tinkering of the girl, who had never stopped, finally

convinced the Superplexor that the President was right and that he widely underestimated his temper as an old man over 80 years old, and vowed to take every opportunity, during that conference, to look for other evidence to that discovery.

The conference continued at various levels, with characters of equivalent power exchanging cordiality lying on the beach while the service staff provided to relieve them of tensions, unfortunately also obtaining a marked listlessness with respect to the complexity of the topics that should have been discussed, demonstrating that the President's thesis about the link between serenity and arguments was not so correct. In the end all they got was the exchange between them and their young assistants on the beach, of a complete collection of nonsense of no practical significance.

For example, while suffering the attentions of two superlative naked girls, a couple of them came to discuss the nature of the space and concluded that an embargo did not exist for the simple reason that the Arms and the Nucleus occupied the same space. Others agreed that the embargo was just a moot point and that in essence it was just a couple of closed spaceports and a handful of reports from some hysterical navigational director. Finally, there were also those who argued that from the point of view of navigation in variety, the Arms were inside the Nucleus and therefore if there was an embargo, it was because of the Nucleus to the Arms and not the Arms to the Nucleus.

In short, because of the innumerable presence of all those beautiful women, in front of whom every man sees his own capacity of reasoning disintegrated, no conclusion was reached, except for the one by the President of the Federation of Arms and the Superplexor of Nucleus to put the question to the two directors of GNA of Nucleus and Arms, without realizing that it was precisely the existence of two directors instead of one, to determine the existence of the embargo itself.

The two directors, individuals on the contrary a little dark and shady, met in completely opposite circumstances.

Sitting opposite each other, at the two ends of the table in the command room of a GNA spaceship, the two looked at each other in furtively, each trying to guess what the other was thinking.

"So what do we do about this embargo?" said finally the GNA director of the Nucleus.

"As far as I am concerned there is no embargo" replied the other.

"I agree, I meant what we say to our two governments" insisted the GNA director of the Nucleus.

"We tell them that as far as we are concerned there is no embargo" stubbornly replied the GNA director of the Arms.

"But our ships actually can't pass" opined the nucleus director.

"Neither can ours, for that matter. Anyway, that's fine with me" replied the Arms director.

"Well, I'm fine with that too" concluded the Nucleus director, as relieved.

"So we agree, the routes are closed and everyone has their own territory. Anyhow, no one goes hungry or suffers economic damage."

"In fact, I really don't understand the reason for this protest" replied the Nucleus director.

"Neither do I, dear friend, however, as long as we maintain the status quo, we keep our two chairs. If things change and the GNA will be unified again, in all likelihood a new director who is not pro one or the other side, as we are, will be appointed.

"So it's best to keep things the way they are. In fact, let me tell you that perhaps it would be appropriate that the embargo be made official."

"Officialized seems to me too much. Until now we have implemented it with gimmicks, I think that from now on we could instead implement it with a real regulation, of course something that would not be so evident."

"Do you have any ideas?" asked the nucleus director.

"Yes, one of my navigation technicians suggested that a

radial tax could be introduced."

"A fine idea."

"Then we agree?"

"We agree."

"Of course this understanding must remain secret."

"Of course."

"And of course you will also realize that such a measure will produce a flourishing smuggling activity and a consequent loss of movement of the spaceports."

"Of course, but that will be largely offset by the fee you were talking about."

"True. So we're done with that."

17 CHATTERING FROM THE NUCLEUS

The gunnery AGRE sergeant puffed drowned in sweat. "Damn battle, the things we do for women eh?" he said to his assistant to the piece, a young artillery rookie weighing a two hundred pounds, like all artillerymen.

"They say they are beautiful and also very sweet, unlike ours which look like assault infantry units" said the assistant. "Those who have had to deal with them, they said that they are great lovers and always want to!"

"Have you talked to anyone who has seen them?"

"No, they just told me" replied the assistant.

"Ah well, there seems to be a lot of talk about them, but in reality I've never really met anyone who has. I wonder if they really exist. The big shots say that we are going to war because of the embargo, but in reality even a child would understand that it is an excuse. It's as if a man protests because he can't go into women's toilets; so what?! We never went in the Arms."

"The big shots must have thought so too, obviously they know something more than we do."

"That's for sure" concluded the sergeant.

"But couldn't we just skip the Arms and go straight into the halo?" said the assistant to the piece.

"Boy, you don't know anything about the war yet and even less about space. Even if we did, we would find the Arms glued to our asses like crabs. The battle must be fought in any case, where it is not important."

"When you fight, you don't necessarily win" said the assistant with unexpected wisdom.

"Yes, so what? Do you prefer to live the way we live now?

Have you ever had a girlfriend?"

"What exactly do you mean *to have a girlfriend?*"

"That's exactly what I wanted to say; you don't even know what I'm talking about. I come from a planet inside the core, where life is still what it used to be. For a while I had a girlfriend, then I enlisted and that story was over. Or maybe the opposite happened, I don't remember well. When I returned to my planet, that too had changed and had become like everything else in the galaxy. No boy, doing as we do now is not the same as having a girl, something is missing."

"What?"

"I don't know, but I'm telling you something is missing and those in the halo still have it."

"And how do you know this?"

"That's just the point. It is more than a century that the Arms have become a sort of solid wall. Those bastards must be hiding something of great value and don't want to share it. What do you want it to be?"

"Women, nothing else can be, we have the bulk of the resources in the Nucleus" replied promptly the assistant.

"Good boy, you know how to use your head."

14th interlude

"So what did you find out?" asked the Ethics Systems Engineer to the Social Systems Engineer.

"I found out that we were completely off track. The war has nothing to do with the perturbations of the core."

"The Wizard said so."

"We don't call him Wizard for nothing, and he was also right about the reason for the war, it's always the same."

"So what happened?"

"There has been a change of cultural circumstance, a real change of boundary conditions. Ironically, the expression is to

165

be taken literally: there is another species in the halo."

"Oehi?!" exclaimed the Ethical Systems Engineer.

"Oh yeah" echoed the other one.

18 THE PLAN B

"Gentlemen, circumstances have changed unexpectedly because it seems that some of us have acted outside of the Project" said the General Operations Director opening the restricted meeting of the Project Committee. "Before reporting to the Chairman of the Absolute Order of Space-time, I would like to be clarified the circumstance, the reason and the substance of this change."

"It was an experiment and at the same time an emergency solution in case we had failed with the Project species" the Biologist replied promptly getting defensive, "it is a fork of a species that has always been present on the planet since the very beginning of the Project, a species known to them, even if given its shy nature, present only in mythological tales; therefore it was not really a subterfuge."

"Engineer, in their mythology there are many species but not because of this they exist or have really existed, or not?" replied the G.O.D. sharply.

"Well..." replied the cautious biologist, "let's say we experimented a bit, but they were all little amusements destined from the beginning to extinction. Beautiful species but clearly useless. Jokes of nature, you could call them."

"You played with fire" said the G.O.D.

"No Director, in no case those species have intervened in the Project. In fact they have always been relegated to their fantasy, nothing has been left to chance" replied the Biologist.

"So I wonder who and with what purpose has that species arrived in the halo, since nothing has been left to chance" said the G.O.D. with an inquisitorial tone.

"As I have just said, we thought to foresee a contingency plan in case of failure of the Project close to the intersection between the two galaxies, when at that point it would have been too late to take remedial action."

"I understand Engineer, but your department should have informed the Project Committee. Incidentally, this one of a contingency plan, an alternative plan, let's call it plan B, doesn't seem to me a bad idea and therefore I don't see why hide it."

"Yes Director" assented the Biologist.

"Now I would like to understand if this species has influenced the development of the Project in some way and what the consequences will be if it has happened" asked the G.O.D.

To the request of the G.O.D. replied the Evolutionary Systems Technician. "This new species, even if in reality it is ancient, is known to the main species since their appearance on the planet, but the fact has never produced any deviation from the Project. The new species has minimized any contact with the Project species. Not having an aggressive nature and not sharing the same environment, it has in no way influenced their way of thinking, except by appearing fleetingly in their fantasies because one of its most obvious characteristics is beauty, at least to the males of the species."

"In fact, until now the Project has not suffered any deviation" the Wizard intervened to sum up the complicated dissertation of the colleague.

"Until now, Wizard" replied the G.O.D., "but now it has become the reason for a war."

"Director" intervened the Evolutionary Systems Technician, "war has always been inherent in the nature of the species and consequently, no war can change the Plan. On the contrary, the presence of a war is the confirmation that the species behaves as always and that therefore it is still within the Project. As far as reason is concerned, you know well that no war has ever had one, if not the outburst of repressed aggressivity. We know very well that the species sticks to any excuse in order to put up a fight. "

"In fact, Director" added the Biologist, "one could consider the whole thing as a second species discontinuity, an evolutionary leap, and no discontinuity has ever put the Plan out of the way, indeed, in its essence the Plan is just a long line of evolutionary leaps."

"You could Engineer, but it is not. I remind you that a discontinuity is an evolution of the species itself, not the appearance of another species. Anyway, I turn to you Social Systems Engineer, have you noticed any effect on the species?"

"No Director. If there had been cross fertility, it would have had a devastating effect since the males of the species seem to prefer by far the females of the other species, especially for the more willing behavior, and I can well understand them. But even if this had happened, it would have led precisely to a discontinuity of the second species, since the intraspecies fertility would have led to the fusion of the two so that the Plan would have been undisturbed. Interfertility, however, is not there, so the new species is comparable to a leisure and nothing more. To the effects of the Plan is therefore irrelevant. However, I believe that in the long term, it will have a conciliatory effect between the two genera. For now, males are more interested in the new species than their females and of course the latter are very upset. But I am convinced that they will soon take a more lenient stance, after all they have treated their mates very hard, perhaps too hard, even though we know that we have programmed them precisely for that purpose."

"Will this conciliation has an effect on their evolutionary drive? Will it stop it?" asked finally the G.O.D., still reluctant to convince himself that there was no cause for alarm.

"It doesn't matter anymore, Director" assured him the Diffused Systems Technician. "In the condition in which they are now, the evolutionary push is no longer necessary. The only indispensable thing is that they survive the remaining fifty microcycles which are missing at the intersection, less to be precise."

"Fifty microcycles are not few. Given the current crisis, I wonder if they will make it" the G.O.D. asked.

"They have the same probability to survive with or without this crisis" replied the Evolutionary Systems Technician, then he added "But in all this there is also a positive fact."

"And what would this positive fact be?" asked the G.O.D.

"Recently the species had gone towards a demographic stasis, a worrying thing that we had already noticed because if a species stops reproducing or reproduces too little, it means that it has a serious problem. In the case of an intelligent species, it means that it no longer looks to the future, because it is clear that a species that has not offspring cannot have a future. Now instead, the demographic stasis is restricted to the nucleus population only, while that of the arms has started to reproduce again, even if with a still insufficient rate."

"Good. At least a solution to a possible problem has come out of this entire obscure affair" said the more peaceful G.O.D., "even if it seems to me that it happened almost by chance rather than by a well-designed plan and this is not honorable for beings like us, that everything should we foresee. Having ascertained this, can someone summarize what has happened?"

"I can do it" replied the Wizard.

"I listen to you" replied the G.O.D.

"It all started with a fork of a species also mammalian, albeit aquatic. This species inherited the behavior from its ancestors, a species called dolphins, among other things much loved by the Project species. The new species, moving by nature in a three-dimensional way, has independently developed a correct theory of space, without incurring that temporal oversight of the species. From the correct model of space to moving in space itself, it's a short step. In the meantime we had arrived at the conquest of space by the Project species, even if only with our help. The second species, which has always tried to keep its distance from the first, headed immediately to the halo where it settled. The contact between the new species and the population of the arms then happened by chance. At that point the emotionality entered, since the new species has the particular characteristic of looking very similar to the females of the other species, so the males were terribly attracted by them. The rumor spread, even if it took several microcycles, and in the end the species reacted as during the first discontinuity of second species, if you remember, that of the clubs: they thought well to appropriate the new females keeping away the others, hence the war."

"That's all?" asked the G.O.D.

"That's all'' answered the Wizard.

15th interlude

"Did you like the story I told the Director?"

"Very. It seemed true" replied the Biologist.

"It could have been."

"Not for those who know Plan B well. They have a life too harmonic to devote themselves to technology even if it is true that in that field they would have the intelligence to have a great success.''

"But that the war is for females is true, as it has always been."

"Undoubtedly"

"You transfer them, didn't you?"

"No, I just gave them the means. It was the Joker who told them where to go. He also gave them the coordinates of the planets suitable for them."

"Anyway, the Director bought it. I saved you."

"Saved from what?"

"You don't think the old man would have been as forgiving as he was, do you?"

"Well, the old man is disinterested in our stories, it's enough for him that in one way or another we populate the universe."

"Yes yes, but the last time he got angry, damn it, we had to do it all over again."

"Yes, it's been a hard job, but an even universe is a boredom, sometimes a big bang is healthy."

"Sorry but I prefer that boredom, and then there's always something to do for those with a bit of imagination" said the Wizard smiling.

19 THE HEROES OF BETTIE PAGE

As a matter of women, if there is one thing the men have never been lacking, this is the fantasy of the gimmick. In the middle of the galactic war, officially never fought, an enterprising owner of the Swan-Regolo Arm thought well to modify a cruise ship with a swimming pool, in a vessel with external water compensation accesses, directly connected to the pool.

After several sightings of halo vessels and after numerous interviews with the crews present at the sightings, the shipyard was able to reconstruct with a certain precision the shape and the mechanism of the hatchways of the halo vessels and to design a suitable connection flange accordingly. In fact, without such a mechanism, it would have been impossible, or at least very complicated, to pass from one ship to another, since the different fluids in which the two species lived did not allow the construction of an airlock that could be used by both.

The newborn was launched under the name of Bettie Page, with even a drawing of her, dressed as a mermaid under the name, because according to all those who had met the mermaids, she was the image in human history that more than any other resembled to them. Curious that in millions of years another woman of equal charm had not appeared, as proof of the extraordinariness of that famous Bettie and it was for this reason that those who chose the name claimed to have done so more for the biography of the character than for the appearance itself.

The maiden flight saw the entire ship occupied by war veterans who had taken precedence on the long reservation list at exorbitant prices, while the crew, excluding officers, was entirely made up of volunteers who might even have paid to have any job on board.

The great excluded were only the scientists. First because

they would have certainly pretended to be transported for free with the excuse of embarking for work, second because the Bettie Page did not leave at all for a research mission, but for an outing organized by a ship-owner for profit, taking advantage of the fact that to continue to support the groundlessness of the accusations of the Nucleus, the Arms had to formally deny the existence of any form of life in the halo. Of course, the Arms government was very happy with the initiative and contributed financially in a covert way, paying extra tickets to some agents of the information services, and since they were also veterans, the thing was formally unassailable.

The third and most important reason why the scientists were completely excluded was that with their pedantic mania to study everything, they would certainly have ruined much of the program that the veterans had in mind, if there had been the meeting.

The Bettie Page left the armament station in a blaze of fireworks, which to be visible in the vastness of the port in space, were made with thermonuclear devices of several megatons, now produced only for this purpose, which in the absence of gravity formed large luminous discs and pretty colored bubbles.

"Katjusa, route to the halo, galactic zenith, let's offer to our passengers a show not to be forgotten" ordered the Commander when the launching procedure was completed.

Since the times of the famous Admiral Berg, myth of every Arms man, the central computers of every Arms vessel were called Katjusa and they faithfully reproduced also the erotic pin-up voice, a voice that in the case of the Bettie Page was the most appropriate. The habit was so widespread that in the common speech the name had become synonymous with computers, and even something else.

The Bettie Page's Katjusa immediately responded to the command. "Calculated course, AGRE engine active, standby for destination, ETE in variety forty-eight minutes and twenty-three seconds" she said in a languid voice that in the Captain's imagination made her look like a perpetually naked woman.

"Activate" said the Commander, "Officer of Navigation, Commissioner, come with me, let's go to meet our passengers."

When the Commander began to speak, the Bettie Page's ceremonial hall was packed with noisy veterans.

"Gentlemen" began the Commander, "this is an inaugural flight that will hopefully become the first actual contact with the people of the halo."

A murmur and some irreverent comments on the expression *people,* winds into the hall.

"No one can assure that the meeting will actually take place, but we are all convinced that with a little patience the odds are in our favor" continued the Commander. "Of course, you will certainly realize how important it is to make a good impression this first time, if it ever happens. There will hardly be a second chance if we do not all behave well, always keep in mind that we have this great responsibility. So please leave your barracks habits and battle language in your cabin. Commissioner, you go ahead" concluded the Commander as he walked away.

"Welcome aboard the Bettie Page" said the Commissioner in a lighter tone, "you will find everything you need in your cabin, as no baggage is allowed on this maiden voyage. Surely you will understand that it was not appropriate to risk unpleasant accidents with some nuts carrying a weapon. You will also find underwater swimming equipment simplified, i.e. contact lenses for refractive correction to see in focus underwater, for those who did not understand it ..."

"We're not fish!" exclaimed someone with the tone of a precisely barracks joke.

"Here you go, this is the classic gag that will ruin the whole trip" said the Commissioner smiling, "try to let off steam now and remember that who we are going to meet will maybe look like a fish or an erotic dream, depending on the way you look at them, which is the reason why we are all here on this ship, but it is also an advanced civilization that travels in space, and feel mocked maybe they won't like it very much. Also because they are not fish."

With a whisper of assent the room became quiet.

"So we were saying" continued the Commissioner, "contact lenses, fins of various lengths that you will need to keep up with them, a rechargeable scuba with an hour's charge that you will need to have their own dive time, which is about ten minutes. All cabins have the recharging system. Be aware that it is useless to look for a BC[9], we have tried to keep things as simple as possible. To move up and down, you're on your own in there. On the other hand, you will only have to deal with thirty feet of water. Any question?"

"Yes, I have not seen bathing suits" said one.

"You did not see them because their use is not planned. We thought it appropriate to present ourselves exactly as we are to a species that presents itself exactly as it is. A sort of declaration of equality. They are naked, we will do the same. It is useless to bring our paranoia with us, accept it or not show up at the pool. The use of the pool has rules that you will have to respect and that I will now summarize quickly, but in each cabin you will find a detailed copy. Outside the pool room, you can continue to be what you are, a bunch of scoundrels."

A thunderous laughter broke out in the hall.

"So here are the most important rules. If and when the meeting will take place, as many people as our guests must enter the pool. We will not take them on board and leave them there all alone, right?"

"Nooo!" replied the audience in chorus.

"For hygienic reasons, especially towards our guests, anyone who pollutes the water with their own manure will suffer a fine that I assure you will be completely unaffordable, so before entering the water, go to the toilet. And finally here is the most important recommendation."

The Commissioner paused to emphasize what he was about to announce.

---

[9] Buoyancy Compensator

"We don't know if it can work between us and them because what we know about them are just uncontrolled rumors, so we are pioneers on this journey. Each of you has been carefully examined by a host of psychologists, but as we know, psychology is more an art than a science, so no one can be sure of his own behavior when in the presence of a mermaid. I have seen them, and I assure you that none of your best dreams come any close to them. If I have the chance to touch them, I do not know what I will feel and I do not know how I will react. That's why there are tranquilizers in all the cabins; use them. I recommend everyone to use common sense and remember that the future, and perhaps the fate of all the men of the Arms, depends on you."

The speech was followed by applause.

"I forgot" said the Commissioner again when applause and vocalizing were appeased, "your personal hygiene in the pool is irrelevant, the entire volume of water is reclaimed in just twenty minutes. This means that although it is a swimming pool, you will find yourself swimming in a very fast current, after all our guests can move even at twenty knots and maybe a nice current will be a great fun for them. But my advice is to try not to smell anything. Contrary to what you might think, in the water the smells propagate very well, maybe even better than in the air and with this I wish you a good stay on board the Bettie Page and I remind you that after dinner, in the main hall will be projected an ancient film, kindly provided us in copy by the Department of Expressive Paleography of the University of Honky Tonky, of the real Bettie Page, entitled *Bettie Page revealed.*"

When the Bettie Page arrived at her destination in the halo, warned by the officers everyone rushed to the ship's observers to see the spectacle of the galaxy in its entirety. It was like a large pinwheel with a bright white central bulb and the five spiral arms wrapped around it like ribbons attached to a moving wheel. It was a grandiose spectacle for which even the most hardened veteran remained open-mouthed.

There were those who tried to identify the position of their planet or at least of the Arm's sixth of their origin, but soon everyone discovered why computers were needed to avoid getting lost in space and why the Course Officers were so important.

The Bettie Page spent long days standing in the same spot of space, among observations of the galaxy that soon became for everyone just a huge chandelier suspended above the windows and buffet to pass the time, waiting for contact with the people of the halo that the experience had taught, did not take long to show up if one stayed still long enough.

Finally after twelve days of waiting and boredom, with her usual voice full of eroticism that contrasted with the coldness of her technical language, Katjusa announced the contact.

"Unidentified contact at four o'clock, elevation minus twelve, distance one hundred and forty miles, galactic coordinates alpha 2 degrees 12 minutes 1 second, theta 89 degrees, 59 minutes, 58 seconds. Communication channel open, synchronization performed, relative motion: zero" announced his sexy voice on the bridge out of the blue.

The sleepy Bettie Page woke up with a bang.

"Good morning men, do you have problems? Are you in trouble?" said a mermaid's voice from the speakers.

"Good morning, I am the Navigational Officer, the Commander has already been called to the bridge, will arrive in a moment. We are happy to see you and no, we don't have any technical problems."

Before leaving there had been a discussion among all the officers about how to present to the mermaids the news of the possible contact. Someone had proposed to lure them on board with a stratagem, in the doubt that given their knowledge of mankind they did not trust them, but in the end the common sense had prevailed to tell them the simple truth and then let things go their way.

On the screen, the mermaids stood still in midwater smiling, waiting for the arrival of the Commander.

"Here I am" said the Commander with a firm and cheerful

voice, "we were waiting for your contact."

"Were you waiting for us?"

"Yes, we want to show you something new."

"Yes?" replied almost in chorus the curious mermaids.

"It's called a superbaric trans-fluid airlock, or at least our technicians called it that way."

"And it would be?" asked a mermaid.

"In practice, we have the pool too" the Commander carelessly announced.

"Splendid!" exclaimed a mermaid clapping her hands and making a spin in a cloud of bubbles, imitated by her companions.

"It looks like we won't have much trouble getting them on board" the Commander whispered to the Commissioner.

"It was to be expected" replied the Commissioner whispering, "after all, are they or are they not the kind species that everyone has always told us about?"

"Yes yes, they are like that but it is we who are wolves. If you were a lamb, would you accept to enter the wolves' den if they invited you?"

"I doubt it" replied the Commissioner.

"Well, then let's try to appreciate them for that too" said the Commander, then raising his voice he turned to the mermaids.

"Would you like us to meet?"

"But it is obvious Commander, if you were waiting for us for this purpose, it would not be polite to refuse. Let's hope that your new coupling works."

"It will work. Let's proceed. Katjusa, pull over."

"Yes, Commander" replied the computer in a tone that seemed reluctant to someone.

The maneuver ended with some metallic screeching due to the tolerance of the mechanical steps of the flange, built with a design based only on hypothesis and visual memories of devices seen from a distance and it was a real miracle that the seal was perfect. A whistle and a gurgling that spread throughout the structure of the ship could be heard and from that moment on, it was as if the mermaids' vessel had penetrated the Bettie Page with a liquid appendix.

It didn't take long before the hydrophones in the pool transmitted the lapping sound of the water and the amused screams of the mermaids.

"Commander, to you the honor of the first contact" said the Commissioner.

"Ehm..." muttered the Commander.

"Well?"

"Do the rules apply to everyone?"

"Of course, Commander."

"Um..."

"You won't have any problem jumping into the water naked with the mermaids, will you?"

"In fact, it's a problem I've been thinking about" replied the Commander.

"Look, Commander, pretend they're dolphins, go for a swim, they've never hurted anyone."

"This is also true Commissioner" admitted the Commander. "I go" he said resolutely.

Leaning on the shoulders of two mermaids, his torso out of the water under the powerful thrust of the two tails, and four large breasts crushed on his hips, the Commander of the Bettie Page had the face of the happiest man in the galaxy.

"This water is perfect Commander and this current on the skin is delicious, you were really good. How did you guess the exact salinity?"

"They told me it is the average salinity of the Earth's seas. Since you also come from there, we thought that no matter how much you change, you always keep the memory of the origins" replied the Commander.

"It's true, we would have adapted even to fresh water if it was necessary, but to discover it so marine was a real surprise."

In front of them appeared a tail that flashed on the water with a sharp thud and from the wave generated appeared the long hair of the owner of the tail, then the face, then the shoulders, then the big breast.

"You're not coming to meet us alone, are you?" she told the Commander.

"Would you like to meet the men of this ship?" the Commander dropped in as an answer.

"Sure" said the mermaids emerged in chorus, some even adding a pretty pirouette to the answer.

"In that case we thought that ... how many of you are now in our pool?"

"Ah ah, then you had planned it all!" exclaimed one of the two mermaids he was hugging, laughing, then splashing some water on his face with a tap of his hand.

"Sure "replied the Commander with an amused grimace and his eyes half closed, "to be honest, and I don't know why, here among you I feel that the only thing I want is to be honest, we hoped, so hoped that we could meet."

"Commander, it's nice what you just said, but why? What do you hope to get from us?" asked a mermaid.

"I don't know, I think we all hope for something different. Now that I am here I understand that what I was hoping for was serenity, and that is exactly how I feel now. I don't want to leave anymore. Do you know that our history is full of legends of sailors who met you and then died? Now I know that those legends were true, but those sailors did not die by your hand, but by the sadness of having to leave you."

"You are such a sad species Commander, always in conflict between males and females. You have been thrown into an excessively harsh reality, despite yourself. No one can do anything about it but we are very sorry, we are always sorry and..."

"We've been thrown?" the Commander blinked, interrupting the mermaid.

"Oops" replied the mermaid with a big smile, "Sorry Commander, silly me, I misspoke."

"Oh well, it doesn't matter" replied the Commander pretending to forget the expression.

20 FIESTA IN SPACE

The Bettie Page's swimming pool had become a permanent party, with buffets continuously supplied on the edge of the pool by the diligent kitchen attendants, who did not feel excluded from the event at all because the whole crew had also been included in the mermaids' meetings. The mermaids fell in love with the music as soon as they heard it and promptly developed timed movements, which often synchronized in jumps and somersaults out of the water and in rapid dives and slides, delighting the men who could follow their elegant movements even underwater, also because it was underwater that the mermaids gave the best of themselves. With rock the hall was transformed into a circus act, but it was Chi Wun Chao's melodious and abstract arpeggios that were more successful among the mermaids.

"Would you like to give it a try?" said a mermaid hugging a massive veteran.

"It's obvious, isn't it?"

"Oh yes, it is! In you, nature has made it so evident! Sometimes we can't understand why there are so many misunderstandings between your genres. I mean, you males are so clear in your intentions, your females can always understand what you want and this should give them a sense of tranquility, a sense of trust, instead it is not so. Well, as far as we know, it is not so."

"No indeed, in fact, we have even to hide it or else they get offended. It is a paradox that they get offended just when we give them the most sincere compliment, because on that side we have no way to lie, as you can see. What is it like among you?"

"Between us it is not evident, we recognize each other by

smell more than anything else and we never know if a male has desire, and vice versa. So we ask ourselves, as well as I just asked you."

"Don't you stand out? You mean that males and females look the same?"

"Sure, including long hair."

"Are there your males here now?"

"Of course there are, but don't worry, I'm a female."

"Really?" asked the veteran, suspicious.

"If you want, you can check."

"Ah, umm, oohhh, I mean, ehmm, sorry eh, check you say."

"It's really true, you are so repressed!" exclaimed the mermaid with a laugh, followed by a spin underwater amused. "Look, it's easy" she said when she resurfaced, "come down and stick your penis where it needs to go."

The mermaid gave the man time to put the respirator between his teeth and drag him underwater. She assumed a slightly inclined position with his belly upwards so that he could see well her long body, then released the muscles closing the vaginal orifice which opened like the pupil of a cat's eye from which came out a row of tiny air bubbles.

On seeing the maneuver, the man emitted a series of tumultuous bubbles and perhaps his eyes turned into those of a frog but then he gathered up the courage and slipped over the mermaid to which he anchored with a hug. The mermaid, for its part, swayed weakly to facilitate the maneuver. She remained motionless when this happened and at that point, after tightening the penis firmly closing the muscles of the opening and embraced the man too, began to vibrate his vigorous tail. Pushed by the powerful six feet long caudal fin, the two started at full speed cutting through the water like a torpedo and when they reached the surface of the pool, they lifted a trail of splashes like a speedboat would have done.

After a couple of whirlwinds in the pool, the mermaid headed firmly and at full speed towards an edge where she stopped, suddenly projecting the man out of the water onto the floor of the hall. The man thus thrown did a long slide and drift on his belly.

"Woooow!" he shouted while still slipping, "what a buzz!" Some janitors rushed towards him anxiously.

"What happened? Did you make her angry?"

"Not at all! Fuck fuck fuck fuck. It was like surfing, water skiing and built-in fucking, fucking spun me! These are from another galaxy! Never done such a thing! I'm not going back in the Arms, I'm not going back in the Arms anymore!" he screamed almost to the edge of hysteria, while the mermaid responsible for the fact, half emerged in the middle of the pool, looked at him slyly with a big smile.

Half the dozen men in the pool were equally lucky. They asked their mermaids for an explanation of what happened, and those of them who were female immediately gave a practical demonstration with an equally scenic ending. Within a few minutes they were all expelled from the pool, including those who accompanied the male mermaids, who entrusted them to the females who remained free for the demonstration.

The news of the event traveled the Bettie Page at the speed of lightning, arriving perhaps even faster on the bridge.

"Communication officer, call the mermaids" ordered the Commander as soon as he heard the news.

"Yes Commander" replied a mermaid immediately appearing on the screen.

"Have you heard what happened?"

"Sure, at the same time it happened. The vibrations of the tails and the pleasure of our friends spread through the water."

"Do you have anything to tell me about?"

"Is something bothering you Commander? It was what you expected, was it not?"

"It was what we ..." put out the Commander without finding the words to conclude the sentence.

"Don't go on Commander, we know how much you have been used to lying about everything related to sex, so we all thought we had to force your hand a little. Don't worry

Commander, we did it gladly."

"Did you do it for us?"

"No Commander, do you see? It's still the habit that makes you talk: that belief that if a female gives herself, she does it only to do you a favor. It is not your fault, your reality is like that, but for us it is different. We have even more fun than you do, and the feeling is not different from what it is with our males, after all we are very similar."

"I knew it!" exclaimed the Commander, tapping his hand with a fist.

"Did you know what?" asked another mermaid that appeared on the screen.

"That Admiral Berg was right centuries ago. In the beginning nobody believed him. He did not talk about it willingly, only with a few trusted friends, but the rumor spread. You are a dream beyond human dreams."

"Thank you, Commander."

"What do we do now?"

"Let your men have the freedom to do so, it will be a memory that they will carry within themselves forever."

"When we go back, word will spread and everyone will want to come to the halo."

"We know, Commander, but don't worry, there's no way this is getting out of hand. We still live well hidden in the halo. But keep in mind that we are much less numerous than the human species, we could never give this gift to everyone."

21 THE GNA REACTS

Following the return of the Bettie Page in the Swan-Regolo Arm, the galactic war hardened and the blockade became a siege of the Nucleus. As had always happened in human history, the ultimate reason why men were fighting each other was the females, although in this case of another species.

The human females, powerless, stood watching, without really knowing what was happening. Partly because the event in the halo and all those who followed it, were perhaps the best kept secret in history, and partly because they were unable or unwilling to accept that they were no longer at the center of their men's world.

Unlike the war of resistance, whose events could be distinguished in bureaucratic, when the off-core routes were refused, or accidental, when those who adopted an unauthorized flight plan disappeared without return, the siege war also formally closed the commercial exchange between Arms and Nucleus.

Even with this turning point, however, the war was never official. Its beginning was included, or better to say, hidden, in a tariff measure introduced by the GNA of Arms that said: "To make date from the publication of the present measure (U.G.T.S.[10] introduced with single measure from the U.T.G.[11] n.5234.137) on the Bulletin for Interstellar Navigation, is introduced a transit fare on each flight plan, proportional to the full load weight according to the attached Table A and corrected with the radial anisotropy coefficient of the route expressed in

---

[10] Universal Galactic Time Standard
[11] Unified Terrestrial Government

thousandths, relative to the three-dimensional space only, except for the exemptions mentioned in letters F (diplomatic transports) and H (political transports) of article 57bis of the Unified Regulation of Galactic Navigation."

In essence, the GNA of Arms, immediately followed by the GNA of the Nucleus with a similar measure that had actually been agreed, introduced a progressive tax to the radial component of each route. As a consequence, each route tangential to the galactic circumference was tax free, while each route along a radius was burdened by a tax so onerous to be higher than the load value of any spaceship. As a matter of fact, all trades continued only on routes that kept constant the distance from the galactic center, or deviated a little bit from it, so all the Nucleus routes remained in the Nucleus, and the Arms routes remained in the Arms.

Naturally, a special commission was set up by both governments, Federal of Arms and Central of the Nucleus, to assess the effect on trade of such a tax measure, issued by the two sections of the GNA without their knowledge. Since, in fact, the two economies could easily be conducted autonomously, the commissions concluded that the measure would have a negligible economic impact, over and above the fact that the only ones who could afford the economic burden of a radial trip, were those same politicians and diplomats who had exempted themselves from the measure. Another constant in human history: who decides on taxes is who never has to pay them. An unpleasant forgetfulness of all the ethical philosophies appeared in history that never introduced the simple principle "whoever proposes a law, must also suffer its effects". Naturally there was, as always, an unassailable justification: for the institutional tasks of maintaining relations between the two governments, it is necessary to travel from the Arms to the Nucleus and vice versa.

As a result of such a tightening of relations between the two areas of the galaxy, the cultural boundary between the Arms and the Nucleus became sharper as the time went by and in a few years it became a de facto boundary.

16th interlude

"How is Plan B progressing?" asked the Social Systems Engineer.

"It is bringing unforeseen disturbances" replied the Wizard.

"Is the Project in danger?"

"I don't think so, by now we are close to the intersection and also there is a war going on. War is the reality that the species recognizes as its own, so as long as there is war it means that we are in the path of the Project" replied the Biologist.

"Then everything is fine, what would be these disturbances?" asked the Social Systems Technician again.

"The perturbation is only one, but the secondary effects have spread to the whole domain of ideas, with important long-term changes" replied the Wizard.

"For example?"

"For example, in half of the population of the galaxy, the peripheral one to be precise, the conflict between the two genders is disappearing. This has almost eliminated the programmed evolutionary push, which had exhausted its function but paradoxically the species has induced a new push itself."

"How would they eliminate the evolutionary drive?" the Biologist doubtful asked.

"Still they have not made it, but now it has irrelevant intensity to the effects of the Project. One genre has done so, directing its interest elsewhere. At first the other genre resented it, then protested, then became angry but little by little it is learning that dumping an avalanche of insults on someone, is not the best way to mend relationships. Well, it has always worked that way, but only because there was no alternative, now there is."

"But how is it possible, they are blocked by intraspecies infertility!" exclaimed the Biologist.

"Oh for now they don't worry about it" assured the Wizard, "another side effect is precisely a demographic decline but considering the galactic population, there will be no need to worry about for many millicycles."

"When a species does not procreate, I worry more than anything else!" exclaimed the Biologist, alarmed by the news.

"We subjected them to too much tension, in the end they collapsed, this is the truth" said the Wizard.

"Odd anyway, the equations of progress did not lead to this result" considered the Social Systems Technician.

"The equations are precise and would have continued to be valid if that perturbative force not included in the model had not appeared" replied the Evolutionary Systems Technician.

"What about the central population?" asked the Biologist again.

"It is apparently in stasis, but soon the migration will be triggered because a high pressure gradient is forming between the two zones, that is: they are more and more unhappy" replied the Social Systems Technician.

"But they have not yet noticed the intersection? By now in the nucleus should be evident, it seems as if they didn't care at all" said the Wizard a little annoyed.

"No wonder, they have always been very lazy" said the Biologist, "until the drama falls on them they do nothing. Don't worry Wizard, when the time comes, they will react. Instead tell me about this new evolutionary push. It interests me."

"Oh well, it is a bit improper to call it evolutionary, because it is obvious that it cannot lead to any effect properly evolutionary, but the encounter with the new species has reanimated them. They had become stagnant, now they are studying gimmicks, plotting, ingenious, as on the other hand they have always done in the relationship with the other genus."

"In short, they behave as they have always behaved under their evolutionary drive, except that they do not obtain any practical results" summarized the Biologist.

"Yes, it is more or less exact" confirmed the Wizard.

"I have always said that it is not an intelligent species" concluded the Biologist.

22 THE JOURNEY OF THE VIE EN ROSE

"What is the purpose of this route?" asked the Second to the Captain, observing on the three-dimensional model of the galaxy the curve tangent to the Nucleus that ended at the lower galactic pole.

"Just follow it" cut the Captain short.

"Captain, do you have something in mind? We are not going to load emigrants up to the Pole, are we!"

"I'm sick of carrying stinking stowaways and also we've done so many of those full load trips that we can even afford a vacation."

"A vacation? It's the first time I've heard you say that word, and for that you want to go to Pole? Have you heard of any new brothels?"

"Don't play dumb, among us two, the most up-to-date one on the maps of the brothels is not me" replied the Captain. The Second sneered inwardly.

"I'm going to do something illegal" added the captain, "after all we are still a pirate ship but if you tell the crew I'll throw you out of an airlock."

"I don't understand you Captain, here we are all in the same boat and we do nothing but illegal activity, so where is the novelty?"

"This time is different; we will do something really very illegal. Look Second, I'm getting tired of all this mystery between the Nucleus and the Arms and I don't think at all that all the missing vessels have really disappeared. In my opinion it's because they never came back."

"Saint Rose and Saint Mildred, you want to go into the halo!"

exclaimed the Second.

"Once we get to the pole, let's jump straight to the Galactic Nadir and see what happens. Yes, that's the plan" admitted the Captain.

"We will be intercepted and destroyed instantly by a fleet of the Arms, that's the way it is for everyone."

"No, it's just a *rumor*, nobody knows for sure."

"And you want to risk all our lives to find out?"

"What is so precious about your life that you do not want to risk losing it?" asked the Captain sharply.

The Second opened his mouth to answer but then closed it immediately, remaining pensive a moment before answering "in fact, nothing. And how about the crew? Don't you think it is right to tell them?"

"Fair would be fair" admitted the Captain, "but no one must know anything. To have any chance of success we must do something totally unexpected. If I tell them and let them decide whether to come or not, someone will get off and talk. The Arms secret services is everywhere and in no time we will be intercepted. If I tell them but I prevent them from disembarking, I find myself with mutineers on board and it will be like being intercepted, because surely someone will do sabotage."

"There is always the possibility that they all agree" opined the Second.

"And when has a crew of pirates like us ever agreed on anything?"

"A point in your favor Captain."

"That's right. So you see, if I don't tell them and everything is fine, they will have no reason to complain. If, on the other hand, they destroy us, well... in that case they will have no way of complaining anyway" concluded the Captain with a sinister smile.

"Fair. And what do you hope to discover?" asked the Second.

"I have no idea; the rumors going around about the halo are totally absurd. It is always the same mythology of sailors since men began to sail the seas of the Earth. Impressive, millions of years and the stories are always the same."

"Whales, monsters, mermaids, sea gods and the like?"

"And such things indeed. Can you imagine if terrestrial monsters, which, by the way, never existed, or mermaids, arrived in the halo. And how did they get there, with canoes?" said the Captain with a sarcastic tone.

"So what?" asked the Second.

"Bah, maybe riches, maybe naked women, like those who found the first explorers in the remote islands of the Oceans. Wait, how did they wrote it in history books ... oh yes, *wild women in various states of nudity*. Or perhaps they were *degrees of nudity*? Never mind, but I think it's unlikely that exists an alien species, but the same as us. Alien but same. Perhaps a very similar one, I don't know, maybe with four tits."

"It would disgust me!" exclaimed the Second.

"Uh-huh, and how is the woman you like?"

"With an ass the size of a house and pointy tits" replied promptly the Second.

"You are lucky; the majority of women are like that. I like the exact opposite, that is very small but with huge tits. Impossible stuff to find, what bad luck! Who knows where our aesthetic sense comes from, it's not rational. Anyway I was just saying that maybe there is nothing out there and all the lost ships, in reality they have only deserted. In the Arms you live better, that's why people emigrate. Less rules, less bureaucracy, everything is more dynamic. The Arms are the Frontier of our time."

"Those must have been good times. Hard, perhaps, one could only count on one's own strengths, but when he had it, he could do anything" commented the Second.

"What have you got, three million years that you remember?" the Captain mocked him.

"No! I went to university, I studied history."

"Ha ha ha, you never told me that, and you ended up being a transporter of illegal immigrants, with me?"

"I don't know if you realize that every offense you do to me, you do to yourself too" replied the Second, acidic.

"You're right, sorry. So are you with me?"

"As always Captain, shall I proceed?"

"Proceed."

On board the Vie en Rose the maneuvering alarm sounded. Except in battle, no alarm had the meaning of real alarm anymore. The AGRE propulsion was completely inadvertent and a trip presented no danger except to arrive at a point in space already occupied by another spaceship, but in that case the bang would be so instantaneous that no one would have time to hear it, so no one would think about it. If it had to come, it comes period and that's it. But the chances were very low. In fact, in all the history of galactic navigation it had never happened, so the crew of the Vie en Rose continued quietly in their occupations.

"Computer, new route to the South Galactic Pole, broken trajectory, four splits" said the Second, adding whispers as if speaking to himself, "so we save some of that unfair radial tax."

"Destination acquired, calculation of the broken route made. Anisotropy rate of 12,300 Uni-ISO" said the central computer with a lap-dancer's voice, then added in a somewhat knowing tone "A six-segment split would provide an anisotropy rate of only 750 Uni-ISOs with an increase in transit time and consumption of only six percent."

"I hate her when she's a professor!" growled the Captain.

"Six-leg trajectory. Recalculate and activate, automatic confirmation for all routes" said the Second.

"Good, so she won't bother us at every leg" approved the Captain.

"Coordinates entered, final destination at x zero, y zero, z 89 degrees and 59 minutes, w 212 degrees. ETE five hours and eight minutes. The fee was paid to the GNA with the tele-transaction n.8969.07040.012. AGRE engine active, entry into variety in five seconds, four, three, two, one, entry into variety carried out, time at the first way-point thirty-eight minutes and twenty seconds."

"Well, at least she's efficient" said the Second, "if only she didn't have that petulant tone!"

"Do you think they programmed her that way, or is it just a figment of our imagination?" said the Captain.

"In my opinion, they programmed her for. That voice must have been taken somewhere, and which is the woman who sooner or later does not become petulant."

"Well, when she's in a good mood it's a voice that makes you horny" said the Captain, "maybe that's why they used it. Do you know that the central computers of all the ships in the galaxy have the same voice?"

"Is that so!" replied the Second, looking at the nails of his hand.

"I tell you it is so" continued the undaunted Captain, "I have commanded many ships and they all had the same porn star voice."

At the time declared by the computer, the Vie en Rose reached the South Pole of the Nucleus.

"And now captain?" asked the Second who had just arrived on the bridge.

"Now let's make the jump. Considering that we are at maximum distance from the Arms, a vertical course will not even pass through their space. In my opinion, exactly at the poles there is no one. Let's go down vertical to the halo."

"But where exactly?"

"The halo is diffuse and low density, so we have a very low probability of coming up against something, you won't need a map. We descend for a distance equal to the galactic radius. The halo is spherical so we will find ourselves right inside."

"All right, let's see what the computer says" replied the Second. "Computer, new course, polar G.S.[12] coordinates, alpha zero, theta zero, rho fifty thousand, what a destination!" exclaimed the Second after saying it.

"Destination acquired, calculation of final metric coordinates

---

[12] Galactic System

carried out, radial anisotropy rate 1,245,001,050 Uni-ISO, the rate is higher than available credit, route not possible" said the computer with a voice that the Captain seemed to be what he would have heard in a brothel where he showed up with empty pockets asking for a benefit on credit.

"Damn it!" exclaimed the Second, "She refuses!"

Without commenting on the computer's communication, the Captain took a memory card out of a pocket and inserted it into a plug on the ship's console.

"Computer, upload from port four" he said quietly.

Two seconds of silence passed then the computer voice announced: "Coordinates entered, final destination at x zero, y zero z 90 degrees, w 178 degrees 46 minutes and 2 seconds, ETE eight hours and thirty-six minutes."

"Rapid activation" yelled the captain then.

"AGRE engine active, entry into variety in one second, entry into variety carried out, ETE eight hours thirty-five minutes and fifty-eight seconds" said the computer with voice again persuasive, as if it had forgotten the previous order.

"How did you do it?" exclaimed the Second, looking incredulously at the Captain.

"I met a guy on the last flight. He was a programmer by profession but in reality he was a hacker. He was part of the Great Universal Screw-up, you know, that group of morons who would like to overthrow the whole damn system. As a payment for the passage I accepted a little program that overwrites the permanent provisions of the GNA in the computer memory. He assured me that it will also work with the GNA of Arms. That's what gave me the idea to make a detour into the halo."

"A shrewd for real! And what was he doing on board?"

"He was one of the illegal immigrants. They caught him and gave him the maximum sentence. He must have made a lot of people angry, not even murderers are given such a punishment."

"And that is?"

"They took away his access to brothels for life. A true cruelty. So he decided to need a change of scene and try his luck in the Arms."

"Poor guy, I pity him, I hope he will have better luck in the Arms."

"If you don't get in trouble there too, you know hackers are compulsive."

"Anyway, how could you be sure it would work?" asked the Second.

"I wasn't" replied the Captain calmly. "I'm going to take a nap" he said then moving away, followed by the astonished look of the Second.

The Vie en Rose appeared in the halo in an area of totally empty space. The computer announced the event with a laconic *diagonalized tensor, nominal ATO*[13], without adding anything else because there was really nothing to add. Twenty-eight thousand kilometers away the sensors detected the presence of two hydrogen atoms that the computer considered irrelevant and therefore did not even mention them. Through the windows it could be seen only the absolute darkness and some bright dots of weak and distant stars, maybe twenty in total.

"What a desolate place" the Second was saying when the deck chief got in the command bridge with a big breath for the run.

"Captain, did you see outside?"

"There is nothing to see" the Captain replied calmly.

"Not from here, from underneath!" insisted the deck chief.

All three rushed to the lower deck. Through a service window, in front of them shone the whole galaxy.

"Marvelous!" exclaimed the Captain.

"I had no idea it was so beautiful!" echoed the Second, stunned.

"Captain, where are we? Did we take a wrong course? We must re-enter the galaxy immediately before something happens to us" shouted the deck chief apprehensively.

"Easy chief, we're exactly where we wanted to be, and we're

---

[13] Actual Time Over

too out of Arm's reach for anything to happen to us."

"And what are we doing here?" asked the chief.

"We enjoy the show" replied smiling the Captain. "Second, go back to the bridge and rotate the ship, I want the galaxy suspended above the panoramic dome. Tonight, gala dinner with a chandelier."

When the activities on board were suspended for rest, which in space was equivalent to the concept of an evening, the crew warned by the Second gathered in the panoramic dome, where the cook on board, by an order of the Captain, had prepared a sumptuous dinner to say the least, in case someone got angry.

When everyone was present, the Captain stood up to speak. "Gentlemen, forgive me if I did not warn you before, as you can see with your own eyes we have left the galaxy in order to ..."

A red light flashed on the dashboard communication panel hanging on the wall in front of him. The Captain stopped and looked at the Second who had assumed a worried expression.

"Go ahead, tell them" he whispered to him and running away.

"Computer, what is happening?" asked the Captain when he arrived on the bridge.

"Fleet of Arm approaching, twenty-two units, communication channel opened" replied the computer with a satisfied tone like saying *I told you!*

"Bitch" hissed the Captain, then speaking normally added "Open communication."

On the dashboard screen appeared the imposing half-bust of a man in uniform.

"Hi, you're a little off course don't you think?"

"Uh, yeah" the Captain found nothing else to answer.

"I am Admiral Oost of Sagittarius Arm, I must warn you that if you try to maneuver we have twenty-two bullets ready to launch."

"Given how you put it, I don't even think about maneuvering, but anyway it wasn't in my plans" replied the Captain.

"Better, to whom do I have the honor to speak?"

"I am Captain Mbuen of the Vie en Rose, cargo vessel, currently empty."

Admiral Oost made a half smile.

"Don't worry Captain, we're not pirates trying to rob you."

Meanwhile, the Second had reached the Captain on the bridge.

"Have you already met them?" asked the Admiral.

"Meet who?" asked the Second, then added addressed to the captain, "and who would he be?"

"It doesn't matter" the Admiral said, "now you have two choices, follow us or be destroyed."

"And why? As far as I know it is not forbidden to travel in the halo" replied the Captain dryly.

"In fact it is not forbidden" replied Admiral Oost, "and yet what I said are the only possibilities you have."

"It looks like an act of piracy, Admiral, despite your initial statement, and wearing a uniform does not change the nature of what you are doing" replied the Captain.

"Call it what you want Captain, nothing changes. So, what is your decision?"

"Mmmm, let me think about it" replied the Captain in a sarcastic tone, "a very difficult choice."

"Captain!" exclaimed the Second.

"Shut up, of course we're following them, don't get involved."

"Be aware that whatever happens, you will not be able to return to the Nucleus" said the Admiral again while the two were confabulating, "but on the other hand I don't think you will want to" he added almost in a low voice.

"How can you say that?" hissed the Captain annoyed.

"You will find out, and there will be no need to convince you. It happened to all of us, you will not be the exception. We will escort you to a rendezvous point."

"Rendezvous with whom?"

"Rendezvous with them."

"Them who?"

"You'll see" replied the Admiral with a mysterious smile.

"Hey Admiral Oost."

"Yes?"

"How did you find us in such a short time?" asked the Captain.

"Oh it's always very easy. The polar routes are the most used by those who try to evade the Arms, or escape from the Nucleus which is the same thing. They all arrive here, or at the other galactic pole. We found it convenient to keep a minimal fleet stationed around here as a welcome. You thought you were the smartest, didn't you? It is the vice of us men, we always think we are the smartest. Unfortunately humility is an uncommon virtue" replied the Admiral in a dry tone.

"Welcome, he says" murmured the Second tight-lipped, "a warm welcome with guns pointed."

"I heard you" said the Admiral, "but weapons are only needed until you know. Trust me; if you do not try to escape, we have no intention of harming you, neither now nor after the rendezvous. The Arms gladly welcome people with a bit of resourcefulness and a certain sense of risk, as you proved to possess when you arrived here."

"You heard him? I told you the ships couldn't all be gone!" said the Captain.

"We'll see" replied skeptically the Second, "it could just be a trick to keep us quiet until it's time to take us down."

"But come on! If they wanted to take us down, they would have done it the moment they intercepted us. And by the way, I would like to know why we did not intercept them" said the Captain with a slight tone of reproach.

"Gentlemen, the rendezvous point is close by, we will go there in three-dimensional navigation so you can't get out of range. Course Officer, transmit to the Vie en Rose direction and thrust intensity."

The Arms fleet, with the Vie en Rose in the center, set in motion keeping exactly all the relative distances and the effect in the empty space of the halo was as if they were not moving at all. But the powerful inertial thrust of the AGRE engines made them accelerate up to 45,000 kilometers per second and in a few hours they moved several hundred million kilometers.

When they reached the rendezvous point, they found two ships stationary in space and connected to each other. One was perfectly recognizable as an Arm's one, the other was not.

"Here we are" said the Admiral reappeared on the screen."Some of you have to get on that vessel, our vessel of course, the other one you can't."

"What will happen?" the Captain gasped almost exhausted by the tension he had suffered throughout the long transfer, during which his imagination had explored every possible scenario of what awaited them.

"Do not worry Captain, I assure you that I would like to be in your place. Above all I would like to relive my first time, as you are about to do. We will wait here until you return."

"I'm coming too" said the Second.

"Good idea" commented Admiral Oost from the screen.

The Captain glared at his Second, thinking that if anything happened to both of them, no one would be able to pilot the ship, then he looked at the Admiral on the screen and from his firm and at last honest gaze, he understood that the Arms fleet would have never abandoned the Vie en Rose to itself.

"All right, let's go" he said.

"Better not move the ship, my gunners may misinterpret the gesture" warned the Admiral, "go with a maintenance shuttle."

When the shuttle returned to the Vie en Rose after six long hours, during which the crew had done the same thing as the Captain during the first transfer, the Captain gathered everyone in the ship's common room.

"You have to go too" said the Captain with an unusually quiet voice, "four at a time, the maximum allowed by the shuttle."

"What's on that ship?" asked one of them, suspicious.

The Captain and the Second looked at each other.

"You wouldn't believe me, you have to see it by yourselves" replied mysteriously the Captain, with a smile on his face.

The crew of adventurers, suspicious by nature, did not take the order well, but since there was no other choice, they did what the Captain had asked them. With each voyage the resistance diminished because of the evident state of euphoria of those who returned. Those who had not yet gone, asked insistently what was on that ship, but the only answer they got was "The captain was right, you have to see it with your own eyes."

When it was all over, the admiral reappeared on the screen of the Vie en Rose and said smiling: "Welcome back to life, new men of Arms, now you are free to go wherever you want, even to return to the Nucleus, if you really want to" and without giving anyone time to reply he said, "Katjusa, activate", disappearing with the whole fleet in tow.

"Who the hell was Katjusa?" said the Captain.

"Their central computer," replied the Second.

"And they call it Katjusa?"

"In the Arms they all call it that, who knows why. I think that by now we should call it that way too" said the Second and then asked the Captain "what do you think about all this matter?"

"What do men say?" asked the Captain as an answer.

"The Admiral was right, nobody wants to go back to the Nucleus anymore and it doesn't surprise me at all, I don't want it either, to be honest."

"Go figure!" said the meditating Captain, "you know what I think? I think someone is playing with the destinies of us all."

"Someone who?"

"Someone out there, somewhere. Come on, how is it possible that the mermaids have populated the halo so by accident. Now it's all so clear to me, so obvious. People leave the Nucleus and never come back. Of course they don't come back, after what they found, but leaving is not the right word. Who challenges the galaxy in this way, is fleeing. Evidently I wanted to flee too, only now I have understood it."

"From what, after all, you didn't lack anything" replied the Second, then he added as if speaking to himself "and in any case I should ask it to myself too, I gladly accompanied you."

"I thought it was because we are eternally dissatisfied" said the Captain, unloading all his little knowledge of human psychology, "but it is not so. That of the eternally dissatisfied is a cliché and that's all. We seem to be eternally dissatisfied but because it is true that we have always been missing something, and given the effect this meeting had, that something had to be what we found in that pool in space. Ha ha ha, but think about it, a pool with a blue bottom and trampoline, floating in empty space fifty thousand light-years from the galaxy, stuff from Ron Goulart."

"And who would that be?"

"One that millions of years ago wrote novels of the absurd. He was hilarious, really, but I don't think he ever came to imagine a swimming pool in intergalactic space, with even an orgy inside. Now that I think about it, I think that someone must have imagined it, but not in intergalactic space, and there is a big difference. Here there must be someone with an excessive sense of farcical, a joker deity, I don't know, a Joker"

"All right, now what do we do?" asked the Second.

"Going back to the Nucleus is not an option; I just have the doubt that maybe it would be right to let them know."

"To whom, to those of the nucleus?" replied the Second.

"Yes."

"I do not know. I believe that many, if not all, of those who have fled have had such a doubt. Who knows how many friends they have left behind."

"Yeah, us too, I guess" said the Captain.

"You guess? What do you mean you guess? Don't you know if you have friends?" replied the Second.

"I certainly do not. I was talking about the crew; there will be someone among them who will have friends or even family."

"Captain, on a ship of pirates like us, friends are only those who share your destiny, that is, those on board."

"Right. However, if any of us had any friend, the fact remains that you can't go back and tell them that you met the mermaids, leave everything and follow me into the halo, they'd take you for crazy. If they had told me, I would never have believed it, not even if they had shown me a hologram. A trick, I would have thought."

"Let's see, you who are a historian, according to you what would be the consequences if somehow we could make ourselves believe" said after a while the Captain.

"I think there would be a worsening of the war. If they knew, everyone would want the chance to come here to see them or even better to meet them. After all, that's what the Congress is trying to get, perhaps without even knowing why or at least that's what they say; we are fighting an unjustified embargo, they say. In my opinion they knew it and they also knew that they could not say it. I think there would be a kind of revolt on a galactic dimension, this as far as men are concerned."

"You bet!" exclaimed the Captain, "the women instead would raise an anti-mermaid campaign and take the opportunity for yet another battle against the males. Wondering *why they like those more?* they wouldn't even think about it. I once read a sentence about women, I can't remember where and when, or maybe it just came to my mind; creatures with an innate overestimation of themselves..."

"Easy, Captain, you're getting warm."

"Yes sorry, it happens to me when it comes to this topic. Moreover, I didn't think well about them before, after this meeting you can certainly imagine what I think about women. So what would women do in your opinion?"

"I don't think they would be very happy, as you say, and a nice protest movement would be unavoidable. I wonder how they dealt with the problem in the Arms."

"You could have asked Admiral Oost, he seemed very well informed."

"I would have asked him if I knew what question to ask"

replied the Second in a dry tone. "Before the meeting I didn't even know of the existence of the mermaids, you can imagine if I thought about the consequences, and afterwards, the Admiral disappeared with the speed of lightning."

"So what do we do?" the Captain asked after a while.

"Are you asking me for advice or making a decision?" replied the Second, then added "would you like to go back to the Nucleus and tell all around wouldn't you?"

"No, if this were to produce an unsustainable situation, and all things considered, there is no way to be believed unless you bring one with you."

"No Captain, nooooooo! Pray it doesn't even cross your mind. I warn you that if you even think of kidnapping one, I'll stick a knife in your back while you sleep, and believe me, the first thought that came to mind was much worse" exclaimed the Second in a visible state of alteration.

"Don't worry, I wouldn't hurt them even if it was about my own life, on the contrary, I would gladly sacrifice it if one of them was in danger. It's weird that they have this effect on us after seeing them only once, isn't it?"

"There you are, that's better" said the Second, calming down immediately.

"But you could always ask one to come" urged the Captain again, reluctant to abandon that idea.

"And do you think the mermaids stand in the halo because they love to be visible? Why, according to you, have they not populated any internal world of the galaxy?"

"You're right, forget everything. I would say that going back to saying it is useless" concluded the Captain.

"Yes, that's what I think too, and I also think that this discussion has been made by all those who have arrived here before us and who have come to the same conclusion as us. That is why there is no news of anyone who has ever returned, now it is all clear. Well, now what do we do?"

"We head to an Arm planet and find ourselves a job, the Admiral downloaded the Arms maps to the central computer, or rather now I should say in Katjusa. I also asked him to pass the registration of the ship to the GNA of Arms; I think we are now registered. But first we could wander around a little bit here in the halo and see if we can meet them again. Wouldn't you like that?" asked the Captain.

"You bet on it, but you saw what was like that spaceship we were on. It had a very special docking gear and anyhow, first of all we should have a swimming pool. Do you think they are just as much fun in a bed?" opined the Second.

"I don't think so" answered the Captain cheerfully, "the pool is essential, you're absolutely right" concluded with a big smile, and then continuing "let's go to a dockyard and get it on."

"And on credit where are we?" replied the Second who had a little more practical sense.

"Before leaving, I transferred all the credits to the ASB[14], so we can use it everywhere."

"Cool!" said the Second smiling.

"I had a plan" replied the Captain.

After a month spent in a dockyard and a couple of months spent wandering around the almost empty space of the halo, on the Vie en Rose there was no longer that great enthusiasm of their first days as citizens of Arms. Mermaids they hadn't found even a shadow of them, even though they had spent their time bouncing around the space and some of them were getting tired of it. Then finally the computer announced with its almost irritating voice to the men who had been in space for two months that something had appeared within the range of the sensors.

"Contact at alpha 132 degrees 12 minutes and 27 seconds, elevation 62 degrees and 43 minutes, distance twelve million kilometers. Arm's ship, Kobayashi class, communication established, synchronism in stabilization, relative speed zero in eight seconds, orientation minus 28 degrees, minimum rotation

[14] All Star Bank

for rendezvous 18 degrees" said with the exaggeratedly cheerful tone of a circus performer.

"It's not what we were hoping to meet" considered the Second, awakened from his numbness by the computer voice.

"Katjusa, what would be a Kobayashi class?" asked the Captain in the meantime.

"Exploratory ship fully automated, equipped for earth-formation. The crew has exclusively tactical tasks" the computer immediately replied in a petulant tone as if it were explaining universally known facts.

"I will never get used to that prig tone of her" grumbled the Captain.

"Hey there" said a man who appeared on the screen as soon as the communication was established.

"Hey" replied the Second, "here is the Vie en Rose, I am Yuri the Second on board."

"Hey there Yuri, I'm Jack and he's Bob" he said pointing at someone off camera, "or maybe I'm Bob and he's Jack, we get confused sometimes."

The Captain and the Second looked at each other puzzled then the Captain asked "how long have you been in the halo?"

"Bob, how long have we been in the halo? I don't think he remembers either, I'd say for a long time, and what are you doing here? You are looking for the mermaids, aren't you?"

The Captain and the Second still looked at each other puzzled.

"I think they're a little crazy" said the Captain whispering, then turning to the screen he said "Yes, that would be the idea."

"Ah ah, sometimes we meet someone who tries but it's not that easy. We have been working in the halo for twenty years and we have only met them twice."

"Anyway it was enough" said Bob who had entered the screen. The two started giggling like idiots.

"The first time we were together with them for almost eight days" Bob continued, "but if we had known it was so hard to find them, we would have been there a lot longer and the second time we were there for almost a month and we lost 20 pounds."

"Heh heh heh" chuckled Jack.

"And how did you find them?" asked the Second.

"Oh, it's not you who find them, they find you. Finding them on your own is practically impossible. Here in the halo they populate several planets but, made the appropriate proportions, is like finding a sardine in an empty ocean, there is a lot of space here" replied Bob.

"Hey, speaking of sardines Bob, tell him about that sardines planet thing."

"Now I'm getting there Jack. You must know that we go around looking for T planets and then we colonize them with everything that grow there. Well, in short, there aren't many of them around here, I mean, of planets I say, we find maybe one per month, for the rest of time we stay in space waiting for the results of the sensors."

"Yes, but tell him about the sardines, and also mackerels" Jack intervened.

"Now I'm getting to it Jack, do you let me to tell this story or not?"

"You tell them the story of your life Bob! Do you think they give a shit about?"

"But I have to explain otherwise they will not understand, so I was saying...what was I saying?"

"Stopped in space to wait for the sensors" said the Second exchanging with the Captain a look more and more perplexed.

"Oh yes. So once, and mind you, it was only once, the sensors tell us that there is this planet, or rather two, because they were two in the same system, and we went there immediately. They were two beautiful planets, perfect for life and with a lot of oceans and what do we discover? That the planets were already full of life, understand? Then I said to Bob, it must have been a bureaucratic oversight and this planet has already been earth-formed by another ship like ours, because we are several down here understand? I mean, the halo is very big."

"Yes but the sardines Bob."

"I get there now Jack, I mean, I tell myself, someone has already gone through it and forgot to register it in the GNA database. Then this planet has seas full of sardines, and also other things but mainly sardines and listen to this, the other planet, which was practically the same, had mackerels instead. Do you understand? On one sardines and on the other mackerels, but I say, who colonizes a planet only with sardines or only with mackerels. It must have been to make a joke, what's the point, you know? But you want to know about the mermaids, don't you?"

"Yeah," said the Captain, barely holding a yawn.

"So when we found out that that planet was full of sardines we immediately thought it was one of the mermaids' planets, right Bob?"

"Yes yes" intervened Bob, "we thought, well, how about this lucky break, we finally found them..."

"... but no" continued Jack, "there was no trace of the mermaids, in short it must have gone just as I said that someone had formed the planet before. So we recorded it, location and everything and then of course we never went back."

"The halo is too big to go back to the same place twice" explained Bob while nodding.

"So how did you find the mermaids?" asked the Second.

"Ah, straight to the point you eh? But you're right, sorry, it's just that we don't meet people often here and Jack and I have already told each other everything, so much so that sometimes we think we are the other one, so we like to have a chat with someone, when it happens. So, it works like this: you stand still in space and if you're within their radius they come because they think you need help or that you want to meet them. If you move all the time, you never find them. I mean, you never find them anyway, whether you are moving or standing still, they find you if you give them a way to find you, do you understand?"

"Did they find you?"

"That's exactly what happened" Bob said.

"And how did you make contact, as far as we know, you

need a specific equipment" the Captain asked them.

"Oh well, that's not a problem for us, we have practically everything here, even diving equipment. After all, we are still an exploratory ship. But have you already met them or are you on your first time?"

"A certain Admiral Oost introduced them to us" replied the Second.

"Did you hear Bob? They know the Admiral Oost. A badass that one, he is a legend here in the halo. He's the only one who always knows how to find them without fail. But Admiral Oost is also a hunter of illegal immigrants of the Nucleus, I guess you come from the Nucleus" concluded Jack suddenly becoming serious.

"We were, now we are Arms men, don't worry" replied the Second.

"Bravo, good choice. And then we have the mermaids, even if we don't see them much."

"So what do you suggest us to do to find them?"

"Depends on how much time you have. How long have you been in the halo?" Bob asked as a reply.

"About two months."

"Not much. If you have a couple of years you can try to wait here and there, everybody do this way and at least half of them succeed. If you have less time, then give up, even if it is not excluded that you may have a damned stroke of luck."

"But one of their planets has never been found?" asked the Captain again.

"No, never" said Bob and Jack together.

23 THE DECLINE OF THE NUCLEUS

The galactic war, the only war in human history in which not even one battle was fought, lasted several millennia. A war made of intimidation, blockades, acts of piracy, masked incidents, sometimes even sporadic guerrilla warfare. It ended spontaneously when the population of the galaxy was so radically transformed that the regulations of the GNA that had been its engine, fell into disuse.

The population of the Arms had suffered a slow but steady demographic decline, due to an increasingly hostile attitude on the part of women, something that men in the end did not care about anymore. The tendency to demographic decline, already present at the time of the discovery of the mermaids, suffered a marked worsening when men began to travel more and more frequently in the halo.

However, the demographic decline was perfectly balanced by Nucleus migration, either in the form of authorized migratory flow or in the form of illegal flow. The Federal government, aware of the decreasing trend, very appropriately authorized anyone who wanted to immigrate, within the numerical limits to keep the population constant and modulating the authorizations in number inversely proportional to the age of the migrants.

With such a shrewd policy, they not only prevented the decline of the population of the Arms, but also stopped its aging, which strengthened their economy because they acquired labor force instead of costs, as would have happened if they had instead imported old people.

For its part, the Nucleus government stood by and watched as its population seemed stable at first. Then, as the Arms admitted more and more immigrants, the Nucleus began to empty, especially of young people, and as a result the Nucleus population aged even faster than it would have done with the demographic decline already underway.

Ageing led to an increasingly conservative population, a typical characteristic of old people, who elected governors who made quiet living, order, cleanliness and security their strong point in electoral programs. And the governors in turn favored the emigration of young people who would never vote them for such electoral programs. A negative spiral that dragged them towards extinction. Their economy went from a phase of subsistence to a phase of mere survival based on stocks, and in the end not even that, when the electoral programs began to include among their fixed points the reform of cemetery spaces with the introduction of large plots of land parceled out at popular prices.

Entire worlds emptied and when the GNA's measures were suspended, no one noticed.

And nobody even noticed that, because of the deformation of the galaxy, many worlds that had belonged to the Nucleus were now in the Arms.

24 THE WRATH OF THE CH.A.O.S.

Everyone was present at the Project Committee meeting. The Chairman of the Absolute Order of Space-time, as always spoke first.

"We have reached the final phase of the Project. I know that there have been some unauthorized variations during its development, but I also know that until now the Project has not suffered any damage and that's enough. The events of the universe are now beyond our power to control, if not that of destruction, but of course, this is still a very distant subject. General Operations Director, give us an overview of the current situation."

"Sure Chairman" replied immediately the G.O.D. "First of all let's see what the current situation is. The intersection between the two galaxies is near, the two halos are now almost in contact. However, compared to the predicted trajectory, galaxy 2 will not exactly cross galaxy 1 but will pass only tangent. The Physicist says that the different trajectory is due to the perturbation of two other galaxies in the area that have deviated a bit the galaxy 1. However, since during the close passage a bridge of stellar matter will be formed between the two galaxies, there will be no obstacle to the passage of the two species from one to the other."

"Two species?" asked interrupting the Energy Systems Engineer.

"Oh yes, not everyone is informed" replied the G.O.D. explaining, "in the galaxy there are currently two species, one that populates the galaxy itself, one present only in the halo. The second species has developed unexpectedly starting from a species already present in the Project or at least this is what the

Biologist assured us."

The G.O.D. looked at the Biologist with an air of complicity and the concerned expression of the Biologist relaxed.

"The two species are in contact and influence each other. However, the influences have not affected the Project, but we will talk about it later on" said the G.O.D. and continued.

"The physical situation within the galaxy is that the core has begun to deform significantly due to the gravitational attraction of galaxy 2. The induced motions have caused considerable disturbances in stellar orbits with obviously disastrous effects, so the species has progressively left the nucleus moving into the arms."

"It wasn't like that at all!" exclaimed the Joker, "if it wasn't for the war they would stay there until the earth burned under their feet."

"Wars have never changed anything in their history, their ridiculous brawls are not the forces that governed them on their way to the galaxy. The existence of a war at the moment of abandoning the core is a pure coincidence" the G.O.D. replied, "on the other hand there has almost always been a war, so the coincidence is not at all surprising."

"Mmmmm, maybe it will be so" replied a moody Joker.

The G.O.D. resumed his speech after looking askance at the Joker. "The arms instead have not suffered any disaster but only changed a little bit of shape. During the intersection, nothing will happen inside them and this is the physical situation. Almost better than expected."

The G.O.D. took a break but nobody took the opportunity to intervene.

"So, to summarize, the galaxy is now populated by the first species in the arms and the second species in the halo, while the core is empty, as the Project foresaw. So far everything is clear and we can also say that everything is ready for the intersection. The only point that falls outside the parameters of the Project is that species 1 has a very low reproduction rate. Considering the galactic population, they will be able to arrive in sufficient number at the intersection and also to cross it, but if this trend of population decline is not interrupted, the species is destined to extinction and the final outcome of the Project, even if successful, will be unsuccessful."

A whisper ran through the meeting.

For the first time the CH.A.O.S. intervened during the discussion.

"This result is unacceptable" he slowly said in a low, roaring voice that rumbled around everyone, like coming from the entire surrounding space.

The oldest among those present were terrorized, while the others discovered with sudden horror how terrible and powerful the CH.A.O.S was. Around them, the galaxies suffered the shock wave of its voice and not a few stars exploded into supernovas.

The first to recover from the scare was the Evolutionary Systems Engineer who had, or thought he had an explanation.

"Don't be alarmed, Chairman, the reproduction of species always has ups and downs, it does not depend only on the drive to reproduce, but also on circumstances, energy and environment."

Even the G.O.D. took a little while to recover from the CH.A.O.S.'s reproach.

"We will do everything to ensure that this does not happen Chairman, we will intervene. First, however, it is necessary to understand exactly why this demographic decline. Who can tell me something? Biologist? Social Systems Technician?"

"I speak first" said the Biologist, "although I don't have much to say. As far as I am concerned, the species works well. It is healthy and consumes the nominal energy of metabolism at regime. That is to say, there is nothing wrong with them, they are fine, in fact, never been better."

"All right, thank you" said the G.O.D., "Social Systems Technician?"

"For me instead, it's not going at all. Let's begin from the consideration of the Biologist who assures us that the species is healthy. Since it is a fact, the species must reproduce. Since it does not, and this is another fact, there must be some impediment at work. In the case of any animal species, an impediment is a lack of resources, i.e. food, or a predator too numerous for which the species reproduces but the predator exterminates it with a higher rate. The Project species has even too many resources and as far as predators are concerned, it had many in its initial phase but now it has none, so the impediment is not biological."

"That's for sure" said the Biologist.

"An impediment can also be physical or cultural" continued the Social Systems Technician, "physical if the two genders are for example separated, i.e. divided in space. But for the species this is not possible because they can move freely."

"But they are divided in space anyway" said the Diffused Systems Technician, "one genus lives on some planets, or at least most of them, the other genus lives in space and on other planets. The joint presence of the two genus is sporadic and to statistical effects, almost irrelevant."

"They are divided because they have decided to live like that, not because they are forced to, so division is not the real obstacle" replied the Social Systems Engineer, "and this leads us to ask why they have decided to live like that. The answer is that the impediment to reproduction is cultural. They have decided to live separately. Why? This is the problem and the answer is not easy because it is obvious that it is an unreasonable attitude."

"It is" said the Wizard, feeling called into question, "unreasonable I mean, but it could only end like this. I remind you that in the species acts from the very beginning an irrational impulse, which is then what determined its evolutionary drive. They do nothing but behave according to that program, but the circumstances for that program are no longer there. We created them to be unbearable to each other, but forced to live in the same reality. Now, forced are no longer and therefore separation was inevitable. In other words, they used to live together because the brutality of one gender has always overwhelmed the reluctance of the other. Now that they have another choice, the brutality induced by reluctance has disappeared, so reluctance can no longer be overcome. To keep the species balanced, the reluctance should have disappeared along with the disappearance of brutality, but this is impossible because the reluctance is genetic."

"Why did we not foresee such a situation in the Project and did we not plan for the disappearance of gender reluctance?" the G.O.D. asked.

"Technically we could and we also thought about it" replied the Biologist, "but we would have had to program a feature with a deadline without knowing exactly the deadline, with the risk of making it disappear when it was still necessary and at that point, evolution stopped and goodbye Project."

"Right. So Wizard" resumed the G.O.D., "why the brutality has disappeared, what other choice you was talking about?"

"The other species, the halo species."

"But with that species there is no fertility, so how can they prefer it?"

"You all think only in mechanical terms" replied the Wizard, "that is, in biological terms of reproductive drive that governs all species, but in the Project species, that is only one of the forces at play. They are also governed by other forces, by irrationality above all, or to put it another way, by feelings. The second species does not satisfy their reproductive drive, but satisfies the emotional one. In the end this last force had overcame the first."

"It can be deduced that as long as there will be the second species, the first will not reproduce again, is that correct?" asked the G.O.D.

"I wouldn't be so sure" replied the Wizard, "the species had entered into demographic decline immediately after having occupied the whole galaxy, when they decided to live separately and with that the wars disappeared, but anyway before meeting the second species. There was a recovery when the galactic war began, of course, but now that it has run out, the decline has started again. So the second species has only emphasized a trend that was already in place. I repeat, the second species has nothing to do with it. We created them this way and this is how they will be throughout their existence" concluded the Wizard.

"Then they will reach the intersection only because they are quite numerous, but then they will disappear" said the G.O.D. sadly, but immediately recovered.

"But we have a second species" he exclaimed.

"Yes" replied in chorus the Biologist, the Joker and the Wizard.

"Are they able to move through space?" the G.O.D. asked.

"Yes" replied the Joker.

"Do they reproduce?"

"Yes" replied the Biologist.

"Then we can think of an alternative plan" said the G.O.D.

A murmur ran through the meeting while the CH.A.O.S. listened attentively.

"After all, isn't this second species coming from the same planet, didn't we create it?"

"We certainly did, like every other form of life" replied the Biologist.

"Then I would say that since there is no way to correct the sad behavior of the first species, we will act on the second one."

"We have called the B species, but there is an if" said the Biologist again.

"And it would be?" asked the G.O.D.

"They know of our existence."

"So we can't manipulate them because they would resist, is that what you're saying?"

"Yes."

"But we can get their cooperation" said the G.O.D.

"They are a species with a very balanced thought, they will know how to evaluate our intentions. I believe therefore that everything depends on what they are" replied the Biologist with a neutral tone.

The Diffused Systems Technician asked for the floor.

"There is a way to achieve our goal. Let us communicate to them our desire that they populate other galaxies. We will warn them of the intersection and I believe that they will gladly pass to the other galaxy. If they wish, the first species will be able to do the same, but it will extinguish anyway. If we also suggest to the second species to abandon completely the galaxy where they now live, there is also the possibility that the first species, lost contact with the other one, will find again its balance and will not extinguish itself."

"We would need more than a *believe that*" said the G.O.D.

"To get a certain answer, just ask them" said the Wizard.

"True" replied the G.O.D. "Wizard, you think about it, when you have the answer we will meet again."

17th interlude

"The whole meeting was a lie" said the Biologist bitterly.

"When you start lying, you have to continue" replied the physicist dryly.

"It is not true that the species has abandoned the core because of the deformation, the Director has made a blunder. The species is not intelligent, it's just aggressive, proof is that they didn't even notice the intersection. They are only extinct" said the Joker.

"In fact, but the result is the same and then let the Director think that his species has migrated" said the Biologist, then added "and that thing of high or low reproduction depending on energy? Life reproduces anyway, if they had to stand there and watch if they had food for their children they would never reproduce. For example, they would never have survived their prehistory if they had reproduced according to the availability of food, and even in the midst of the most devastating wars, they have always reproduced more than enough. Speaking of lies, that matter of the galaxy diverted by a perturbation?"

"I was just wondering if someone understood that it was not true" grumbled the Physicist.

"And how did you do it? The original trajectory had to lead to the full intersection, the two galaxies had to cross each other" the Biologist asked him.

"Ask your friend here" replied the Physicist indicating the Joker.

The Joker began to sneer.

"So?" said the Biologist.

"Oh, a simple drift current, you know that bridge of matter the Director was talking about. I've been diverting galaxy 2 since the beginning. I had it ejecting stars for almost half a cycle so it lost momentum and deviated."

"And where did the stars end up?"

"That's the beauty, to get away from galaxy 1, I made it expel stars in the opposite direction to the motion and a bit sideways. So it missed the target, but the expelled stars have simultaneously formed a bridge between the two galaxies, so you can pass anyway, but not on the whole volume, only in the bridge. In this way we can let pass whoever we want" said the Joker ending with a bad smile.

"What else do you have in mind?" asked the Biologist.

"For now nothing" replied the Joker with a neutral tone, "but it is always better to be prepared for everything. I'm used to sudden requests. For example, if we didn't do that operation in the halo, they would have gone off a long time ago. As a species they worked only as long as they were giving clubs between males and females, but since they did not do it anymore, they have become an endangered species" concluded the Joker.

"Damned cultural influences" the Biologist considered acidly, "I've always said; life works better when the brain is minimized."

"Sure, the great reptiles of the previous project had been made just like that, but with what result?" replied the Physicist.

"The truth is that after that stupid galactic peace, by inducing that war we gave them a shake, but it wasn't enough" said the Joker.

"At least we tried" said the Physicist.

"Anyway, you don't have to worry, when the old man will discover that the species will become extinct anyway, the second species will be beyond the intersection and since, unlike the first, it cannot become extinct, at that point he will be happy" said the Joker.

"So we will populate the universe with harmony instead of war" added the Biologist.

"We did good, didn't we? We've got it on the G.O.D. and the CH.A.O.S." said the Joker.

"Sure, after all we are Gods" ironized the Physicist.

"Ah ah, or at least there are those who have thought it" added the sneering Joker.

18th interlude

"However, it is not true that the reproduction of the species depends on the circumstances. It is true for any species, but not for them" said the Social Systems Technician to the Evolutionary Systems Technician. "They have always reproduced in the most difficult conditions, in lack of energy, even lack of food. They have never suffered birth rate decreases during wars, famines, epidemics, no matter how hard they have been. They reproduced well even during the initial period, when they were subject to all predators. They also successfully passed the glaciations and those were really hard. No, they simply don't reproduce anymore only when they don't want to anymore, and you know it."

"I know it, you know it and the Biologist knows it, the others don't. In the meantime I calmed the old man down with that argument" replied the Evolutionary Systems Technician.

"Did you say it just for that?"

"And for what else otherwise, did you see what happened when he spoke?"

"I saw. I didn't know what to do anymore, I was as if paralyzed by terror."

"I know, the only ones who didn't break down were the Director and the Physicist, maybe even the Joker but you know, he is always very ... altered. It's hard to say what is going through his mind."

"Anyway, you told him well, it's a miracle he believed you. Even the last of the technicians knows that demographic curves are governed by exponential equations and therefore cannot have ups and downs. Once they start a trend, be it positive or negative, they can no longer change it. If a population reproduces little, it just disappears" said the Social Systems Technician.

"I know, I just wanted to postpone the problem to a quieter moment, this meeting was really hard but let's hope in the second Plan and also that we do not have to face that problem anymore."

"How did he call it?"

"Plan B seems to me. Or maybe it was species B?"

25 INTERSECTION

The General Secretary of the Arms Federation, Yo-Ho, received with cold courtesy the astronomer who presented himself with a bundle of star maps and holographic cubes in his arms, after making him wait more than six hours in the cramped antechamber of his huge office. Six hours at the end of a bureaucratic process of requesting an urgent hearing, which had begun three years earlier.

What will an obscure astronomer ever want from me, the secretary Yo-Ho had asked himself; *money for sure. Why doesn't he make a request to his department*, he said to himself. So he had refused the interview for a long time. The astronomer, however, had not given up and gradually broke through the various layers of secretaries, even giving in to the attentions of two morbid officials and an unpleasant secretary for whom he was still wondering how she got the job, since the career of women to prestigious positions is usually determined primarily by their appearance. In the end he was allowed to wait for the Secretary in his antechamber, if the Secretary ever had time to receive him.

The temperance and determination of the astronomer, in the end, had won over the prejudices of uselessness of the Secretary, who on the other hand would have received instantly any woman if she had been available to the unexpected or even more simply with a deep neckline, as all the powerful had always done since the beginning of human history.

This is what the astronomer, calm and silent, thought while waiting. He bitterly thought that if he had a great breasts he would be received immediately. And he also thought that maybe all that effort, all that humiliating himself to give humanity a new course, maybe humanity didn't really deserve it.

"What can this humble servant of the government do for such an esteemed scientist as you?" Secretary Yo-Ho began with that greasy tone of all powerful men and one had to wonder why, despite the fact that that unbearable greasiness was so evident in all of them, they had never been stuck in their climb up the social pyramid. A position from which they mainly exercised the personal power they had so laboriously conquered through blandishments and flattery, that is: copulating with the highest possible number of females, as had always happened in human history. Of course, some claimed that power itself was the purpose of that kind of men, or even more concretely to accumulate wealth, but in reality both were sought only to achieve that first goal which, on closer inspection, was the only real purpose.

The astronomer had all this well in mind, like all men of science who, in spite of a behavior often distracted, as if human events did not matter to them much, inside were a fire of frustrated desires that sublimated in devoting themselves to abstract problems. Despite the fact that Secretary Yo-Ho and what he represented, he did not like at all, he had persevered in his intention because, perhaps, there was still a part of humanity worthy of a future.

"Your Excellency, I'm sorry to have disturbed you, but recently my group and I have made a very important discovery that no one wants to hear about, as if it were unimportant."

"But dear sir" replied the secretary with a round mouth, "I am only a humble servant of the State and science I know very little about. If people more competent than me have decided that it is not important, who am I to contradict them?" concluded the secretary by joining his fingertips and emphasizing that attitude with a false smile.

"The fact is that for the scientific world it may not be important, although I would have much to say on this point, but for the Federation I think it is important" replied the astronomer with the most diplomatic tone possible, so as not to arouse the anger of the Secretary with his insistence.

"So tell me, tell me about this concern of yours" said the annoyed Secretary, while his mind closed behind *what this one wants to know about the Federation.*

"Thank you Secretary. So it is soon said. There is a new Arm, we have called it Virgo Current because it is a stellar flow directed to our galaxy, placed in the homonymous sector" said the astronomer with dry tone, "of course I have all the star charts to prove it."

The Secretary's mind suddenly reopened.

"What? A new Arm? And how is it possible! The Arms don't sprout like mushrooms! I won't be an astronomer, but I'll get there!" he said, raising his tone as he spoke, and concluding almost with a shout.

"Absolutely right Secretary. In fact, it is an Arm of another galaxy. Our galaxy has approached another one and an Arm has formed between the two, perhaps by perturbation, perhaps by attraction. The formation mechanism is mysterious because the stars are moving too fast towards us but anyhow ..." the astronomer began to explain with a tone that manifested the serious intention to launch himself into a conference. The Secretary Yo-Ho immediately cut short.

"And how come we didn't notice it before? A galaxy doesn't move from one day to another!" interrupted him the Secretary still incredulous, who didn't know much about celestial mechanics, but he was still a man of a galactic civilization for which the size of the galaxy was a known fact.

Sure of what he was saying, the astronomer did not lose his temper in front of the almost hysterical reaction of the Secretary.

"This is also true, in fact, it is a phenomenon that has been going on for a long time but as you certainly know, astronomy and astrophysics do not receive a lot of funds, so there are few who dedicate themselves to it. We didn't discover it before because there is a lot of space to watch and few people who do it, and anyway our presence towards the edge is minimal, so the phenomenon has not been noticed until now. That's all."

"Yeah, yeah, you're absolutely right" replied the Secretary

who became calm again, "and are those of the GNA informed? What do they say?" the Secretary investigated in the end.

"When we let them know, they said it wasn't their responsibility. They said that the Current is still outside the galaxy so their statute does not provide for it. They are a little bit bureaucratic, if I may say so, but in their defense there is also the fact that the continuous movement of the stars in the Arms keeps them more than busy in the constant updating of maps and navigation metric tensors."

"Yeah, yeah, they have quite a job too" replied the pensive Secretary. "And where exactly would this new Arm be?" he then asked the astronomer.

"The Current unites the other galaxy with the Unicorn Ring" replied the astronomer.

The news was the final blow that finally made the Secretary lose control.

"Straight to the edge?" he exclaimed, squinting his eyes.

"Directly to the edge" confirmed the astronomer with careless air.

"Shit!"

"Excuse me?" said the astronomer.

"Oh nothing, I'm sorry for the expression" said the Secretary, coming to his senses and suddenly changing his tone. "You did well to come and report this fact to me" he said smiling and standing up, as if to say that the interview was over.

"Don't you want to see the charts?" asked the astronomer reluctant to leave.

"I trust you dear sir, I trust you, you seem to me to be such a good and competent person" replied Secretary Yo-Ho as he pushed him out the door.

The first thought that came to Yo-Ho's mind was to make the astronomer disappear in order to keep the news secret, but later he considered that after all, that bookworm had wandered for three years through all the offices of the Federation and no one had given him the slightest consideration, so he dropped the idea, judging the disturbance useless. Then he thought that it was worrying that no one in the entire bureaucratic apparatus had understood the importance of the news and put in the back of his mind the intention to launch a personnel reform as soon as possible. Finally he called his secretary who arrived preceded by the ticking of her heels, a shift of air caused by the impressive geography of the hills and valleys of her figure and finally a blaze of perfume, whom the Secretary began to dictate a long series of measures.

26 THE FIRST TRUE GALACTIC HERO

At the meeting called by the Secretary Yo-Ho, were present all the Super-Admiral of Arms, some high officials of the information services, in addition to the canute Superplexor of Nucleus, whose position was now only honorary because the Nucleus, although formally still existing, had in fact been reduced to a colony of a few billion individuals in need of health care.

"Gentlemen, I have just been informed of the existence of a bridge between the outer rim and a galaxy that has approached our" the Secretary said. "Leaving aside the fact that the phenomenon must have started thousands of years ago but so far no one has noticed it, and wondering why it would be tantamount to opening a useless process to the past, I believe that the reports of recent times of information services, about the increasing difficulty of contact with the population of the halo are related to this novelty" concluded the Secretary the preamble of the meeting.

The admirals looked each other perplexed.

"They're moving" said an intelligence officer, accustomed from his job to quickly draw the consequences from the strangest and most unexpected news.

"Or they are running away" added another official.

"In fact, for some decades now, encounters with the mermaids have become increasingly rare, as if they didn't want to be seen again" added a third official, "something we started to worry about because we had reached a certain balance with them and now, I believe that our social peace is closely related to the mermaids. In short, let's face it, they are now part of our in quotation marks *leisure-cultural offer*, so to speak. If they were to disappear, I think we would have to deal with a big problem."

"So what do we do?" asked the Secretary.

"We stop them" said immediately the Super-Admiral of Orion.

"Bah, they are not our citizens and do not respond to our laws. To stop them you should use force. Have you really thought about this, Admiral?" said the Secretary, who was still a man of common sense.

Understanding the stupidity of his sentence, the admiral silenced.

"We could follow them" suggested then the Super-Admiral of Shield-Cross.

"And do we populate the other galaxy too?" asked the secretary thoughtfully.

"I don't think it's possible, Secretary" said an official of the information services, "since the collapse of the ... excuse me Superplexor, I mean since the decline of the Nucleus, the entire galactic population has been reduced to only one hundred billion, we are simply not enough to populate two galaxies. We are already few for this one galaxy."

"Then we could move en masse too" insisted the Super-Admiral.

"Ah, Admiral, it's easy for you to say that" the Secretary intervened. "You are too accustomed to deal with the fleet with which you only need the order to mobilize and everyone goes where you want, but to transfer a population is another thing. People are rooted on their own worlds, attached to their homes. And then what about the women? Do we move them too, explaining that we do it to follow the mermaids?" said the Secretary with a hint of sarcasm, "or do we leave them here, definitively decreeing our own end? "

"If they have decided to go, there is nothing we can do about it" said the first official.

"We'll see" concluded the Secretary. "Anyway we have time to decide what to do. That Arm will last centuries, if not millennia, so there is none in a hurry. We have to think it over and then decide on a serious long-term policy, including the problem of demographic decline that it is time to face. In the meantime someone would do well to go and explore this new Arm, Virgo Current or whatever the hell it is called" and saying this the Secretary stood up, thus closing the meeting.

19th interlude

"So what did they say?" the G.O.D. asked.

"They will do it, but they are in pain for the first species" replied the Wizard.

"Why?"

"They believe that we were too cruel, that we forced them to live in a reality that was too difficult."

"What does it matter to them?"

"Compassion is what governs them, Director" replied the Wizard, "so they decided not to abandon them. They will leave someone behind to maintain contact."

"Let them do as they please" concluded the G.O.D. dryly.

27 THE REBIRTH OF ARMS

During the following centuries, the Virgo Current was like the subtle link between the two vessels of an hourglass, through which the species B poured into Andromeda, the approaching galaxy then identified by a comparative study of paleo-astronomy. Switching from one to the other galaxy was only possible through the Current because in intergalactic space, the space was not bent by the masses and consequently the metric tensors did not offer shortcuts. That is to say that the distances were insurmountable. And also because no spaceship could do without a periodic supply, especially of chemicals for the life support of the species, which despite the watertight hulls, to some extent were always dispersed in space. Chemists that could be collected even in the immensity of the interstellar void, where there were still a few atoms here and there, but impossible to be found in intergalactic space where the only thing that existed was space itself.

While the migration of the halo people proceeded, the men on the Arms faced first of all the demographic problem, since from it came the limitation to be able to colonize Andromeda, which eventually became their long-term plan.

Believing themselves to be evolved men, as men had always believed since the Stone Age, they tried the path of information campaigns, then that of economic incentives and all the facilities they were able to invent, and finally that of social alarm by hammering the population with statistical data that eliminated any doubt about the next extinction of the human race. But the fate that had suffered the Nucleus was there to show that no argument, however reasonable, could overwhelm that intrinsic reluctance from which, without realizing it, half of the human race was dominated.

In the end men faced the problem in the only way that had always proved effective, and that was a club in the head. Naturally the club had evolved a lot since the Lower Palaeolithic times and with it the means to use it.

The long-term plan began with the first century used to expel from the Government institutions, pretending not to, the female component that had infiltrated them over the millennia, in most cases exploiting their low maneuvers of sexual blackmail, and had reached a presence almost equal to the natural percentage of its kind in the species. It was in fact perfectly clear to the men that the club could not have been used if it was held by a female as well as male hand. The result was obtained with a great sacrifice, perhaps the most honorable sacrifice of the whole human history because it involved, above all, men who were strongly refractory to the sacrifice.

For economic reasons not better specified, they said, to all government positions will be progressively reduced the emoluments, until making them pure volunteer positions, whose burdens would fall on the volunteer himself and continued with the abrogation of all gratuitousness and exemptions from which they benefited. In other words, no wages, no privileges and no hidden fringe benefits whatsoever.

Of course, since women were much more pragmatic than men, as they had always shown by carefully avoiding all activities from which they could not gain any personal advantage, they spontaneously withdrew from public administration, also because, in fact, no one had told them to leave and therefore their fighting spirit was not awakened.

The sacrifice of men, which lasted a century, was the most difficult part and the most brilliant victory of the entire long-term program.

When the Assembly of the Federation was constituted by men only, the club was finally given in the style that had characterized the galactic civilization for millennia, that is a law that seemed to be written by the GNA's managers. "It is introduced a tax of social charge equal to 85% of income, declared or presumed on the basis of inductive assessments, for anyone who has not reached by adulthood a natural heterozygotic replication rate of 2.1. Such tax will be progressively reduced by a percentage equal to the fraction, expressed in hundredths, exceeding the said limit up to the maximum of the percentage capacity, while it will be increased by one percentage point per year for each year beyond the adult age in which the same limit is not reached, up to the maximum of the effective income capacity, ascertained directly by the tax offices of the district. For the purposes of the calculation of said rate, procreations obtained by non-natural methods will not be considered valid."

On a closer inspection, the last apostille was not really necessary, since its substance was already present in the word *natural,* referred in the law to the rate of procreation. It was introduced only to reaffirm the undeniable impulse of men not to see themselves excluded from the process, but above all, both introduced in the law a fundamental asymmetry, which at first sight was invisible. Even if in appearance the law applied to everyone, it was in fact more than obvious that only natural fertilizations could be taken into account to calculate the rate of procreation, from which it followed that those who by nature could not be fertilized, could not be subject to such a law.

The law was promulgated quietly and passed for years under silence, a technique always used by legislators to introduce controversial laws. When sixteen years later, the first women born under this law and in that year became adults, realized that their entire income was directly forfeited by the public administration according to an obscure law sixteen years earlier, they could do nothing more, and were forced to work almost without wages. Finally touched in the only thing that mattered to them, they began to procreate in a hurry to reach, and in many cases exceed, that threshold of two point one child each. It took almost thirty years for the law to come into force, i.e. the initial

231

sixteen plus fifteen that served to reduce by one percentage point per year that 15% of the surviving income, which the more leathery, i.e. the majority, insisted on making enough, until they realized that from the age of thirty-one they would have to work for free forever, because even that 15% had disappeared in the folds of the law. In the end, they all learned and, even if with gritted teeth, they got busy as soon as nature allowed them.

Of course there was not a resounding population explosion because the effects of a law, whether natural or artificial, always tend to be the least possible. The vast majority only exceeded the threshold of two point one, i.e. three. In fact, the law spoke of a two point one in the statistical sense, but when it was applied to individuals, the real rate was obviously counted, so they all had to make more than two children.

This was enough for the Federal government that, in order not to antagonize half of the population, had adopted in the law the reasonable minimum rate of demographic constancy and hidden in the obscure method to count the much more expensive rate three to achieve demographic expansion.

In the second century of the plan, the galactic civilization saw a slight demographic recovery that over time became more and more vigorous. Of course the recovery did not mean at all an immediate growth of the active population, since every human being needs time to reach the adult phase. For women, that time was very short because at the age of fourteen they had to get busy fast, as in reality nature expected, not to reach adulthood, that is at sixteen, without children. Even if the majority exceeded that limit of a few months. For men, instead, that time was a little longer, because their classification as active population did not depend on whether or not they had children, but on the job or assignment they took on in galactic society. Job or assignment that was usually very complex, since technically complex was the civilization of the time.

Paradoxically, an important side effect of the club was also the fall into disuse of the brothels. Since, in fact, women were forced to reproduce, they had to play along, and the alternating phases of human history, with the dark and sad periods of their prohibition and the equally dark periods of their adoption on a large scale, became part of the past. Within three centuries the galactic population increased from one hundred to one hundred and fifty billion individuals, the most brilliant result in all human history, and in the end women were also satisfied because they realized that to give birth as soon as they were fertile, gave them a long and serene life without any more serious worries. They all finally understood that Nature is much wiser than human reason and that if it made them fertile at the age of fourteen, it was because that was the right age to have children and in the end those who appreciated the club the most, were the ones who would never have wanted it.

Secretary Yo-Ho, who had long since passed away, was proclaimed a posthumous galactic hero and in his honor were erected on many worlds, all equal monuments on which was engraved in place of epitaph his most famous phrase: "If you want to do good to a woman, do not ask her opinion" and finally the renewed Federation prepared to move in the Current.

28 IN THE CURRENT

"These maps are two centuries old" complained the Route Officer.

"They are the most updated ones of the GNA, they cannot update the whole galaxy every ten years" replied the Navigation Officer, "do the best you can with them."

"Easy for you to say that, but it's not that easy. Here everything moves at a different speed than in the galaxy. I can't find one just one reference point. To have these charts or not is almost the same."

"As a generic reference there is always Andromeda in front of us and the Ring behind us."

"Beside from the fact that neither Andromeda nor the Ring are exact points, I would gladly do it if only I could see them" replied the Route Officer with annoyance.

"You don't see those either?" urged the Navigational Officer.

"No way, dense fog, there will be a density of at least one hundred atoms per cubic kilometer and maybe even more" replied the other, desperate.

"And what about in the radio field?" insisted the Navigation Officer.

"In the radio field, sure! And what do you think I should be looking for, a VOR[15] station?" replied the Route Officer with a sarcastic tone. "If I put on the radio telescope, and I've already tried that, it's like I'm tuning into every rock radio in the galaxy."

"Then on the 21 centimeters, all the stars emit on the 21 centimeters, you will see something for sure."

"Yes yes, go figure what I see in the 21 centimeters, with all

---

[15] VHF Omnidirectional Range

the free hydrogen around here. As soon as I tune in, the whole screen turns white. We are practically blind, we travel totally in IFR IMC[16], as if we were a plane in a cloud, just to give you an idea."

"Never flown an airplane" replied the Navigation Officer.

"And you call yourself navigator?" the Route Officer mocked him.

"Katjusa what does she say?" asked the Navigation Officer passing over the irony of the other.

"Ah ah, yes, that's the one. You know what computers are like, either you give them precise coordinates or they are incapable of any calculation. I asked her to find a radial of any NDB[17] station, do you know what she told me? ADF[18] for 180! the bitch! Translated: go back, and she even told me as if she was suggesting me to put a condom on before doing it."

"I know, she always has that unbearable tone when she's trying to tell you that she thinks you're incompetent."

"Yeah, she can't admit her limitations. Or perhaps it is only we who attribute tones and intentions to her. What good times I had when I navigate in the halo. There everything was crystal clear. Visibility for thousands of light years."

"Did you really navigate in the halo?"

"Yes."

"And what were you doing there?" urged the Navigation Officer, intrigued and a little envious.

"I used to bring around tourists who wanted to meet mermaids."

"Then you must have met the mermaids, quite often I mean."

"Not as much as I would have liked" replied the Route Officer almost in a low voice.

---

[16] Instrumental Flight Rules/Instrumental Meteorological Conditions
[17] Non Directional Beacon
[18] Automatic Direction Finder

"I regret that I never went there" complained the Navigation Officer, "I used to say to myself you're young, you have time, blah blah blah, then it became more and more difficult. And have you ever brought women in the halo?" he asked again.

"No never, not that someone hadn't tried, also because it was not formally forbidden. But as soon as they set foot on board they were disgusted."

"And why was that?" asked the Navigation Officer.

"Trick. Dirty toilets. If there is one thing a woman cannot stand, these are the dirty toilets. We used to shit out on purpose, you should have seen what filthy latrines they were, so they either had to wash the toilets for as long as the trip lasted, or gave up. Needless to say, they always gave up."

The two began to sneer.

"We could jump out the Current and take a look around" the Navigation Officer then suggested.

"Sure, and which way?" replied the Route Officer with a still sarcastic tone.

"What do you mean with which way?"

"I tell you that we are like blind. Except for the nearest stars, which I can't identify on the maps, I don't even know in what direction we are oriented, I don't know what direction the Current has, I just know that we are in it. So don't ask me which way to go because I have no idea which direction to take to get out of it."

At that moment the Commander of the vessel arrived on the bridge.

"Gentlemen what happens? I haven't heard the maneuvering alarm for a while now."

"Commander, after the last leg we found ourselves right in the middle of the Current and we have only an estimated position. We have no way to check where we are, so according to annex 12 of the GNA navigation rules, we cannot proceed to the next leg" replied the Navigation Officer.

"Navigator, it is good to quote the regulations with such a precision, but we are an explorer vessel and those regulations were made only for vessels navigating in known and mapped areas. So proceed to the next leg."

"Commander" said the Navigation Officer.

"Yes?"

"If from an estimated position, at the next leg we will not be able to find our way, we will be definitely lost."

"It's a risk we have to take" replied the Commander cutting short, "communicate the coordinates to Katjusa and proceed."

"Yes Commander. Katjusa, new leg, same direction as the previous one, extension one hundred."

"Course calculated" Katjusa replied almost immediately, "coordinates x 47 degrees, y 282 degrees and 30 minutes, z 2 degrees 45 minutes and 15 seconds, w 185 degrees and 57 seconds, ETE eight minutes and twelve seconds, AGRE engine active, standby for destination."

"Activate" said the Navigation Officer.

"Entry into variety in five seconds, four, three, two, one, push. Entry into variety performed, ETE eight minutes and ten seconds" Katjusa said in a honeyed voice.

The two Officers remained silent for the few minutes that the new leg would last, a silence that was interrupted shortly after by Katjusa's whiny voice.

"Exit the variety in three seconds, two, one. WARNING, metric tensor NOT diagonalized, AGRE engine off, ATE[19] seven minutes 48 seconds, ATO unknown, end position unknown, local variety topology disturbed, three-dimensional references none, three-dimensional position unknown, contact not identified at alpha 4 degrees theta 6 degrees 12 minutes moving, distance 238.000 kilometers increasing, class unknown, synchronization performed, communication channel opened, answer none" she said in a tearful voice as if she had announced that she had been repeatedly subjected to violence, which perhaps, in the evaluation parameters of a computer, was exactly what that occurred to her.

---

[19] Actual Time Enroute

"Damn, there's someone else and we narrowly missed them" exclaimed the Route Officer.

"I wouldn't say we did" replied the Navigation Officer we a forced smile, "In space 238,000 kilometers are less than nothing! Damn!"

"Call the Commander" muttered the Route Officer as he turned on all his instruments.

"What's going on?" asked the Commander who rushed on the bridge.

"I'm trying to determine our position, Katjusa is just talking nonsense bullshit and there is a vessel in front of us on a similar route. It's not one of ours, definitely halo's" the Navigation Officer quickly informed the Commander.

"Call them!" ordered the Commander dryly.

"Katjusa has already done it but they are not responding, they are disappearing from all our instruments. I saw them for a moment at the telescope but now they have already disappeared. They are still on long-range radar ... Here, go from there too!" yelled the Route Officer, knocking violently on his console.

"But where are we?" the Commander asked.

"I do not know Commander, I cannot find any reference. We are definitely lost" replied the Route Officer.

"Even the mermaids must have gotten lost then, kind of odd that they didn't answer" meditated the Commander. "Do you still have the direction in which they left?"

"They were straight ahead when we came out of the variety, but as if it was done on purpose, in this area we came out of the variety with a slight angular momentum that without references I cannot quantify exactly, so who knows how we are oriented now. We should have followed them immediately by inertial engine, but it took just few seconds for them to disappear and we had no time to maneuver. Anyway, maybe we would not have reached them even that way" replied the Route Officer, "It's a real nightmare to navigate here, it's like being with a boat in the middle of the whirlpools" he added annoyed.

"In fact, it's odd" said the Navigation Officer, "as far as I know they've never behaved this way before."

"We need to find out where we are" said the Commander cutting short, "let's go back and find a fix."

"I don't even know where the back is" complained the Navigation Officer.

"Which back are you talking about?" said the Route Officer with a clear tone of mockery.

"Mine! Are you insinuating that I do not know how to govern this ship?" cried the other one.

"It didn't even cross my mind, I thought you were talking about Katjusa's back, with that whining voice it sounded like you raped her."

Both of them laughed like idiots and also the Commander joined in the laughter.

"Katjusa, reverse course of the last leg, activate" finally ordered the Commander.

"Current position unknown, destination calculation impossible. Absolute destination calculation, impossible. Relative destination calculation, possible," Katjusa replied in an even more whining tone, as if the chatter of the two officers had really been put into practice.

"What say you?" asked the Commander.

The two officers looked at each other for a moment and all three realized that they were in the most feared position of all navigators of all time, on land, at sea, in space or in variety: they were lost. As for anyone lost, even in space there was only one way out: go in a fixed direction and hope for luck. After all, it was in that way that the most important discoveries in history had been made.

"After we left the Ring, we made three legs, one a thousand, one five hundred and one hundred light years. In the worst hypothesis that we got lost from the very first leg, we cannot be more than a thousand, six hundred light-years away from the halo. If we make a straight leg of equal length and in a random direction, we will be almost certain to leave the Current, so we will be able to see something" proposed the Navigation Officer.

"All right" replied the Commander, "let's do it."

The Navigation Officer took action. "Damn, I feel like I'm like those who made the first voyage in the variety. Reckless really. They literally slipped into the unknown without knowing where they would end up."

"They also had luck to find the way back, at that time the maps had not yet been made" added the Route Officer.

"Maybe, or maybe the first ones didn't come back at all. Maybe they tried and tried again until someone managed to come back and say: it can be done! " considered the Navigation Officer by manually entering random coordinates into the computer.

"Katjusa" said the Officer to call the computer's attention.

"I followed the discussion" replied the computer with a laconic tone which seemed not to miss also a slight tone of annoyance and continued "entry into variety in seven, six, five, you can still override the order, four, three, two, one, push, entry into variety done, ETE unknown."

"It's as if I had put my hands in her panties against her will" sneered the Route Officer.

"Uh-huh, yes, and that can still override meant *get your dirty hands out of my panties*" the Navigation Officer ironically said.

"And now how long do you think we will stay in the variety? I'm worried about that unknown ETE" said the Route Officer.

"Who knows, if in this area the variety is flat instead of folded, we could be in it even sixteen hundred years, but on the other hand it is very rare that the variety is flat."

"Then I have time to go and have a snack" concluded the Route Officer.

"I'm coming with you" said the other.

The blind leg brought them close to the halo, hovering several hundred light years outside the Current that stood out in the black of intergalactic space like a faint veil of light that faded away in the distant Andromeda.

"So beautiful and so difficult eh?" said the Route Officer.

"Yeah. If we don't find a way to navigate through it, we will never be able to cross it" replied the Navigation Officer.

"But what was that halo ship doing in there, and how did they know where to go" asked the Route Officer.

"They are moving to Andromeda, by now it is well known fact even if officially everybody deny it" said the Commander who arrived at that moment, "It's obvious that they must have a more updated map than ours and this doesn't surprise me at all, after all they started to cross the Current long before us. We will have to ask the GNA to make a request for updated maps to the mermaids. Anyway, now that we are here, it occurred to me that we could follow the Current just a little on the outside rim, navigator, what do you say?"

"You cannot Commander. The space in the optical field is very different from the space seen in the whole electromagnetic spectrum. The current that from here looks like a beautiful strip of light, is in fact surrounded by X and Gamma fields of very high intensity, due to the *bremsstrahlung* radiation inside it, and it is needless to say that they are all lethal radiation because you will know for sure. To add difficulty to difficulty, the sensors tell me that they are also unstable fields. No instrument would work. We could navigate visually, that's for sure, but visually we could only proceed in three-dimensional navigation and the distance to travel in this way is two hundred and fifty thousand light years. I would say that is excluded. In short, the Current is a tube that can be navigated only from the inside, Commander, and it is also a cloudy and muddy tube if I may say."

"You mean a real asshole, don't you?" the Route Officer echoed him. All the three began again to snigger for the row of the filthy jokes with which they had defused their dangerous situation, from which fortunately they had escape unscathed.

"It's also excluded to arrive to Andromeda in a single leg outside the current, a distance that goes far beyond the autonomy of any ship and anyway on a similar distance the variety makes so many folds that it's impossible to calculate any leg and in the end we could find ourselves totally somewhere else" meditated the Commander aloud.

"Gentlemen, we are facing an insurmountable difficulty. But after all we are just an exploratory ship, we are not adventurers, so let's go back and put an end to this story with a nice report" the Commander concluded dryly, moving away from the bridge.

According to the report of the exploratory vessel, the GNA requested updated maps of the Virgo Current to the halo. To obtain them was not immediate because with the people of the halo had never been established a real channel of official communication, the mermaids had always limited themselves to be found at the occasion. The request was then transmitted by sending a ship into the halo and hoping for contact, but contacts had become very rare, because after three centuries of migration, there were not many mermaids left.

Anyhow, after two years of wandering, they finally came into contact, as always announced suddenly by a laconic Katjusa whose voice, after centuries of software improvements, had almost lost that petulant disapproval like she was feeling jealousy for all human activities that had to do with the people of the halo.

"Contac at alpha 178 degrees 32 minutes 6 seconds, elevation minus 46 degrees 38 minutes approaching, distance 1,225,143 miles, speed 18,200 miles per second, halo class, synchronism performed, residual spin two degrees per minute, eccentricity zero point two, communication channel opened" recited the computer out of the blue with a sweet and persuasive but still neutral tone, like a sex pro would have had in saying *I love you* to a man who she will see only once in her life, a tone that in the end seemed even more irritating than the previous one.

The crew, consisting of the minimum possible to stay in space for a long time without going mad, namely two men and a large library of play material, woke up from the torpor.

"Damn, just now that I had gotten to the point where they were undressing her and they were doing her in three" exclaimed one of the two, stretched slouched in the pilot's seat, throwing the portable viewer on the console.

"Come on! Are you telling me that you prefer that stuff to

flesh and blood mermaids" ironized the other one all excited about the event, pulling his feet down from the ship's main panel and putting himself at the controls. "They're coming right at us from behind, if it wasn't a halo ship it would look like a hostile action."

At the same time the man was talking, a mermaid appeared on the screen of the room.

"Hello men, do you have a problem? Can we be of any help?" said the mermaid elegantly circling on the screen.

"How about that, that's exactly why we are here" replied the man. "I introduce myself, I am Captain Somchaiputisawan, briefly Somchai and he is my second Anarasti or more simply Ana, we have been here looking for you for a long time."

"Nice to meet you Captain, I'm sorry for your long wait, but you know, the halo is very big and we are not many... but you will have a reason to look for us" added another mermaid entirely covered with tattoos that entered the screen.

"That's exactly what I wanted to tell you. We have an official request from the GNA, you know what the GNA is, do you not?" said the Captain.

"Yes, we know" replied the second mermaid, "even though we've never had anything to do with it."

"Of course it is only a request, or rather, a request for a favor. It is obvious that no one expects you to give the GNA authority over you" the man pointed out.

"But of course, Captain, don't worry, we will gladly fulfill all your requests if it is within our possibilities, with the only limitation that does not put us in danger. We have children on board and we always feel very protective with them and we tend to become unreasonable if we feel that there is danger, you understand me right?" replied a mermaid.

"Oh, interesting, I've never seen mermaids babies before!" exclaimed the Second, "but I haven't seen mermaids often either" he added.

"Our little ones are never seen because they usually stay on our planets until they are adults" explained the mermaid.

"And how come you have them with you now?" asked Captain Somchai with an indifferent air.

"Oh, a trip around" answered vaguely the mermaid all tattooed, "but tell us your request, Captain."

"Yes, it is soon said. Do you by any chance have updated maps of the Virgo Current?" the Captain asked carelessly, as if to try to hide the importance of the thing and not to raise the alarm of the mermaids about human plans, or at least so he thought he should do.

"Are you talking about the new galactic Arm?" replied the tattooed mermaid.

"Yes, that's the one."

"We have maps, do you need them?" asked the tattooed mermaid with a big smile but an almost chilling gaze, very unusual for a mermaid.

"So the GNA asked us" replied the Captain in a neutral tone.

"All right, we'll give them to you," replied the tattooed mermaid.

"Thank you, I open the data transmission channel" concluded Captain Somchai.

"How comes Captain, do you want us to just transmit them? Don't you want us to come along and bring them to you?" said then the first mermaid.

The two men looked at each other with stupefied air for the proposal that they couldn't believe it was happening, then the Second nodded like a lemur in heat.

"We will gladly welcome you" replied the Captain with a smile, trying not to give in to the frenzy that had suddenly taken him.

Of course, the spaceship sent on a mission with the purpose of making the request to the mermaids, was equipped with the right swimming pool to accommodate them as well as an approved docking flange.

"We spin our ship for docking" said the Captain, "your approach course has a radial of eccentricity of zero point two, is that right Katjusa?"

"Right" he heard the computer say.

"Yes, zero point two, can you correct it?"

"Certainly captain, I'll do it right away" replied the first mermaid.

With a perfect maneuver, the outcome of a written procedure in every detail that was the result of centuries of meetings, even if sporadic, with the ships of the halo, the two ships hooked up and the compensation whistle announced the passage of the mermaids from one to the other ship.

Floating on two inflatable mattresses, now standard equipment of every swimming pool in space, along with balloons and inflatable ducks because of the mermaids' marked attitude to everything that was play or playful, the two men lacked only the sunglasses to feel inserted in an extra-luxury vacation.

The two mermaids arrived, were the ones that appeared on the screen. After having both played for a long time with the two men, and also done the everything else, one was half up on the mattress, stretching between the Captain's legs, the other, the tattooed one, did the same thing with the Second.

"But would you have really taken the maps via transmission?" the mermaid asked.

"It's a way like any other" replied the relaxed Captain.

"And didn't you also wish to meet us, in short, to do what we are doing?" insisted the mermaid.

"We wanted it very much, but being on an official mission I didn't dare to ask. As if I wanted to take advantage of it" replied Captain Somchai.

"Ohi Ohi captain, centuries of meetings and still you have not learned. You have really been heavily conditioned. But haven't you understood that we like to play with you? If we don't when we meet you, we miss it!" exclaimed the mermaid.

"Really?" replied the incredulous captain.

"Really. It's just that you're always there with that equation that we are women and in the end you always think that we act like them. We are not women! We are not human beings!" said the mermaid in a well-spoken voice.

"But you are females" opined the Captain.

"Yes, I am a female, but we are not all females, it's clear, and you don't know how to distinguish us" replied the mermaid.

"So even the males like to do it with us?"

"Yes of course, after all it's just a game and the character of our species is that. As soon as we see a ball, we have to give it a tail swing, we can't do without it" said the mermaid giggling, "and you are an even more fun game."

Captain Somchai dropped the subject, also because, reassured by the mermaid, it was a subject that did not concern him.

"But listen, I have a curiosity" continued Captain Somchai, "the maps, where did you get them?"

"I don't know; they are part of our on-board equipment" replied the mermaid cautiously.

"But someone will have plotted them down" insisted the Captain.

"I think so" replied the evasive mermaid playing with the Captain's floppy penis.

"And who plotted them, considering that the current is a new formation?" insisted the Captain trying not to pay attention to the maneuvers of the mermaid.

"New is for you who have recently found it, as far as we are concerned, it has existed for millennia. After all, out here in the halo we really saw it coming" replied the mermaid trying to end the discussion by making his maneuvers more vigorous.

The Captain was satisfied with the answer, in the end reasonable, as any other man would have done in that situation and let the mermaid finish what she had in mind.

Shortly afterwards a bubbling appeared in the pool and with a lapping like a waterfall, the surface of the water was shaken by a whirlwind of rapid movements.

"I present you our children" said the tattooed mermaid, in whose eyes a joyful light suddenly appeared, but of the little mermaids only the shapes that flickered at full speed underwater could be seen. Then, one after the other, the children emerged halfway out of the water with their tails supporting them frantically beating almost in sync.

"But they have breasts!" exclaimed the Second.

"Sure, why they shouldn't have them, they have them as we all have them" replied the tattooed mermaid.

"But don't they grow later on?"

"Later on, when?" asked the mermaid.

"In our women grow later" explained the Second.

"There you go again with this story of your species" said the tattooed mermaid, "we are not human, even if we half look like it. We are more like dolphins, when we are born we are small but perfectly formed. After all, as soon as we are born we have to breathe like you, but being born in the water, if we don't know how to swim right away, we will drown, do you understand?" concluded the mermaid, splashing water in the face of man with one hand.

"Yes but the breast is a sexual character that therefore develops only in reproductive age, don't tell me that you can reproduce yourself as soon as you are born" continued the Second laughing at the sketches, but reluctant to convince himself.

"And who said that the breast is a sexual character? For me the expression makes no sense, and anyway the breast has nothing to do with reproduction. In the same way I could say that the legs are your sexual character, would that means something to you?"

"Yes, you're right, nothing, it means nothing."

"Exactly, and then we all have breasts, male and female, so why should it be a sexual character."

"Yes you're right, forget everything" admitted the man finally convinced.

"That's good, now be good, I want to show our children how a man works" and saying this the mermaid began to do the maneuver that her companion had just done to the Captain, while all the little ones were arranged around them carefully observing the maneuver, as if it were a lesson at school.

At the request of the two men, the two ships stayed docked for several days, because they knew perfectly well that in their lives they would never had another chance like that. When at the end and reluctantly, and it seemed to them even for part of the mermaids, they separated, the mystery of the origin of the maps had remained as it was.

"Where do you think they've got the maps?" said Captain Somchai after they were detached.

"They will have drawn them in the long run exploring the Current, you heard what they said, the Current has been there for millennia" replied the Second.

"Yes, I heard" nodded the Captain. "An explanation that at the moment I bought but think about it a little bit, the current is constantly changing, even if on the scale of galactic times, so I do not think that a few millennia ago it was the same as it is now. I've never been there, but I've heard many people say that everything moves there."

"You think?"

"Look, don't you know that we have to redo the Arm's route charts at least every two centuries! And the galaxy in comparison is moving slowly. You can imagine how long the Current's charts can last!" exclaimed the Captain.

"So?"

"So the explanation that they explored it a few millennia ago does not hold up, period. Now the Current is completely different and then to map a place you have to explore it, but a place like the Current cannot be explored without a chart, in short, a perfect stalemate!" concluded the Captain.

"And what would be your conclusion, Captain?"

"I don't know, at a certain point while we were conversing afterwards... well, afterwards, my mermaid let a sentence slip out of her mouth but then she pretended not to having said it, and I didn't insist, also because my thoughts were somewhere else and I just stored it in a corner of my memory."

"And this sentence would be?"

"She said *we had them*" said the Captain.

The Second sighed. "As usual, as mermaids always do. As adorable as they can be, they always remain vague. You always get the impression that they know something more than you do, but they don't think you're up to be told, and they hide behind the pretending to be silly."

"It's true, they're really playing dumb, but in my opinion they're not dumb at all" admitted the Captain.

"But I like when they play dumb "said the Second quietly.

"Me too" added the Captain who then concluded, "anyhow, we had the charts, hoping that they are up to date. I would say that our mission is over".

"And also in a good way Captain, also in a good way. For my part I will never again look at a woman who is not covered by tattoos."

19th interlude

"It was a hard job" said the Joker half annoyed, half radiant, "but I must admit that the species knew its stuff, stopping them was not easy at all. Luckily when they got going, the B species was largely gone, but getting the rest through without letting the others through was like playing a game trying to win and lose at the same time."

"And you want me to believe that you didn't have fun?" the Physicist asked him with a critical air.

"Out of curiosity, how did you do it?" the Biologist asked him.

"I asked the arsonist for a hand" replied the sneering Joker.

"He means the Energy Systems Technician" explained the Physicist.

"Yes, exactly him. Also because by now there is nothing to hide anymore, the passage of the species B at the intersection is part of the Project, so I asked him to make some fireworks, a supernova here and there in the bridge."

"And how did you convince him that it was necessary?" asked the Biologist.

"Oh, to convince him there was no need, when I assured him that whoever had to pass by, had already passed by, he couldn't wait to make some bang. He likes them very much, he said. He also said that they have beautiful colors, but they do too much damage in the galaxies."

"You cheated" said the Biologist.

"Yes, so what?" replied the resentful Joker.

"So how exactly did it go?" asked the Biologist again.

"I gave them the maps of the bridge, and behind every group that passed, we blew up a few stars so the maps had to be remade. New map, new group and new explosion, only the others were getting closer and closer and in the end we had to blow up the whole bridge. Now it's just a big fuss."

"How many have passed?" asked the Biologist.

"Of the B species ninety-eight percent, of the others, zero point zero" said the Joker with a satisfied expression.

"Great. Now, how do we tell it to the G.O.D.? He wanted his species to be free to pass if they wanted to."

"When you start lying, there is no other way but to continue" said the Physicist gloomily.

29 MYTHS AND LEGENDS

When a ship tried to use the new maps of the current recovered in the halo, it soon realized that they too were obsolete, which produced not only disappointment but also a vague suspicion of sabotage.

When questioned on the matter, the mermaids assured that not only were they sorry, but they were also very sad that they could no longer reach their people on the other side of the current because it had become completely impassable. They explained that at the beginning of their migration the Current was quite stable and that the transfer had taken place with a long line of ships passing the coordinates to each other, like a row of ants in which each one just follows the one in front of it, without having any idea what the way is. Then the row had become increasingly sparse while the current was changing faster and faster and for some time they too were no longer able to pass.

Pitying the fate that had separated them from their people, the men believed that explanation without investigating further because they believed that the fact that the surviving mermaids were stuck behind, was a demonstration of their good faith.

With the Current became impassable, men quickly forgot about its existence, which after all had always been only one of the many future possibilities, and armed of the new technically advanced and socially paleolithic social order, which in fact, turned out to be the best combination they had ever had, they cheerfully devoted themselves to repopulating the lost worlds of the core and to the systematic exploration of the halo, where they were occasionally gratified by meeting some mermaids, always very happy to see them.

Since very few were the lucky ones who met them, they returned to the mythology where they had come from and within a millennium no one believed in their existence anymore, despite the abandoned vestiges of their civilization that the explorers of the halo found every now and then under the seas of beautiful worlds hitherto unknown, which in time they learned to identify because they were all full of sardines and mackerels.

Lost the habit of meeting mermaids, compensated by a renewed balance with women, the human species eventually considered it useless to expand into another galaxy given the abundance of worlds in their own and when after other centuries the Current began to fray like clouds after a storm, becoming passable again, they did not even notice. And they also didn't notice, until decades later, that the mermaids had all disappeared from the galaxy.

30 BIRTH OF THE UNIVERSAL SPECIES

At the last meeting of the Project Committee there was an almost festive atmosphere. The news of the success of Plan B had spread and no one showed up with the fear of facing the CH.A.O.S and its wrath once again.

The Chairman of the Absolute Order of Space-time opened the meeting with a good-natured "To you" with which he concluded his intervention.

The General Operations Director was radiant when he asked the Diffused Systems Engineer to summarize the situation.

"Technician of Diffused Systems, please describe the happy

conclusion, which we should actually call the real beginning, of the Project."

"With pleasure Director" said the Diffused Systems Engineer.

"The B species, strong of our help in exchange for their willingness to follow our Project, has already spread throughout the new galaxy of which we have provided the mapping as requested by them, while the Project species has, against all predictions and bio-equation, resumed to be vital, abandoning that cultural behavior that had turned it away from its essence and starting to behave as its nature intended. This proves once again that no species can move away from its nature for a long time, on risk of extinction, and that the equations of behavior are inexorable necessities that, except for transitory deviations, cannot be avoided."

A whisper of assent spread through the meeting.

"And now let's come to the development of the Project, which, with the start of the B species, has started its true beginning. The Project species, revealed to be not up to its aims, will remain confined for seventeen cycles in its own galaxy, since only in seventeen cycles will the next intersection take place for them. Intersection to which we certainly all wish them to arrive and to which, with some help from us, they will surely arrive if they lose the vice of being ruled by culture instead of Nature because as we well know, Nature, that is us, is much more powerful."

The Technician's speech was interrupted by the noise of those who expressed their consent with vigor.

"And now we come to the most brilliant outcome of the entire Project, for which we must pay all our compliments to the far-sightedness of the Director, the Biologist, the Physicist and the Kinetic Technician."

"But not in that order" hissed the Joker tight-lipped.

"Shut up" reproached him quietly a strangely smiling Physicist.

The meeting was filled with a loud shouting of compliments.

"The far-sightedness, the genius, the brilliance hidden in the Plan from the very beginning, imagine that, from the very beginning" repeated the Diffused Systems Technician to underline its importance, "and which has been invisible to all of us and for which we can only feel admiration, can be summed up in a single sentence" said the Technician, then taking a long pause that muffled the shouting until silence, waiting for the announced revelation.

"Gentlemen" said the Diffused Systems Technician, "the species B will have a new intersection in only half a cycle!"

The silence exploded in an ovation for which the Chairman himself felt surprised, because everyone understood instantly the enormous consequence of what had just been said.

"I consider myself honored" continued the Technician, thundering to be heard over the now unstoppable uproar of enthusiasm, "to have the privilege to announce the birth of the Universal Species!" shouted over the turmoil that at that point exploded in a deafening ruckus that completely overwhelmed the words that followed. Words that therefore were heard by almost no one. "It will fill the universe with beauty and harmony. Thank you, Director!"

"Director thanks, my ass" growled the Joker.

"Shut up" said to the Physicist.

ABOUT THE AUTHOR

A.Bagus is a baby-boomer of 1962. Ph.D in Astrophysics, aircrafts pilot, traveler, he has been always fascinated by the mechanics of social behavior thus looking for mathematical models for History. The models used in this book to describe the behavior of the human beings are an actual example.

Printed in Great Britain
by Amazon

70760818R00156